Witches
&Warriors

A SIRENS BENEFIT ANTHOLOGY

Witches & Warriors

A SIRENS BENEFIT ANTHOLOGY

EDITED BY JESSICA CORRA

Witches & Warriors: A Sirens Benefit Anthology
Edited by Jessica Corra
Copyright © 2017

Introduction © Cynthia Porter
The Price © Cass Morris
The Witch of Fal Lanrei © Lyta Gold
Quietus © Lola Lindle
Withdrawal © Rook Riley
The Archivist's Lesson © Cynthia Porter
Mastery of the Mind © Nivair Gabriel
Under the Hunter's Moon © Darian Lindle
What the Future Holds © Kallyn Hunter
Storm's Daughters © Kristen Blount
Witnessed © Jessica Aelwood
Counterclockwise © Kate Larking
The Nine Trials of Ullah Du © Edith Hope Bishop
Feathers and Thread © Jennifer Adam

Cover design by Amanda Lewis

Published by Leftover Wine Publishing in partnership
with Astres Press
ISBN (print): 978-1-988313-24-5
ISBN (ePub): 978-1-988313-25-2

Contents

Introduction

Cynthia Porter

Sirens Conference is a small conference dedicated to women in fantasy literature. All the participants in this anthology have attended the conference. We are writers, readers, editors, and illustrators.

All of us experienced a moment in our lives where we realized that women can wield swords and magic. We can create worlds and stand our ground to protect them.

Witches & Warriors is that realization brought into words.

A benefit anthology is born out of love and inspiration. It is achieved through a lot of work. When the idea of our first anthology, *Queens & Courtesans*, first came along, none of us had any idea what we were doing. We did have an experienced editor and some of our authors were already published. However, none of us had ever written, assembled, formatted, and published a benefit anthology. We all learned a lot during our mad-cap rush from idea to publication in seven months.

The biggest question, did we want to do it again?

The answer was a resounding: Yes!

We chose the theme Witches & Warriors to reflect the 2017 Sirens Conference theme: women who work magic. Jessica Corra again agreed to edit. Pooling our talents along with the lessons learned from last year, we have assembled another anthology with strong, well-developed female characters.

Like the first anthology, all profits from the sales will be donated to Sirens, our gift to the community that brought us together.

Come, share the magic we have found at Sirens. We would love to see you join us there.

Sirens Conference can be found at:
www.sirensconference.org

The Price

Cass Morris

Tala tied up the sachet with a blue ribbon, one of many she'd taken off the last peddler to come through town, then dropped it into the girl's waiting, chubby hands. "Go on home, then, and tell your mother to put this under the babe's pillow. They'll both be able to get some sleep."

The child was halfway out the door before she remembered to call, "Thank you, miss!" over her shoulder. Shaking her head, Tala put away the payment the girl had brought—a basket of fresh-baked rolls. Lyddie Mercer used the same bake-oven as half the town, but something she put in her dough made a difference—a sweet and crispy crunch to the crust, but so soft inside, with an earthiness that seemed to warm a person from the heart out.

Tala tucked a blanket around five of the rolls and put the basket in her cupboard—but the sixth, she popped straight in her mouth. "Rosemary…" she murmured. "Rosemary and… something." She chewed on the bread and the mystery as she tidied up her worktable. Her own sort of herblore, had

Lyddie Mercer. '*And in another life, she might have been of my profession…*' She had the look of it, sometimes, a wildness behind the eyes, like a horse about to buck and jump the pasture fence. A flash of temper, Lyddie had, too, along with her dough-kneading hands, dazzling smile, and excellent baked goods. If Tala had not filled the place first, it might have been Lyddie who took herself to the edge of the town and set up the trade. It might have been Lyddie, paying the price.

But that wasn't the life Lyddie Mercer wanted for herself, and so Tala supplied what she needed to keep an even keel: a shoulder to cry on, sometimes; solid advice, when called for; a cup of tea, at any hour; and when nothing else would do, a charm.

Tala brushed the bread crumbs off her hands and checked the height of the fire. Satisfied with it, she knelt on the flagstones before the hearth, hiking fabric up around her hips: first the heavy green canvas of her kirtle, stained and practical; then the fine linen of her skirt, a gift from Tomas Boran, when she'd found his child that had gone wandering off into the woods; and last, the thin layer of underskirt, peeling up like onion skin.

Her legs were latticework from calf to hip, the white lines of old scars laying gentle and passive underneath half-healed pink stripes and angry red slashes. Tala ran her hands over them, slowly, lovingly, caressing each ancient welt, each dappled weal.

With her eyes fixed on the flames, Tala reached to the side and grasped the familiar bone of her dagger-hilt. Her other hand took a pinch from the pot of spices beside the flagstones, rubbed it between thumb and finger for a moment, then sprinkled it into the embers.

"For the babe," she whispered, drawing the dagger-point over her outer thigh," and the mother. Let them find the respite they so desperately need." Three short crimson lines felt like enough. She wiped the blade off on her skirt, staunched the slowly beading blood with a bit of moss, then threw the moss on the fire. A surge, a heat inside her veins, pooling in the palms of her hands. The sacrifice accepted. The charm would work.

Tala stood up, let her skirts fall back around her ankles, and went about her morning chores.

She hadn't been looking for power, the first time—or, at least, not the kind of power she had ended up getting. A broken-hearted girl with a dagger in her hands, tears burning, legs shaking. A pain so great she didn't know what to do with it, but fell to her knees, begging the gods for help. Cold steel followed by a hot rush, the beauty of blood on a blade.

Through pain, she had found a profession.

Summer seemed to have turned to autumn overnight. Parcee Caden came into the village on the heels of the chilling breeze, pushing straight into the Vellen kitchen, issuing instructions to Tala, and ignoring the panicked protestations of her mother. Like most of the village of Ethrein, Mae Vellen was terrified of Parcee, the grizzle-haired woman who lived on her own up in the mountain pass—but there was no denying her, not when she crooked a finger at Tala and said, "You'll feel it too, someday, when a girl wakes to magic. Someone else will be your problem, as it seems you're mine."

She waited until Mae left the room, though, to grab Tala's chin and ask, "How, then, girl? You did something last night, something you hadn't done before. How?" Tala hesitated, unsure how to explain her broken heart to this gusting woman. Her fingers twitched at her side, though, and apparently that was enough to give her away to Parcee. She snatched at Tala's skirt, wrenching it up to her thigh, and when she saw the dried pips of blood, the still-swollen slashes across otherwise unmarred skin, she exhaled through her teeth. "I should box your ears."

"Why?" Tala's mouth said, before her brain could stop it.

"There's better ways to power than spilling your own blood, girl."

Tala's cheeks flushed; she hadn't known it would buy her power, she had only been seeking relief, but now that it had...

"Something has to pay for it. That's right, isn't it?" So the stories said, and Tala felt the truth of it, heavy on her tongue. "Something has to pay. Why not me?"

Parcee's lip curled. "On your own head be it. Not my place to care where it comes from, just to make sure you don't lose control of it now it's here. I'll teach you what I can. The rest is on your own neck."

She had come to teach, and Tala soaked in her knowledge, drowned herself in it. She did not stay long, though. She hated village life, the comings and goings, the people prodding into each other's business. Parcee liked the quiet company of the pine trees, the chattering of red-tailed squirrels, the songs of starlight. "Too loud here," she would grumble, when some younger sibling started squalling or streetside gossip wafted in the windows. "You'll see. The power's not a companionable thing, girl. You can't keep people close with it. They want too much from you. You'll find a nice homestead in the mountains yourself, someday."

By that time, Tala had known enough not to contradict Parcee out loud. Her heart, though, stamped and screamed and swore its defiance. That was not the life she wanted.

Strange, to think of Parcee, to think of that time. She had only seen the older woman once or twice since then; Parcee claimed it itched for her to set foot in another witch's territory, though Tala had never found it so. Parcee would make excuses for her solitude, and she had always turned up her nose at Tala's desire to stay in the village, to stay among people. 'To be loved...' she thought, as she set water to heating so she could clean her instruments. 'A child's wish, that I never could set down...'

Her thoughts were interrupted by a banging on the door.

***

"Captain Kerramy."

"Sir!" Jess shot to her feet and stood at attention, though the sudden movement made her vision swim red again, and she felt Healer Sarel's hand jab between her shoulder blades to keep her steady.

"At ease, for mercy's sake." As Sarel fairly shoved her back to her seat, the king dismounted his horse and shucked off his helmet. There was a casualness in the gesture, an ease, that reminded Jess that her king was no older than she was, for all the dignity of office that weighed upon his shoulders. "Healer, don't let me stop your work."

"I wasn't going to," Sarel murmured, just low enough that the king could pretend not to have heard.

"Captain Kerramy, how did this happen?" Jess opened her mouth, but before she could respond, the king went on. "I have it from General Greves that you and a pair of scouts surprised a platoon of Yarian soldiers at a campsite on the north side of the Ardreen River."

"Hardly a platoon, sir," Jess replied. "A squadron, at the most. And not as much of a surprise as we might have hoped. Two managed to get their weapons." She nodded at her shoulder, which Sarel was still applying a coagulant to. "One of them caught me in the shoulder. Sloppy of me. Won't happen again."

The king crossed his arms over his chest, taking her in: old scars and new, and the king knew the story of each. Jess bore his gaze unflinching. Every drop of blood spilt was for him, and the nation, shed to defend the land she loved from Yarian incursions. If they had spoiled the physical beauty she had been born with, she loved them all the more for what they spoke of her. This new one would not be so bad—a faint line, usually covered by clothing. Nothing to the wound she had taken at the Battle of Haneb. That had been gruesome at the start, rending a tear clear through her cheek. But the king had good healers, and now the ragged red scar only pained her if she quite literally bit off more than she could chew.

"Three of you," the king said, "against an advance squadron of Yarians. And you think it sloppy that you took a single wound, while the scouts came away unharmed?" He shook his head. "What a mad, reckless thing you are," the king said, and Jess grinned. Bemusement from the king was as good as admiration, so far as she was concerned.

A flush on her cheeks, an iron tang in her mouth, the beauty of blood on a blade, pride in her service. These were the things that propelled Jess through life.

"Healer," the king said, "will she be fit to travel soon?"

Sarel frowned, knowing what "soon" meant when the word passed a king's lips. "She'll be fine today, so long as she doesn't ride hard or go charging into a vicious horde of blade-wielding maniacs."

"I make no promises, Sarel, you know that."

"Nothing so strenuous as that, I should hope," the king said. He waited, quiet, while Sarel finished tending to Jess, watching the swift work of her hands, needle and sinew moving in a flash, dabbing away blood, applying a pain relief ointment, all in a perfect repeating sequence.

When she had done, she nodded to the king and took herself and her supplies off towards the mess tent. Like Jess, Sarel had been working for the royals long enough to pick up on certain unspoken cues.

Only once Sarel was out of earshot did the king continue. "I need to send you home to Ethrein. An errand needs running, and I think..." His pale grey eyes were not quite focused on her, looking somewhere beyond. He might have been look at the muster taking place on the field behind the tents, but Jess knew better. She had been in his confidence long enough to recognize the drift. "I think it had best be you who runs it."

She needed no further explanation. "I'll leave at once."

***

Old Man Derren would, Tala knew, stay longer than his business required, so she put on water for tea. With his wife gone and all his daughters married, he came as much for a natter and some soft-hearted attention as for the tonic for his back.

On the whole, Tala didn't mind. It was part of the calling, as she considered it. Part of the bargain. She gave attention and affection alongside cures and charms, and she received regard, esteem, maybe even love.

But sometimes, she did have cause to regret just how familiar her patients and clientele felt with her.

"Thirty's only past marryin' if a man's a fool," Derren said with a snort, "when the woman's got a business solid as yours." He gave her figure an appraising look, at which Tala endeavored not to take offence. There was nothing salacious in it, but the old man did tend to view all young people, male and female, the same way he viewed his prize studs and brood mares. "Your mam kept on carryin' long past your age. I bet there's fertile ground in you yet that could take seed."

Tala knew how to divert Derren's speculations. "And is it you that's offering for the job, Derren?" she asked, grinning mischievously over at him.

He gave a hearty laugh, slapping his knee. "Oh, lass, to be forty year younger." He waggled a finger at her. "But a man knows when to stop riding the hunters and stick to comfy old nags."

"I think your late wife would not thank you for that comment." And that, reliably, sent Derren down a path of fond remembrance, extolling Ayani's departed virtues. Those who had been young before her death remembered a raven-haired tornado of a woman, who could hold a seat on the fieriest stallion her family traded in from the north—but who showed infinite patience when teaching the village children to hold their seats on gentle palfreys. To Derren, though, she had been a soulmate, a love so great that it had brought them together across half a continent.

After that, it was time for the usual update on each of his daughters—Jorene was breeding again, it seemed, and Kamani was considering taking a second husband to help her on the trails. Then, village gossip, most of which had already been brought to Tala's door by other means, but Derren happily recounted the tales, and she had no objection to listening as she set his tonic brewing.

Today, though, he seemed set on turning the topic back around to Tala. "I worry, girl. Hell, a lot of us do. Grohan and I have wondered at it over many a pint."

Tala's lips twisted slightly, not sure if she liked being a topic of alehouse conversation. *'Better than nothing,'* she reminded herself. *'Better than ignored, forgotten, abandoned...'*

"Plenty of fine lads and lassies in the town," Derren was going on. "But if none of them take your fancy—and I would understand that, sometimes a place can be too familiar to be choosing stock from—then certainly someone with your advantages could look in farther fields." His face folded, not quite in a frown, but Tala saw concern rippling through his snowy whiskers. "And even if it's not in your stars to be foaling, still... We hate to think of you living here, always alone."

"Alone?" Tala laughed. "Most days it's an astonishment if I go three hours together without a visitor. How could I be lonely?"

But Derren's eyes, as he got to his feet and reached for his cane, were too kind, too knowing.

If it had been someone else, one of the village boys, her mother and everyone else would have said he "came courting." But he was the farthest thing from a village boy, and so no one said anything. Not their place to comment. Not their place to express concern. Tala smiled as she ran alongside him, skirts fisted in her hands, and he did look at her with such love in his eyes. No one could deny that.

He never made promises he would be unable to keep, and Tala never asked for them. The words "forever" and "always" were, by silent compact, forbidden between them. And what did that matter, when the sun was high, the streamwater cool, and the meadow empty but for its usual neighborhood of bees and butterflies darting among the wildflowers? They splashed and played like children, then spread a blanket beneath the honeysuckle as the lazy hours of afternoon stretched on. What they spoke of—well, that was for their ears and the gods'. What mattered was the drawl in his voice, the spark in his eyes, the reverence with which his hands hovered over her skin.

They turned up at the bonfire that night, red-cheeked and laughing, and no one said a thing. His arm was about her waist, and all night, he doted on her. No village boy could have been more solicitous, bringing her honeyed treats, taking her hand for a dance every time the fiddlers struck up a fitting tune. Her hair caught the firelight as she laughed and clapped, and the people of Ethrein could almost forget that he was not one of them, for a few moments, seeing their girl in his arms, their girl kissed by his lips.

Was it really the hottest summer Ethrein had seen in decades, or did it only feel so to the love-scorched?

One visitor never knocked.

Tala and Jess had always been in and out of each other's houses. Their mothers had been friends from cradle to grave, and the children of each knew they could always find a meal in the house of the other. Tala and Jess had become closest. Sisters of the heart, happiest when their heads bent to the same pillow, and though their paths had diverged in adult-hood, their souls were no farther apart.

So when the door swung open unannounced, Tala did not lift her eyes from the sigil she was embroidering on a pillow-case. "I wasn't expecting to see you again so soon," she said, as she tucked her needle under a satin stitch. "I thought you had all moved north of the river."

Then, she actually looked up, setting down her embroi-dery as Jess shut the door—and saw the new scar, lancing from Jess's hairline down to her chin.

"Oh, Jess."

Jess grinned, and the action gruesomely stretched the roughly-patched flesh. "Not bad, huh? Don't worry, it hardly hurt after a week."

It had ever been so. Jess had been the undisputed avenger of injustice among the village children, ready to tackle a bully twice her size or chase a taunter all the way from the temple yard to the forest's edge. Hers were the first wounds Tala had treated, hers the first body Tala had protected with a charm.

"You should have sent for me." She stood, came close enough to inspect Jess's face. "I have balms…"

But Jess was grinning. "Are you kidding? I wanted this scar to be as horrific as possible. Shows the troops what I'm made of."

Tala's eyes crinkled in concern. "What you're made of is flesh and bone, Jess, not immortal ichor."

"We both pay for power," Jess said with a shrug. "The coin of my flesh buys respect better than any commission. The sol-diers like seeing a captain who doesn't flinch from the thick of the fight."

"They must adore you, then." Tala's hands were already moving at her spice rack, already plucking down herbs from the strings hanging before her windows.

"They do!" Jess cheerily agreed.

"So tell me how it happened." And as Jess spun out another tale of war and glory, Tala's fingers flew, plucking buds, pinching grounds, crushing seeds. Mortar and pestle moved almost too quickly to be seen. A simple recipe, one she could make in her sleep by now, as Jess's familiar voice rolled over her. The story was nothing terribly new, but Jess liked to recount her fights—and the more Tala heard, the more she knew how to keep her friend safe.

"—and it's not as though we don't have Healers, honestly, Tala, I know you don't trust anyone's work but your own, but Sarel really is wonderful. She's the reason I'm not spitting out the side of my face."

"Yes, you've sung her praises before," Tala said, dumping the mixture of herbs and spices into a small paper packet. "Here. If you won't take a balm, then at least take this."

"Your famous tea?"

"*Your* tea, I should call it," Tala said. "I've blended it more often for you than anyone else." Jess snickered as she took the packet and slipped it into her bag. "So what is it that's brought you back so soon?"

"Ah, we've had trouble pressing north of the river. The Yarians are camped everywhere. We're lucky it's mostly forest there, not farms, else a lot of folk would be in for a lean winter…" Jess cleared her throat. "But the truth is… he sent me, Tal." For the briefest of moments, Tala froze—a flame caught in a sudden chill. "He said he had an errand, and that it had better be me who ran it. I think he must be looking for—"

"Yes." Tala's voice was tight. "Yes, it's finished…" Moving as if in a dream, Tala went to the sideboard, to one of the smallest of her wooden chests: rowan, kept warm with a charm, carved all over with intricate patterns. It eased open at her barest touch. Tala drew out a small iron disc on a long chain and held it out to Jess. "Give this to your king."

"He's your king, too, Tal," Jess said as she took the charm.

Tala ignored the reminder. "Tell him to wear it from the full moon to the new. He must not take it off, not even once, no matter how much… discomfort he experiences." Jess arched an eyebrow. "It may itch once it gets working," Tala explained. "He should take that as a good sign. The traitor will reveal himself before the moon turns again."

"If this works," Jess said, testing the weight of the amulet in her hand, "he'll make you a Duchess."

Tala snorted. "The Witch of Ethrein, swanning about the court? What a fine spectacle that would be."

"You'd do better there than you think." In answer, Tala spread her homespun skirts wide and made a mocking curt-sey. Jess laughed. "Seven hells, Tal, if I can scrape by without embarrassing myself too badly, you'd have no trouble. You have manners and charm. Half the peers would be eating out of the palm of your hand within a week."

Sighing, Tala turned to a small basket with colored glass beads in it. She had not yet decided what to do with them; the tiny treasures were the gift of a grateful glassblower from the village to the south, when Tala had been able to heal his small daughter, who had fallen into the fire. She had been up all the night, gently applying layer after layer of balm, waiting for the skin to refresh itself, and peeling off the ruined flesh. By the time she was done, the child's complexion was as fresh as ever, shining bright as amber and smooth, and her whimpers of pain already forgotten as she laughed to greet the sunlight. *'Children rebound from injury so readily.'*

Mostly to give her hands something to do, so that Jess might not notice their tremble, she took the basket to the kitchen table and began sorting the beads by color.

"If he made you a Duchess," Jess said, voice softer, "he could marry you."

Tala released a long breath through her teeth. Then she

shook her head and gave a mirthless laugh. "And what has our dear queen done that I should wish such unhappiness on her?"

Now it was Jess's turn to snort. "She might thank you for the favor. She's got an eye on a duchess, herself." Tala quirked an eyebrow; a rumor she'd heard, but not confirmed. "He still loves you, Tal."

"As you say." Tala felt a warm twinge on her leg; no doubt one of the lines she had cut that morning, for Lyddie Mercer and her restless babe, and yet Tala imagined it was the oldest of all, so faded as to be nearly invisible underneath years' worth of others. "We all pay a price for power, Jess." She turned to her friend, smiling sadly. "I was his."

Jess was hanging over the backyard fence, wondering when Tala might emerge. That curious princeling had left more than an hour earlier, and Jess thought Tala would be on her way out any moment. She usually was, kiss-dizzy and floating like fairies were carrying her. She told Jess such things—and while Jess wasn't sure she approved, how could she not rejoice in her friend's happiness?

Jess waited until she noticed the storm clouds gathering overhead, infecting what had been, an hour earlier, a bright blue sky. But now the wind whipped at the leaves, warning sensible folk to get inside, and Jess decided she wasn't waiting anymore. Privacy be damned. If Tala wasn't coming out, then Jess was going in.

She vaulted the fence in familiar fashion, but her footsteps quickened as she neared the Vellen house. Something was wrong, the rustling trees seemed to whisper, terribly wrong, and Jess pounded open the Vellens' back door with more than her usual force.

She saw Tala, kneeling before the hearth. Saw the tracks of tears on her cheeks, though the wetness itself had dried. Saw the smeared blood on her hands, the knife hanging limply from her fingers.

Jess's heart froze mid-beat, and only started up again when Tala turned her head, the firelight glowing red on her cheeks. Jess had no need to ask what had happened; she had bit off the warning too many times. Princes didn't marry seamstress's daughters from the middle of nowhere, not if they wanted to stay princes, and Tala wasn't stupid, she knew that. Jess had never wanted to insult her intelligence by pointing it out.

But it seemed the moment had come, when Tala could no longer tell herself convenient fictions.

So Jess knelt beside her, gently taking the knife away, and wrapped her friend tight in her arms.

Parcee Caden came the next day, as though summoned by the storm, and Jess watched as Tala learned how to build something useful from the ruins of a ragged heart.

"There's a blue pouch on the sideboard, there," Tala said, rolling a little red bead between her fingers. "Carry the amulet in that until you put it into his hands."

Jess retrieved the pouch, but she gave the amulet a long look before dropping it in. Simple enough, nothing that would raise many eyebrows even if it were noticed: iron, cold to the touch. A sigil engraved in it. A sigil faintly tinted red.

Jess stowed the pouch in her bag, tucked safely against the packet of tea. "How much did it take, Tal?"

The pause before she responded was a breath too long, and her eyes remained on the beads. "How much what?"

"Dammit, Tala!" Jess slammed a hand against the nearest piece of furniture—a cupboard that proved, fortunately, sturdy enough to withstand her strength. "Don't you play dumb with me. With anyone else, even with him if you must, but not with me. I *know* you. How much did it take?"

"I do *know* what I'm doing," Tala reminded her. "It isn't as though I took it all at once. Why do you think I told him it would take so long to prepare?"

Jess could feel the heat rising in her cheeks, a lancing pain along her scar. She was devoted to king and country, would do anything for him, anything to protect him—but Tala was something else. Tala lay outside those vows. "Do you ever wonder," Jess said, steel in her voice, "why the only way you know to help people is by hurting yourself?"

"You bleed for this country," Tala shot back, finally looking up from the piles of beads. Her eyes were flashing—a good sign, Jess thought. Anger suited her better than the numbness she so often feigned. "I bleed for my neighbors. For people who *know* me, at least. Who show gratitude."

"For the rheumatisms you cure and the babes you quiet?" Jess huffed. "Such little things, compared with what burns inside you—"

"It's not little to them."

"A lesser witch could serve their needs. You, Tala!" Jess's chin had taken on the stubborn set that indicated she was trying not to shake her friend by the shoulders. "There's a reason they speak of you from Tehlin to Parkease." She gestured at the colored beads scattered on the table. "A reason traders travel for hours to bring their children to you, and pay a prince's ransom for your treatments. I swear, I look at you and think you could call down lightning from the heavens if you wanted to." Tala shook her head, but Jess reminded her, "I was there, Tal, the first time. You drew a storm when you had no idea what you were doing. You brought on autumn weeks early. So I know you have it in you, even if you've stuffed it down for years. You—You could summon mists from the ground, change the flow of rivers—"

Tala barked another bitter laugh. "What should I want to do such fool things for?"

Jess's mind was full of a thousand reasons: a soldier knew what such power could do. Jess had spent half her life honing herself into a weapon, and that Tala could forge herself into one with hardly a thought and yet chose not to was beyond her comprehension. With powers like Tal's, Jess's work would never be sloppy again. No Yarian would catch her off-guard; no squadron would slip by her notice. Some legions had hedge witches attending them instead of Healers, sure, but none like Tala, none with the power banked in them, waiting to be more. None who could, if they chose, reshape riverbanks or persuade the sun not to shine. "For the country," Jess said. "For the men and women who die in its name. For the king, dammit, Tal! You could be doing better for him than this little charm!"

"That charm is what he asked for."

"He knows not to press his luck."

"So he has you do it for him?" Tala rose from the table; her hands, Jess noticed, were still shaking, worse than before. "He sends you, to ask me to strike the Yarians down with lightning or set ghost fires to their camps? He has you come a-begging on his behalf, when he won't even—" Tala winced, and when she continued, it was in a low, cold voice. "You know how I buy my power. And I know you don't approve. How you can ask me—how you can imply—Do you know, what it would cost to work magic like that?"

"It doesn't have to be your blood!" Jess yelled, frustration finally overtaking the last of her discipline. "Soldiers bleed all the time, Tal. And since unlike the Yarians, we don't set slaves to do our fighting for us, the blood's far more freely given than one of Parcee's chickens or crows. Hell, Healer Sarel's mopped up enough of mine alone to pay for concealment charms for a whole squadron, by my reckoning. We all bleed for what we love, Tal!" She sighed, like the wind buffeting out of a sail. "So why not make more of it count for something?"

She regretted her temper when she saw the tears standing in her friend's eyes. So proud, her Tala, and so damned stubborn. *'Well. We are friends for a reason.'*

Jess strode forward and folded her arms around Tala.

She felt her friend tense from the shoulders to the face, felt the refusal to weep rippling through her—but then, felt her muscles relax, slightly. "Just think about it, would you?" she murmured against Tala's ear. "Not for him. For the fear of the gods you'd put into the Yarians." Tala snorted into Jess's shoulder, and Jess gave her a good-natured jostle. "Wouldn't you love to see the looks on their faces, as you ride in on the tide of a storm?"

"*Your* face," Tala said, straightening. "Your face when I did is what would make it all worth it."

"There you are, then!" Jess cupped her friend's cheek. "I imagine he'll send me back again before too long. Think on it till then."

"You can't stay for supper?"

"'Fraid not. I promised Sarel I'd be back in time to rest up my shoulder."

Tala's eyes flew wide. "What happened to your—?"

"Oh, never mind it. I swear, between the two of you, I'll be coddled to death."

Tala gave her a pinch. "If Death ever manages to find you, I imagine you'll have given her quite a run first."

Another broad, slightly painful grin. "May my legend tell it thus."

The friends embraced again and exchanged all those small words of parting, so meaningless and yet so weighted. By the time they walked to the door, dusk had nearly fallen, the sky going purple and gold in streaks across the horizon. "Be careful," Tala said. "Or what passes for it in you, at least. Come home safe."

"I will try." Mounting her horse, Jess looked back to ask, "Should I give any message? Besides the instructions, I mean?" But Tala shook her head. "If you're sure, then."

"I am."

And as Jess took off down the village lane, Tala drifted back into her house and collapsed into the chair by the kitchen table. Did she mean to keep sorting the beads? She wasn't sure. Her hands intended so, it seemed, but her mind was elsewhere.

There was no great game that summer, no secret. She knew he was the prince, of course. Everyone knew. But if he felt no need to stand on ceremony when he visited Ethrein, then why should she? And every time he passed through town, there were flowers.

Flowers, to start; bouquets as he went from the palace to the academy; bouquets as he returned. Then other tokens. Handkerchiefs. Bracelets. Ribbons and feathers and other trinkets. All quite traditional gifts. None too imaginative.

How little that mattered. For a few months, Tala had songs in her heart and in her ears, poetry dancing along the curves of her skin. Tala had kisses in the moonlight and laughter under the sun. Tala had a warmth in her like none other she had ever known.

How little it all mattered, in the end.

Princes didn't marry seamstress's daughters from the middle of nowhere.

Princes didn't even keep girls like that as mistresses, supposing their pride allowed such an arrangement.

Princes didn't even know girls like Tala Vellen.

But a king might know a witch.

She had made the charm as though it were for someone else, some nameless monarch in a faraway place. It would work just as well; her blood had seen to that. But she had not allowed herself to think of him while creating it, any more than she let herself think of him on any other day.

Eti, the king.

Eti, who had loved her.

Eti, who loved her still, if Jess were to be believed.

Everything was a choice, and he had made his. He loved her, but not quite enough to choose her, not at the price it would have asked of him—handing the throne to his half-grown nephew, giving up the defense against the Yarians, never again setting foot inside the hallowed halls of the Cemerin Palace. *'Loved, but not enough, not enough, never enough…'*

She could not fault him for the choice he made—but nor could she fault herself, if once in a season, she allowed herself to think of what might have been, had he chosen differently. Of what might be, if she were willing to trade the life she had for the life dangled before her.

It was a flaw in a woman, this wanting to be loved. A potentially fatal one, in a witch. But power came from the heart, one way or another, and it was ever so much easier to bleed than to feel. Since that first storm that she hadn't meant to summon, Tala knew that her feelings were dangerous, and not only to her. So she had dammed them up, working what magic she could from the little pains of the blood, resolving only to touch the greater magics of the full heart when in dire need.

There were other ways to pay the price, though, Parcee had said, and Jess offered a grander stage for those greater magics. Tala had determinedly ignored such temptations, but now, they beckoned.

'Could I even still…?' But that was the wrong question. She knew the power was there, twelve years of it long-banked, if she chose to open that door. *'But could I control it?'*

Was it selfish, not to try?

Tala pried herself from the kitchen table and knelt before one of the many boxes that contained the tools of her art. She opened the wooden chest and sifted through its contents: several blades, some ornate and some plain; a stash of candles; a precious packet of incense; half a dozen ribbons and knotted threads; a seashell from the ocean she had never seen.

And a letter, carefully preserved. The only one she had kept. Not the first, with its awkward endearments; nor the last, the one that came after goodbye; nor any of the dozens in-between, except this, and not for anything it said. She'd kept it for the tiny sun he'd sketched in one corner, brightening her remembrance.

At first, the sun was all she could bring herself to look at. The words cut, deeper and harder than her blades ever could.

The ink had not been exposed to light enough times to fade, and yet Tala knew every word. Her eyes ran over them, only half-seeing, but she heard them in his voice: words of love, but never promises; words of faith, but never fidelity. Then she folded the paper and replaced it, carefully, in the box. In its place, she drew out a single long pin.

One bead of blood at the tip of her left ring finger; that was all she drew. Darker than the blood that sprang from thighs and calves, as though her life-force was more concentrated there. One bead of blood to serve as conduit, and as it blossomed, Tala opened the box in her mind, the one that held at the things she spent so much energy not remembering.

A kiss on Midsummer's Eve.

Racing through the meadow when a thunderstorm broke over their heads.

His fingers, laced through hers.

The scent of him, cedar and lemongrass.

The way her name sounded on his lips, the first time, the last time.

The way his name tasted on hers.

One bead of blood, and an ocean of pain. Tala coughed rather than crying it out, determined to choke on it if she had to; she had to channel that agony, had to make it useful.

She couldn't stop the sharp sting of tears, though, wetting her cheeks and blurring her vision.

Without looking up, she raised her right hand and snapped her fingers once.

A bolt of lightning cut the heavens.

The Witch of Fal Lanrei

Lyta Gold

I wish to clarify the exact difference between the known and the unknown, the true and the false. Too many rumors are breathing through the capital in clouds of courtly poison. They settle around the brow of our Incarnate, as mist around a mountain peak: they are as immaterial, and as meaningless. There are no secrets about the Incarnate's origins. There's no new nightmare descending on our shores. And there's no substance to the stories about the witch.

You might argue that the representative of the divine needs no defense. Sacred authority can hardly be strengthened or weakened by a pamphlet penned by a mere inspector-of-the-faith, even an inspector-of-the-faith recently honored by elevation to the fourth degree. Of course, my readers will correctly note that my domain is punishment, not argument. This much is true. I enforce the laws of heaven; I don't need to understand the burning words inscribed along the brindled branches of the Celestial Tree. We can support knowledge without understanding it, and we can defend reason and good governance without claiming false expertise. If this pamphlet serves any function in these troubled days, let it be to punch the air out of those who speak glibly, dangerously, of events and purposes beyond their understanding.

By what authority do I write these words? The authority of my own eyes and mind. Who else among the royal court has visited Fal Lanrei and spoken with the witch in question? Let me reassure you: the tales you've heard about her are gibberish. As they say in Daxora Province, someone is mistaking a kitten for a tiger. But, if a kitten is mistaken for a tiger often enough, then the kitten might begin to believe itself a tiger; as a lie, repeated often enough, gains physical weight. It grows flesh and leaps out into the world, a mockery of the image of truth.

I repeat: there are no mysteries about the origins of the Incarnate. The God with Two Faces descended from the heavens forty-three years ago; his birth and his divinity were confirmed by the presence of sacred signs. As a child he was raised in the sanctuary of Brenin, as all Incarnates have been and will be in the centuries to come. When, twice yearly, he leaves his holy valley to dwell among us in the capital, his words are etched into obelisks of marble and sandstone so that his genius might live for eternity in the sight of the court and the King. (And, with all due deference to those of greater degree than I, it would be well if some among you would visit the obelisks and read these words, and consider their hard clear truths!)

You remember how the Incarnate rescued our colonies from the Harpy of Eschik, how he brokered the marriage of the King's fractious daughter to the Scarlet Emperor across the sea—though the princess later led us to grief. You will also recall how he cured the paralysis of Admiral Rho with a wave of his hand. Certainly, the admiral died soon after, but that was from too much celebrating. Miracles are meaningless if morally neglected and unaccompanied by sober reflection.

As for the Helleboric plague—yes, the Incarnate may have received some small help from the witch, but those who magnify her role have forgotten the manifest gifts of the Incarnate. They have forgotten his greatest act.

When the eight thousand ships of the Scarlet Emperor appeared on our horizon, many of us surrendered in our hearts. Despair sullied the capital, gripping muddy talons in every mansion, every plaza, every workshop and fruit-stall and counting-house. Soldiers deserted amid a tumult of looting. The Incarnate rode out alone.

At the time, some claimed he was fleeing back to Brenin, or over the mountains into Mazarine, or that he planned to surrender to the Scarlet Emperor in exchange for his meaningless mortal life.

But we all remember what happened. The Incarnate summoned a great wind and darkness. The ocean became a field of golden wrath, tossing like wheat before the harvest scythe. The sky shattered and bled in thunder—and the fleet of the Scarlet Emperor broke upon the waves. He went down with the fleet, as did his traitorous empress, that former princess of ours who dreamed of being a warrior and whose name has been stricken from our histories.

This is the fate of all who oppose the Incarnate, the King, this country of wheat and stone and law like iron, the pivot around which the universe itself revolves.

Even the Incarnate's smallest gestures blaze with light. A single word from his lips, sweet and potent as a drop of rock rose honey, can soothe the most vicious quarrel among court ladies. At other times his voice is a cannonade of thunderclaps, and stiffens the King's stern and necessary edicts. Once, the merest sound from the Incarnate's holy throat above this undeserving head rescued me—your own humble inspector-of-the-faith—from a serious error.

I had in my charge a woman who seduced a monk. She protested innocence and unwillingness. The monk's testimony weighed hard against her, but between her sobs and her feathery, frightened eyes, I began to doubt my resolution. One day, I happened to be passing through the Lapis Garden from the east as the Incarnate spiraled down the terrace from the west. Where our ways crossed, I genuflected, but I confess—and my guilt writhes within me, even now—I failed to contemplate the Incarnate's sacred presence. I thought only of the woman, of her blue and drowning gaze.

As the Incarnate swept past me, he coughed. A light, careless cough, directly above my head. He didn't speak a word. Words weren't necessary.

Because instantly, I knew clarity. I remembered my responsibilities, my duty to the Incarnate, the King, and the law.

I put the woman to death.

Such are the blessings of the Incarnate that they are too many to be written, and even he might fail to notice their effects, as the storm might fail to notice how it strengthens the inconsequential stream!

If the Incarnate is beloved here in the heart of the world, he is even dearer in his native village of Fal Lanrei. The people there are perpetually hungry for stories of the one they call "their" Incarnate. This is blasphemous, and when I was their departmental inspector-of-the-faith, sixth degree, I punished them for their misshapen words. Nevertheless, they savor each new tale of the Incarnate like a holiday loaf of fig and apricot bread.

Fal Lanrei resembles every other village in the eastern mountains: remote, clannish, resentful. The only road to the tumbledown gate is a ragged switchback pass between two peaks. Winters are bitter. Summers are cool and windy and subject to dangerous droughts. If it weren't for the Incarnate, no one of importance would know of Fal Lanrei, and no inspector-of-the-faith above the ninth degree would have been dispatched to its shabby council-hall. The village is no more than a small chaotic overhang of goats and scrub and tamarisk trees, peopled by herdsmen and weavers and drunks. There's a village headman, a council of elders, a blacksmith, one half-literate scribe, and, of course, a witch.

I've heard that in distant countries, witches live apart from their people. Forced into the wilderness, they can only be found deep in the woods, or squatting under a bridge, or imprisoned in some high and lonely tower. This practice is, of course, absurd. The witch of Fal Lanrei lives in the heart of the village, next to the headman and the council-hall. Her home is like any other in the mountains—four narrow passage-ways, a cracked and overgrown courtyard, an herb garden, and an ancient fig tree. From that tree her husband suspends his spindle and his shuttles. Most of their children are weavers, like him; a few are goatherds, and one is a drunk.

Despite what you may have heard, the witch—Sorah Tehn—is not a captivating forest nymph with dancing feet. She doesn't have a cloud of silver hair; her eyes are not as clear and mysterious as moonlight. Sorah Tehn is neither old nor young, neither ugly nor beautiful. A portion of her left breast is missing because it grew a cancer and she cut it out, herself, with the help of her daughters and plenty of whiskey. She brews that whiskey from the barley in her garden —it forms the base of most of her remedies. The people of Fal Lanrei swear by her cures, and the village is strong and healthy, at least in comparison to their neighbors. But they're a florid, promiscuous, dirty people. None are committed to the Rational Dignities, and few of them can read at all. Sorah Tehn herself is quite illiterate. The dullest novice or neophyte philosopher knows more of Measurable Truth than she does or ever will.

By coincidence, Sorah Tehn was born in the same week as the Incarnate. On a pale spring evening of blue and fragile cloud the monks from Brenin came up the switchback pass, searching for the new embodiment of the God with Two Faces. This century's omens were unambiguous: the god had fallen to earth in the cleft between two mountains during the last week of Metaraxi on a clear night when Adarant was in the ascendant. When the monks reached Fal Lanrei, they rang the bells of the lowest and humblest house on the slope, just beyond the splintering gate. This was the house of the Tehns.

This meeting has been recorded in the annals because, for a few moments, it caused tremendous confusion. The monks tell us that as the infant Sorah lay within her mother's arms:

...the clouds melted away from the moon. A light, very pure, very silver, reached out and seemed to caress the child's sickly face. The gleam in her black eyes was that of stars caught in the net of night. Despite all reason, we believed at first we bore witness to a sacred sign...but reason triumphed. This was not a sign, but a puzzle, a test of our credulity. The God with Two Faces is precise about the form of his residency: he has only ever chosen a boy child, unblemished, and in obvious good health.

In adherence to custom, the monks still asked the Nine Sacred Questions. The Tehns' responses are recorded in the annals—the early answers resemble truth, if you squint at them hard enough. The later questions weren't answered at all. Reportedly the Tehns were a nervous, inarticulate pair, unused to monks. Their tongues stilled in their mouths like the clappers of rusty bells. The monks, uneasy inside the silence, asked if any other babies had been born in the village within the last few months. Sorah's father answered that yes, a boy had been born to the headman and his wife on the cusp of the last week of Metaraxi, though these ignorant villagers failed to note the exact position of Adarant.

An answer to the mystery, clear and piercing as an arrow. The light we beheld in the eyes of the child Sorah was only reflected glory from a different house, a little higher up the road.

The infant Incarnate was a fine-featured boy, red and wailing. He wore silver-threaded wrappings, a torque of aventurine, and bracelets of solid bronze. His parents answered the Nine Sacred Questions correctly, without a single misplaced word. The monks note that they sobbed through the exchange, clearly overwhelmed by the honor. When all the right words had been spoken and recorded, when all the correct signs had been seen and sanctioned, the monks were able to declare that the child was indeed He, the Sun and the Moon, the Dawn and the Evening, the Young Man and the Old, the Hero and the Sage: the God with Two Faces, returned to us at last.

The Incarnate was whisked away to Brenin where he grew to manhood in robes of gold and silver, memorizing the Twelve Burning Texts, the Forty-Seven Rational Dignities, and the Eight Hundred Responsibilities of Man. He returns to Fal Lanrei once a year, to pay his respects to his adoptive family as is required by the Rational Dignities. (I regret that I was not present for any of these visits in the short months when I operated as the local inspector-of-the-faith.)

Sorah Tehn stayed on the mountain, and grew older. She told me once that she learned her craft in the way of witches —that is, from her grandmothers and from observation. Her lessons were in the ways of water, the uses of plants, and the numberless voices of the rain.

Her talents, such as they are, lie mostly in the realm of healing and purification. No doubt her life has been enhanced by the rubbed-off luck of the Incarnate. Every single one of her children was born alive and has lived to adulthood. The women of Fal Lanrei, eager to share in her secondary luck, demand Sorah's services as a midwife. They say that under her care every woman and infant in Fal Lanrei has lived through childbirth—this has to be a lie, but a gentle one, and we can see why they might wish to believe it.

A favorite rumor among the women of Fal Lanrei concerns the blacksmith's daughter, born feet first and twilight blue, cruelly choked by her own birth cord. Sorah Tehn took the tiny body away, but didn't bury it—instead she carried the dead child up the mountainside. According to village legend, a secret spring descends from that mountain, manifesting only in darkness and running swift and invisible through the hard black night. At the mouth of the river of night, the witch bathed the infant over and over, dabbing its frozen lips with her special whiskey, all through the long hours until sky and water faded, growing grey and haggard in the endless procession of shadow after shadow. By the time an arc of fire wrote its name across the peaks, Sorah was seen descending into Fal Lanrei. Against her heart she cradled the baby, who stirred in her arms and cried a little.

I've met this blacksmith's daughter. She has a limp and slow speech but is otherwise healthy, with a rosy face and a smile of such sweet radiance that I can't believe she ever touched the waters of death.

Little fables of this sort spring up in the eastern mountains like patches of clover. They are harmless, and easily tended, unlike the forest of lies that ensnares the capital.

Certain members of the court must be composing their refutations of this pamphlet already. They will correctly note that I wasn't actually in Fal Lanrei during any of the events now disputed. It's true: I obviously wasn't present for the birth of our Incarnate. Nor did I witness his unexpected visit to Fal Lanrei during the Helleboric plague—by that time I had already been honored with the fifth degree and posted to the capital, a just reward for the swift enactment of my duties. And no, I wasn't a member of the sacred band chosen to accompany the Incarnate and the witch on their desperate journey. But what was told to me of that time came from the lips of men who were present, men of high degree and holy status. I warn my readers that to doubt the honesty of these men is a verbal act-against-the-faith, of the sixth inclination, and is morally intolerable even if one's degree of rank prevents punishment.

Let us not forget the horror of the Helleboric Plague, the fatal nightmare that leaves purple-black bruises on the eyes and mouths and genitals of its victims. The capital, as we remember with sorrow, was particularly affected. Brenin, however, was safely quarantined, making it all the more remarkable that the Incarnate rode out in the heat of that dead and spoiling summer. He traveled north and east, up to the desolate mountains and Fal Lanrei. Maybe in a moment of noble weakness he worried over the health of the family that was never his, as they created only the earthly wick for the burning spirit of the God with Two Faces. Regardless, when he reached Fal Lanrei he spoke to his family, and then with Sorah Tehn. She left with him, descending the mountains for the first time in her life.

Against the plague, the Incarnate wore a white robe and a long mask stuffed with cinnamon and lavender. His mortal nostrils suffer from allergies, and it's said he frequently sneezed. The witch brought nothing except a simple yellow-wood bow, a quiver of arrows tipped with bone, several bags of medicine, and a one-eyed, sly-spirited goat to carry it all. Twenty of the Incarnate's monks and ten of his guard accompanied them to Kalatha Province, through the villages of the fifth and sixth departments. Here the plague had hit first and hardest. No men moved upon the plains, herding or harvesting or studying the movements of the stars. The company saw only dead villages where hellebores bloomed on every fallen face and all the holy braziers had blown out. The entire world seemed to be rotting, a decadence of decaying flowers, limbs and bellies blackened and split open like poisoned fruit.

The Incarnate and his men kept as far away as possible. They didn't approach the dead, either to count or to bury them. But they killed every animal they could find, from a distance, with bows. They weren't looking for dead villagers. They were looking for a living beast.

Some have claimed that the Incarnate sought out Sorah Tehn because he didn't know the origin of the plague or how to halt it, as if the God with Two Faces could possibly know less of any subject than a mountain witch who'd never left her home! The Helleboric plague was, it's true, unusual. All previous plagues have originated in the western swamps, or filtered through the capital in the filthy bodies of foreign sailors. Consider this as evidence of the Incarnate's wisdom, his resourcefulness, his humility: when he hunted for the beast that caused the Helleboric Plague, he brought along the witch whose children lived, whose sure hand—and whiskey—had, at times, demonstrated authority over illness.

It was a long journey through a desolate country of hot dry grass. They killed every animal they saw: foxes, lapwings, doves, even leaping eland with ebony horns. After a time, the only living creature in the waste was the occasional eagle overhead, screaming in rage at the barrenness below. How the Incarnate, a man of such deep understanding, must have felt behind his protective mask! The witch, it's said, wept unrestrainedly. We're fortunate she was the only woman in the party, or they would have died there, trying to bury every animal, shedding tears over each unpleasant but necessary death.

In a hollow under a hill by a dark green river they found

the beast at last. A whipped and flea-bitten bull, crusted purple around the mouth. He was very ill but his body was too strong, too stubborn, too convinced of its selfhood to die.

According to Sorah Tehn—as relayed to me by a guardsman—the plague wasn't spread by the bull itself, but by its fleas. It was the fault of the master who charged twelve bits to his neighbors to watch the bull battle exotic animals from over the sea, brought in by careless and unscrupulous smugglers. Regardless of the plague's origin, the bull refused to die of it. He snorted and dug at the floor of the hollow under the hill as if waiting for his master, desiring relief or vengeance though misuse is the master's right.

Before the Incarnate could act, the witch fired a bone-tipped arrow at the bull. A bad shot—it only caught the creature in the withers. Evidently the arrow had been dipped in a pain-relieving poison, because the bull sank to its haunches and lay quietly on the floor of the cave. The Incarnate reportedly shouted at the witch to fire again from the yellowwood bow but she refused—actually refused him, Incarnate of the God with Two Faces! I'm told she walked over to the bull even as the Incarnate ordered her to stay. She squatted beside the beast, stroking his side; and after a time, the bull's breathing slowly eased, evening into silence. At last, the creature relaxed his hold on his tormented life.

If the witch's actions appear to you as courage, or compassion, remember the fourteenth of the forty-seven Rational Dignities. "Excess of courage is not courage, but a desire to demonstrate worthiness. Excess of compassion is not compassion, but a lack of resolution."

When the bull's spirit had descended into death, the witch drew blood from his side and siphoned it into a flask. Then she stripped off all her clothes—in the sight of men—and dove into the dark green river. She scrubbed her entire body violently with sand. Rising, she drank some of her whiskey and demanded that each of the men take a swallow in turn. The Incarnate instructed them to do so, and they obeyed.

It may have been the potent whiskey. It may have been the death of the bull. Whatever the cause, some of the curse on the land seemed to lift. The sun beat gold through the heather again, and crickets murmured in the waving wheat.

It was then that the Incarnate wrapped the witch in his very own cloak.

Can you imagine the humility it must have taken, the grace and the forbearance, to wrap a wet and dirty and naked and scar-breasted and not even particularly attractive witch in the gold and silver cloak worn only by the Incarnate of the God with Two Faces? I can't, and neither can you. From this act alone we may perceive that the Incarnate is a god, and the rest of us mere pebbles in the running river of time.

Upon returning to the capital, the Incarnate brewed up a medicine with some help from Sorah Tehn. This was a liquid compound, distilled from the bull's blood and certain mountain herbs before being injected into the veins of the unafflicted. I recall arresting five natural philosophers who protested this treatment as both brutal and ineffective. Publicly challenging the will of the Incarnate, I will remind my readers, is an act-against-the-faith, of the fourth inclination. As you will recall, the Incarnate's treatment was proven correct by Measurable Truth. The preventative worked. The Helleboric plague disappeared.

Here we must consider context. When the Incarnate disavowed his wisdom and his luck, claiming the cure was Sorah's, and Sorah's alone—we must remember how exhausted he was from his journey, how overwhelmed with the stress of curing the capital in an organized way, descending through the ranks from first to twelfth, and down to the boiling unranked below. The Incarnate had to manage Sorah Tehn, who kept sneaking out at night to dispense the cure, out of sequence, in unauthorized districts. If the Incarnate made any peculiar statements at the time, rest assured that it was due to the depletion of his mortal energy.

And if, on occasion, he still makes some startling declarations, the blame lies entirely with Sorah Tehn, and her whiskey.

Undoubtedly driven by envy, and a burning sense of her substandard abilities, the witch brought the whiskey to his chambers. Liquor wraps a veil of desire over the unloveliest of forms; only in this way could Sorah Tehn hope to tempt a living god into indecorousness. When the Incarnate proudly refused her she fled, leaving the whiskey behind. The Incarnate is certainly entitled to drink this whiskey, if he chooses. In small quantities, the liquor lights a candle in the heart, melting illness and weariness throughout the body. But, like all medicines and all pleasures, it can be dangerous in larger doses, an inferno of unsatisfiable desire.

Clearly, the Incarnate has been attempting to master the whiskey's effects on his mortal frame. Who is the Incarnate, who is the God with Two Faces, if not the representative of balance and sober moderation, the bulwark of civilization against the tangled chaos that beckons beyond the sun and moon in the branches of the Celestial Tree? As such, any comments he may have made under the influence of the witch's whiskey should be considered a form of the cosmic chaos as he strives to achieve mastery over it. If his words seem strangled, if they bear no resemblance to the holy syllables that once descended from his mellifluous throat, transfigured by the monks-of-the-record into deep engravings on obelisks of marble and sandstone—let these phrases fade, as the monks-of-the-record have done. Let these ugly words flutter away on the wind where they must scatter and disperse.

Bored clerks and courtiers parrot everything they hear—they are pretty as princesses, and every bit as useless. I will set down a few of these phrases now, not on stone but on mortal paper, so that I may refute them one by one. Yes, under the influence of the hellish whiskey, the Incarnate has "confessed" he never cured Admiral Rho. (Again, I quote this only so we may know its falseness, and avoid the error of repeating it.) When you hear the Incarnate declare that he only waved his hands and mumbled phrases from the Twelve Burning Texts until the admiral believed so strongly in the cure that he leapt up out of his chair and broke his head on the flagstones—refuse to hear, refuse to believe, let the words pass over you as breath and whiskey fumes. Admiral Rho rose from his chair too rapidly, too joyously. He abandoned the dignity of his office, and above all, his sacred duty to fleet and king.

As the death of Admiral Rho directly preceded the Scarlet Emperor's invasion, the Incarnate has taken to blaming himself for that as well. At times—it burns my heart to write this —he has even denied his greatest act.

When the Incarnate claims he was, in fact, fleeing to Mazarine with saddlebags full of gold; when he says the Scarlet Emperor's fleet sank in a sudden storm, a random display of nature's will, and not his own (as if there could be a separation!) —simply recall Sorah Tehn and her muddling whiskey. In this matter, even the King has spoken against the Incarnate, quoting the twenty-fourth of the Rational Dignities, which cautions against excessive self-effacement. The Ecclesiast of Brenin has written an eloquent pamphlet, respectfully agreeing with His Majesty but also noting a relevant passage in the Twelve Burning Texts, which describes humility as the mark of the divine. "What could be humbler," the Ecclesiast has written, "then the denial of great deeds? What could be holier than the denial of holiness?"

The Incarnate, in his battle with the whiskey, seems to take no notice of the debate that seethes around him. Within the haze of liquor, he's backtracked further over his life, saying it was a mistake, a cruel and terrible mistake, to alienate the princess and send her into the arms of the Scarlet Emperor. But no one who remembers the princess will agree. She was from birth a violent-tempered brat, more interested in duels than dresses, and by sending her across the sea the Incarnate did his best to tame her wildness and to force her to appreciate her position. And if her daughter, the so-called Obsidian Empress, the Lioness of Oxara, if she's really accomplished everything that myth-making says she has—forged a new covenant with her rebellious provinces, "liberated" our colonies in Eschik, conquered the Seven Archipelagoes, and all before the age of twenty-one—well, even if true, no one can blame the Incarnate. If a mother warps the mind of her daughter, teaching her the ways of war-making and treachery, do we blame the gods or the woman? We know our princess raised her daughter in hate. We know she tutored the girl in politics and strategy. And then our princess decided to launch an invasion and die, possibly on purpose, just to give her daughter a reason, a weapon, a shining banner in the sky of her presumptive destiny.

I have no fear of this new girl Empress, and you, my readers, shouldn't either. In the stewpot of rumors that is this city, the most outrageous by far is the one about the Obsidian Empress's fleet. Obviously, the new imperial fleet disappeared because it sank in a storm. The ships the Incarnate mentioned in the confusion of whiskey must have been the daughter's, not the father's. On this matter, our admirals are in consensus. We must strenuously refute this fantasy that thousands and thousands of ships somehow evaded our scouts, swinging around and landing in the deepest south, on the edge of the crippling ice.

Listen to this wild nonsense, these blubbering myths, all doom and disaster! The Obsidian Empress survived the sea. The Obsidian Empress brokered a secret treaty with our vassal kingdoms in the south. The Obsidian Empress and her army race up the steppes even now on the backs of borrowed giants! Beasts the world has never seen, has never even imagined! And, scraping the clouds on the back of these beasts which loom taller than a villa of the fifth rank, this infernal army ascends the southern foothills to fall like an avalanche on our nation, very soon, any day now in fact!

Such bizarre tactics couldn't be attempted, let alone succeed. Our generals declare it beyond the scope of Measurable Truth, and therefore utterly impossible. And even if, someday, this girl empress succeeds in landing on our shores through some miracle of luck and prideful exuberance—well, we needn't fear. We're nothing like the other nations that have fallen—or, may have fallen—to her black-and-gold banner. We're blessed. We have the Incarnate.

Remember this when you repeat the rumor that the monks chose wrongly forty years ago; or, that in choosing a single Incarnate they've never chosen rightly at all. If that were true, then our noble clerics would, eventually, have realized their mistake. There would have been direct and unambiguous signs, carefully noted in the annals by the monks of Brenin.

We know what we need to know. We exist within the spectrum allowed by Measurable Truth. We know that once every hundred years the God with Two Faces condescends to walk among us in human form, and everyone who has seen the Incarnate enthroned in golden glory in the valley of Brenin must fall to their knees, stunned in sober silence at the grace of the gods, the beneficence of their gifts!

The witch has no sense of Measurable Truth. She couldn't bear the divinity of this city or the purity of the Incarnate. When she fled I pursued, capturing her along the highway. For all her vaunted power, she was easy to imprison and drag back to the capital in chains. Her acts-against-the-faith were too numerous to be counted. The only appropriate punishment was execution.

Those who bleat against my actions sound like the witch's pet goat, whining and sly, ever concealing their true purpose, their true hunger. They hate the world-as-it-is; they want to burn, to destroy, to create a world-that-is-not. They are in love with wreckage. They believe our nation is evil, and deserves an evil fate. In the twisted caverns of their hearts they love the Obsidian Empress; they desire to be conquered, seduced, enslaved at her feet. When they describe the cities the Empress has razed, the ancient libraries she's destroyed, the shrines and temples broken and dismembered—they speak not in warning, but in lust. Nothing could be more decadent than the love of ruins. They want to see our culture relegated to a golden past, so they may have the joy of mourning it, and themselves. They want to compose a romantic elegy for the Forty-Seven Rational Dignities. They want to watch our nation burn, and toast their sorrow in the ashes.

You may ask—I know many of you have been waiting to ask, chewing your tongues in your haste—why, if the witch is so powerless, so meaningless, so crushed by chains and whips and irons, did she manage to avoid her fate? It was no failure of mine. She escaped due to an unaccountable laziness on the part of a few miserable guards. Who falls asleep in the brightest part of the day, in the middle of a moving army? Who lets a prisoner drop out of a locked carriage and escape without being seen, naked and barefoot through the grass? These miserable guards say it was as though night suddenly fell upon them, a cloudy night of sleepy blindness. Let me assure you: they have been justly beaten and dismissed.

I've heard that the witch has since returned to Fal Lanrei. The Incarnate has ordered all inspectors-of-the-faith to cease pursuit; we will of course obey. Unlike some members of the court, we understand our place in relation to holy authority —as lesser pieces on a chessboard, embodiments of eternal will.

In his wisdom, the Incarnate has chosen to teach Sorah Tehn, not to punish her. Every day he sends the witch letters in which he must describe her moral failings and urge a brighter path. And she must remain a stubborn student, because he keeps sending letters. Certain courtiers whisper that he begs her to return, with increasing desperation.

Lies wither, like birch paper in a brazier. Wisdom remains, preserved forever in the light of Measurable Truth, inscribed in the annals by the monks of Brenin. If, on some distant day, Brenin should fall, its monks slain, its treasures stolen, its libraries incinerated…but that is utter lunacy. What could be madder than to believe that Truth—Measurable Truth—will not endure forever?

To those among my readers who openly hope for the witch to return and somehow mount a defense against this brilliant girl empress who isn't a threat, who isn't racing toward our southern border with some mighty army on the backs of demon beasts, to sack our towns and burn our libraries, rob our harvest and smash our obelisks—lose your hope. I know Sorah Tehn. She will ignore the Incarnate, no matter how eloquent his persuasions, how manifestly correct his lessons. She was trained only in minor magics, and knows no spells that would help against any invasion, even if it were impending. We can imagine the half-literate scribe attempting to read the Incarnate's letters to her, even now, as she gazes down the mountain through the rosy haze, westward across the plains toward the capital which she can't see, can't even comprehend in its brightness, the beacon of heaven upon earth. She's too corrupt to risk herself among the righteous. She will never again descend her mountain. She will never return from Fal Lanrei.

Quietus

Lola Lindle

"I am the Pirate Queen, and you will never defeat me!" Thia shouted from a large, leaf-covered branch, eight feet off the ground.

"You will never win, pirate queen. The Lady Knight shall always triumph," cried Ryia. Thia battled her six-year-old twin with magick and with wooden swords almost every day in light-speckled, deciduous woods that felt more like home than the house they shared with their parents. Mother encouraged the twins to play outside because it kept "the Silver Witches out of the house and out of her hair," a statement made frequently.

Leaping from the leafy branch into the open air, Thia held out her hands and sensed the ground with her fingers. Using this feeling, she pushed off the ground still feet below her and kept herself aloft. She laughed. By continuing to apply pressure through her fingers, she found she could stay up as long as she pleased.

Yearning to try this new trick, Ryia launched herself into

the air. After thrusting her hands too hard and shooting twigs at the ground, she was finally able to duplicate her sister's discovery. Thia squealed with glee. They spent the rest of the day hovering through the woods shooting twigs at each other. Bursting with pride, Thia, the faster of the two, sprinted ahead through the forest to tell her parents about their new talent. Her father, always proud of these new powers, smiled and hugged them both. Their mother only smiled at them.

"Papa, will you tell us the story?" Ryia pleaded with big eyes after they had gotten ready for bed.

"Please, please, Papa?" Thia added. Papa chuckled as he sat down on their bed.

"All right, all right you two," Papa cleared his throat and began. "Many, many years ago, when Kratha was a Kingdom-"

"The first Argentate was born!" Ryia interjected.

"That's right. To the King and Queen. The Silver Prince, as they called him, grew up powerful but he never learned to control his Argentate magicks. He hurt many people as he grew up because of it. He was wild and spiteful. Without the King's knowledge, he led the army to war with the Srila Queendom to the south, because the princess had refused his advances. His untrained powers killed many of the Srilan army and the Krathan army as well. When he returned, the King had no choice but to punish him like any of his other Army commanders. The Magistrate sentenced—"

"The Prince to death." Thia finished in a scary tone.

Papa chuckled, "Yes. The King and Queen were devastated, but could not overrule the Magistrate. The moment the sword severed the prince's neck—"

"The King and Queen were struck down by his magicks." Ryia shook her head as she spoke.

"And the Kingdom only survived because his twelve-year-old sister took up the crown and remade Kratha into a

Queendom to prevent such masculine destruction from happening again. Since then, Argentates have been seen as signs of destruction or death. The new Queen made it mandatory to send Argentates to the academies so that they learn how to control their power and to use it wisely. She also made it illegal to kill Argentate babies. Now it is time to go to sleep, my silver ladies." Papa kissed both of them on the head and snuffed the candle.

Later that night, Thia awakened to yelling. She heard her parents arguing about the girls and their magicks. Thia only understood part of their conversation, but it was enough.

"Why do you keep telling them that story? It only reinforces that everyone hates them." Thia could hear tears in her mother's voice.

"They have a right to know why everyone hates them. It isn't their fault." Papa was rarely angry, but he sounded it now.

"I know that. Don't you think I know that? I can't blame them. But everyone blames me. Everything that goes wrong in the village is my fault because I had twin Argentates. They can't take it out on children, but they can take it out on me. On us. We lost our farm. We lost our way of life."

"They are all fools. I won't send my children away when they aren't even old enough to remember that we love them. I don't care what the Seneschal says. We will send them when they are older."

"They are becoming dangerous; their powers grow every day. They surpassed my powers when they were three." Her mother cried.

"They are not hurting anyone. They are learning with each other—"

"And you are encouraging them. We should send them to the Seneschal now before they have an accident." Thia heard a door slam, and the voices were too faint to hear more.

Thia knew their Argentate magick was different from other children, but she'd never seen it as dangerous before. She decided from that night on, she and Ryia would have to hide their new powers from their parents.

***

"Mama," Thia asked her mother before dinner a few nights later when Ryia was out of earshot, "why did we leave the village?"

"Well, we lost the farm, so we had to find a new home."

"Was it because of us being Argentates?"

Her mother sighed and reached out for her eight-year-old and pulled her into her lap. Thia could count on her hand the number of times her mother touched her in the last few years. She shook with the thrill of the touch.

"Yes. A single Argentate birth is seen as a bad thing. As far as I know, twin Argentates have never happened before. People were scared you would destroy the town. They threatened to kill you both when you were born, if not for the laws preventing the slaying of Argentates, I'm sure they would have done it. Understand, it's not you and your sister they fear, but what you represent. Change. Power. Uncontrolled Magicks."

Thia nodded. "Do you fear us, Mama?"

Mama's eyes widened. "I love you and your sister with my whole heart."

"But are you afraid of us?"

"You aren't old enough to understand my full answer, sweetness," Mama hugged Thia to her. "I don't fear you or your sister. I know you wouldn't hurt someone intentionally. But an accident is always possible. And to the town, they only see your silver hair. So, your father was forced to sell our farm. Now he sells firewood. My apothecary shop used to earn a good living. Now, I barely have any customers, and we barely have any food. What I do fear is that their superstitions will be the death of us. Do you understand?"

Thia nodded. *Why are we such a curse?* "But Mama, why are Argentates forced to go to the academies and through the Quietus?"

At this, Mama paused for a long time before answering. "The academies are there to teach you to control your powers, which are much greater than anyone else's. The Quietus is required for Argentates if they survive the academies. Argentates are very rare still. There have not been any in the last eighteen years." Mama stopped and looked at Thia. She squeezed her tightly before continuing. "Most initiates do not choose to compete in the Quietus. They leave after the sixth confrontation. The Quietus is meant for those ambitious enough to train with and eventually replace the current Queen's Maaj and Queen's Champion. Only two initiates have chosen to compete in the last 15 years. No Argentates have ever completed the Quietus or been the Champion or Maaj."

"So, every Argentate sent to the academies has died. Why does the Queen want us all dead?" Thia suddenly felt her life was meant to be very short.

"I don't think she does, Thia. I think she wants to prevent any Argentates from following in the Silver Prince's footsteps. We are all afraid of war and we are all afraid of how powerful some Argentates can be," Mama stroked Thia's hair. "Enough for now, it's time to eat."

***

"Pirate Queen, the Lady Knight has come to forsake you." There was a pause. "Come on Thia, play with me." Ryia waited. And waited.

"Not today."

"But why? We haven't played this game in forever. It used

to be your favorite. You always love capturing the Knight and turning me to piracy. Let's see if the Knight will win, seeing as the Pirate Queen is rusty."

Ryia's goad worked, as usual, she always could push Thia's buttons.

"Fine," Thia sighed. "I am the Pirate Queen, and you will never defeat me!" Thia shouted from out of the sky, as she floated over the ground from her hiding place. She knew every word of this game and sometimes longed for a new one, but this had been their favorite. This time was different though. Ryia had gotten much stronger with her magicks.

Ryia blasted into the air to attack her. "You can never escape, Pirate Queen, for the Lady Knight shall always win!"

The glee in Ryia's voice made Thia smile. They played and fought with old wooden weapons they'd made when they were small. The mock battle lasted for a long time, much longer than normal. Neither Thia nor Ryia could get the upper hand; they moved through the forest recklessly and loudly.

"Girls," Papa's voice shouted unexpectedly from below. "Don't get too close to the road."

Thia held up her hand to Ryia, and they paused their game to see where their father was down below. He was chopping up firewood to sell in town just beneath where they were playing. Thia hadn't noticed how far they'd traveled during the battle. They had started deep in the woods, but now they were almost to the edge of the birch forest. Neither had been paying attention to anything other than the battle.

"We promise, Da," Thia called to him. Ryia blew a clod of dirt into her face unexpectedly and let out a laugh as Thia coughed and spluttered. Their battle resumed.

Thia climbed a tree to get a better angle. Ryia shook the branch under Thia's legs, knocking her off balance and out of the tree. Thia thrust towards the ground to stop herself, but her panic caused thick pointed branches to fly out of her hands instead.

Ryia screamed.

Thia caught herself just before she struck the ground and lifted her head in time to see her father fall. She sprinted the few yards to him. Her unintentional spikes had impaled him in three places.

"Papa!" Thia shouted. Ryia joined Thia kneeling by their father, and he reached out and took both of their hands. Thia cursed herself that she never thought to learn healing magicks. Now, she could only look on as her father took his last breath. Ryia wouldn't let go of his hand. Her lips were moving; she seemed to have been speaking for some time, but Thia hadn't heard a word. Thia reached up and closed his eyes. Ryia finally tore her gaze away from their father's face and up into her sister's eyes.

"What did I do?" Thia asked, plaintively.

"What did we do?" Her sister responded.

"Girls? Roderick?" Mama called from the house. "I'm back."

Thia couldn't bring herself to answer. After a time, she heard her mother's voice calling from the woods, then the clearing. Thia clearly heard when her mother broke into a run.

Ryia was still holding their father's hand, and Thia had moved around to sit by her sister as their mother approached. Mama sank to her knees and touched her husband's face. She looked from her husband to her girls to the wooden spikes. A change seemed to come over her mother's face, an absence of emotion more frightening than rage or weeping. Thia pulled her sister a few steps away from their father. Their mother suddenly yanked the spears from his body. She stared at the sharp and bloody points for a long moment before raising her eyes to the twins.

"What happened?" Her voice wracked with grief.

"I'm so sorry, Mama," Thia cried.

"You did this?" Her mother was in disbelief.

"It was an accident, Mama," Ryia cried.

Their mother broke then. She began sobbing, but her tears quickly faded and turned to a horrible, mirthless laugh. "They were right. They were all right," she said. Then she raised the bloody stick she still held and swung it at the girls. Ryia screamed as the blunt side of the stick whacked her in the shoulder.

"Mama, stop," Thia commanded. Her mother froze mid-swing and looked at Thia with emptiness in her eyes. Thia ran to Ryia's side. "We didn't mean for this to happen Mama. We love Papa. We love you. We won't let this happen again."

Her mother snapped at this. "Again? You won't have another chance to let this happen again. Obviously I can't teach you. You surpassed my skills long ago. Should I have sent you to the Seneschal? No one would teach two curses like you." Their mother seemed to deflate at this, but as she looked at Papa's body, her anger returned quickly.

"I should have let them kill you. I wanted to drown you, but Roderick wouldn't have it."

Thia held her mother again with magick as she raised the bloody stick again.

Mama strained against Thia's magick and broke free. "He's not here to protect you anymore." She ran at the girls, ready to skewer them on the bloody stick.

"No, Mama," Ryia cried as Thia raised her hand. A half breath later, Ryia raised hers in the same way. Sharp, pointed sticks flew from their hands and embedded in their mother's chest as she ran at them. Thia lowered her hand and Ryia wrapped her arms around herself.

"Mama was gone, Ryia." Thia explained. "Mama was gone already." After a while, Ryia pulled Thia toward the thing that used to be their mother and pulled the sticks from her body. The two girls used magicks to dig graves for their parents. Thia could see the silent tears fall down Ryia's face as they worked and said goodbye. Then Ryia led her sister away from the carnage, and they walked back to the house, together.

"What do we do now?" This asked.

"We wait. Someone will come for us."

"But Papa? It was an accident. And Mama. She went mad, didn't she?"

"Yes. Mama went mad. Now we are all we have left." Ryia hugged her.

***

"It won't be so bad," the Constable reassured the two girls. When Thia and Ryia did not warm to his smile, it seemed to fall from his face, leaving behind a blank expression and a bushy mustache. Thia shuddered and Ryia put her arm around her.

Thia clutched at her sister as they rode in silence in the sheriff's carriage away from their home in the woods. Thia looked out the window. All of the familiar trees were beginning to recede, giving way to the foreign farmland and the outskirts of the town where they were headed. The two had spent the last three weeks all alone in the woods. They had not spoken much, but when they did, it was about their parents and what had happened. They were both determined, nothing like that would ever happen again. They were resigned to their training now.

Not wanting to see her beloved forest disappear, Thia turned to the inside of the carriage itself. The interior was plush with a soft dark blue fabric that felt like the underside of a leaf beneath her left hand. There were white curtains pulled apart at the center of both windows, displaying the outside, but there was a pane of glass between her and fresh air. The glass may have blocked the wind, but it did nothing to keep out the cold. Thia and her sister were only wearing their thin coats and bare feet. Since their parents' deaths, Thia had done her best to keep them fed, and Ryia had kept the house warm. After Ryia had agreed, neither girl strayed far from home except to hunt and gather food. They had fended for themselves for weeks as fall faded into winter.

In the carriage, the cold crept in around them. Thia felt sure nothing good would come from this long ride with the faux-faced constable. She shivered next to Ryia; the unfamiliar landscape making her uneasy.

Thia read her sister's thoughts on her face. We are of testing age. They won't allow us to remain together. The two had talked of the Testing with their father a few times and knew that now it would be forced upon them. With our parents dead, they will blame us for everything that goes wrong. Mother said there had never been twin Argentates before in all of Kratha. It is better to be separated than killed. Thia closed her eyes and touched her forehead to her sister's. She could feel her tears begin to fall. It is better to be separated than killed. Isn't it? Thia felt Ryia's fear as she shook slightly while she held her hands. Tear after tear fell onto their clutched hands. Ryia began humming to soothe them both.

The ride seemed over too quickly. Thia and Ryia were forced into the town Seneschal's office. The sheriff was inside with the Seneschal. Sheriff Clarice had known the girls their whole life, and she had never been scared of the silver-haired twins. Even when the town had turned against them, the sheriff had always been kind.

Ryia ran to the sheriff now and threw her arms around her waist. "Mama and Papa are dead, Clarice."

The Sheriff patted Ryia on the back as she looked at Thia, who came to hug her as well.

"I know little sterlings. That's why you're here. It's time to be tested. I know your Da wanted to delay your testing, but now he's gone, and we haven't a choice. Every Argentate must attend an academy by the rule of law." Clarice gently nudged Thia back and pulled Ryia off her as well. She maneuvered them to a chair big enough for both to share.

"Girls, this is Seneschal Lytton, she will be your tester. You will take turns and the Seneschal will give you your aptitude assignments. Thia, you'll go first."

Something in Clarice's voice made Thia pause. The sheriff was polite and kind, but Thia saw at that moment that the woman would not fight for them. Thia saw the veiled disgust on her face; she wanted them gone as much as everyone else did. She'd just hid it better than most, until now. Thia met Ryia's bright green eyes. Ryia nodded at her sadly; she'd seen the truth in the sheriff's face as well. Thia embraced her sister, the only one who would never stop loving her, and then walked quietly into the Seneschal's office.

The test was easy. The Seneschal used minor magicks to create realistic obstacles like crossing river rapids, puzzles to test strategy, and magickal opponents to battle. All of these were designed to test a potential initiate's magickal abilities as well as her physical abilities and fighting skills. For an Argentate, there was no challenge in it. She and her sister created more dangerous and challenging scenarios every time they played Pirates and Knights. As the test continued, it focused more on magicks than physical challenges. When it was over, Thia was dismissed. She bowed to the Seneschal and left the office.

Ryia sat on a chair facing the door. Her face was smooth and her eyes closed. She looked peaceful, but Thia knew her better. That was Ryia's listening face, she had heard it all. Thia touched her sister's hand, causing her to open her eyes. They embraced again. Without a word, Thia sat in her sister's place in much the same position: body taught, eyes closed, face smooth, and listened.

When the Seneschal dismissed her sister, Thia took a deep breath. From what she had heard, Ryia's test had been very different from her own. Why? She wondered. Ryia sat down beside her and clasped her hand as they awaited their fates. When the Seneschal came out of her office, she wasted no time or emotion on her declaration.

"Both academies train three to four initiates of each level each season to master magicks or warrior skills. The Maaj Academy has four confrontations before the Quietus. Many students drop out after the first or second confrontation to take lesser magickal positions, such as apothecary, healer, curse breaker, metal-charmer, et cetera. In the Quietus, only four initiates out of the original thirty participated. For those who do not have the talent, the teachers do not recommend attempting the Quietus. Consequences for such rashness are final."

Thia knew the schools were brutal, but she wasn't prepared to learn that more than half the class didn't make it. She shuddered and took comfort in her sister's arm tightening around her.

The Seneschal continued, "The Conscript Academy has six confrontations before the Quietus. Fewer students leave, and more give the supreme sacrifice due to the aggressiveness of the battle training. Those who leave tend toward manual labor, or, if they have some minor magickal abilities, they may apprentice with lesser magickal positions. There were four conscript initiates in the last Quietus out of the twenty original students. Both schools are demanding. Those able to win the Quietus are named the new Queen's Maaj or Queen's Champion. No one has survived the Quietus in the last fifteen years."

"Thia Hawtrey," the Seneschal turned to Thia, "as is typical of Argentates, you have shown an aptitude for both magicks and conscription. However, you show particular talent with magicks. You are assigned to the Maaj Academy, to report immediately as the semester has just begun."

"Ryia Hawtrey," she turned to Thia's sister, "as is typical of Argentates, you have shown an aptitude for both magicks and conscription. However, you show particular talent with conscription. You are assigned to the Conscription Academy, to report immediately as the semester has also just begun."

The Seneschal then addressed them both, "As Argentates, you will likely be a favored target for the other initiates. Many are killed during their academy years in accidents. You will be kept in separate accommodations, as the academies do not want to inflict the nature of your Curse on the other initiates more than is necessary. You will not be permitted to leave the academies until completing all confrontations due to your innate and powerful abilities."

She looked from one to the other before continuing, and then gave the customary initiate farewell, "May your strength see you through the confrontations until the Quietus takes you."

And that was it. The twins were to be split up. More than likely, they would never see each other again; one or both probably would die. Thia pulled her sister into a hard embrace. Too soon, the faux-faced constable and the Sheriff were pulling them apart. Thia sobbed as Ryia cried out for her. Kicking at the constable, Ryia ran to her twin and stroked her face, putting her forehead to her sisters. "We will see each other again." The promise felt empty to Thia, but her sister was trying to give her hope, give both of them hope. The constable gripped Ryia's arm again. He and the Sheriff pulled them apart and they were led off to their separate fates.

***

Thia was conscious of Maaj Highmore watching her as she tried to meditate before her Quietus. She stood before the giant door that would open onto the confrontation field. It had been eight years since she had been sent to the Maaj Academy, but today she felt just like that little girl. She knew that she was the best of the Queen's Maaj initiates, but her confidence was quiet today, leaving her feeling petite, unassuming, and seemingly meek. She had tied her silver hair back in the black scarf to hide its color. This had served her well in the past; she had used her hair as a weapon of its own, to distract and frighten her opponents. Would it work for her today?

Thia kept her eyes closed, lost in memory to help calm her breathing. This had never been her strong suit. Living a tumultuous life, Thia had a turbulent mind to match, flitting from memory to memory unable to find anything close to calming. She wondered if her sister had survived the Conscript academy and then alighted on a long-buried time, a sun-dappled forest floor, a warm breeze across her skin, and a high tinkling laugh caught her notice, niggling from a faint, early memory. Thia smiled despite her current predicament. She had very few memories of that time in her life. Most initiates didn't, as they left home at such a young age. With her unpleasant present, she worked hard to bury them because the memories pained her. But not today. She reveled in the memory, sword fighting near the river, soaring through the trees, and casting spells. Surrounded by an evergreen forest and silence, save for the sounds they had made. It had been peaceful and happy, but it did not last overly long. She wanted to stay lost in this memory, as it was what must drive her today. Never before had she been so close to her goal.

"Today is either the beginning or the end, is it not, Thia?" The Queen's Maaj had startled her out of her reverie.

Thia started and opened her eyes. "Yes, Maaj." She had

been ripped away from her memory and it felt just as it had that day ten years ago. Pain momentarily flitted through her usually impassive face. So quickly, it might not have happened at all.

Lady Highmore came to stand by Thia's side directly in front of the doors currently barred shut. No noise had come from behind them all day as the other initiates completed their Quietus. This distressed Thia more than any noise possible. Thia swallowed her fear and looked up at her luminaries' weathered face. Maaj Highmore was the oldest Queen's Maaj that had ever been. At 43, she was well battered and beaten by the castings and conflicts of the Krathan Queendom. She always looked worried, but today the lines on her face looked deeper, more inset. Thia knew from the Maaj's face that none of the other initiates had survived. She was the only one left for the final challenge.

"Maaj?"

"Yes, Thia." Lady Highmore turned to her.

"How did you survive the final confrontation?" This was apparently not the question that Maaj had been expecting and it took her a moment to answer.

"To this day, Thia, I do not know. I don't remember thinking at all, just following my instincts. I was gravely wounded, but I walked out of these doors unaided. May you hope to do the same." Uncharacteristically, the Maaj reached out to Thia and squeezed her arm. Unused to physical contact, Thia felt discomfited by it. But Lady Highmore quickly released her and walked away, climbing the small staircase to the right of the doors so that she could watch the Quietus with the Queen's Champion. Thia was left alone.

Thia reached for a casting stone from a leather holder on her calf. Her belted white overdress split at her legs for ease of movement and expertly hid her power stones while keeping them accessible over her leather leggings. Patting the various pockets in her leather vest for all her necessary pre-made items, Thia ran through several prepared spells, but much like Lady Highmore, she usually depended on instinct rather than preparation for her battles.

Convinced she was ready, Thia pulled the bell chain next to the oversized doors and heard a low bell toll. A moment later, she heard another deep bell toll and knew that the doors would open. She awaited her final task as an initiate: The Quietus Confrontation.

The oversized doors opened slowly, the field before Thia filled with a magick fog designed to lift once both initiates entered the arena and took their positions. There was usually no audience for these confrontations, save for the Queen's Champion and Maaj. No one needed to see the brutality first hand.

Thia walked forward as the door closed behind her. She hung her head so that she might keep her calm. Abruptly, the magickal fog lifted and Thia could see her opponent clearly. The conscript initiate waited, silent and still, in full, well-worn armor, sword and knife strapped at her side, for the fighting gong. Thia could just make out bright green eyes peering out of the helmet's visor, but what drew her attention were the shiny silver threads against the dull metal of the armor. *Do I see this right? Is my mind playing tricks on me?*

The gong sounded, loud and keening. It ripped through Thia as she reached up and pulled off the black cloth covering her head, and her straight silver hair flowed down over her shoulders, ending near to her waist. She tucked the black cloth into her pouch at her waist and took a small step toward the conscript. The conscript mimicked her slight step, not a counter, but an imitation. Both initiates hesitated. Slowly, Thia raised her head, her hair falling back to reveal her face.

The conscript started forward again but stopped. She reached up and removed her helmet. Thia looked into a version of her appearance. She should have expected this.

"Thia," the conscript whispered.

"Ryia," Thia spoke her sister's name like a caress.

Though only one of them was to survive or none during the Quietus, no power would make Thia hurt her twin.

Ryia sheathed her sword and dagger and ran to her sister, who also had begun to run toward her. Ryia embraced her sister in her strong arms. The gong sounded again, a reminder of their purpose. Ryia broke the hug and looked up to where the Queen's Maaj and the Queen's Champion watched them. Lady Nayda's face was red with anger and the Queen's Maaj was glaring at them both. Ryia could feel her power coalescing. This had been the plan, she realized. The Champion had pushed and prodded where she could to make this moment happen. From the look on the Maaj's face, she had too. They had wanted the twin Argentates to destroy each other. Lady Nayda had never made a secret of her hatred of Ryia, but because of the laws, could not outright kill Ryia herself. This was the only way to get rid of them both. Ryia had been silly to think that if she had won the Quietus that the Queen would ever welcome an Argentate at her side.

The Queen's Champion shouted over the distance, "You must fight to the death."

"And if we do not, Lady Nayda?" Asked Ryia, her face hardening.

"Then you will both be killed at our hands."

"How many other students did you kill to get us here, Ysaulte?" Thia bit back, using the Queen's Maaj's first name was a sign of disrespect.

Lady Highmore nodded, "None of them would have made it this far. But you can go no further, either of you."

"Then kill us if you can, Cindra," Ryia pulled her sword and dagger from their scabbards and almost automatically used magicks to place protective spells over her and her sister.

Out of the corner of her eyes, Ryia saw Thia holding a gemstone and taking a defensive posture.

Thia felt the magicks settle over her like a blanket. Her sister still had considerable power despite the strict rules of Conscription preventing their use. Thia could feel the familiarity of the nearness of her sister, and as they readied for battle, she felt a glimmer of hope.

In the blink of an eye, the Queen's fiercest fighters were in front of them, mounting their attacks. Thia let her magicks take over, feeling her way through the battle. Not hampered by only using magicks as had been required in the other confrontations, she struck out at Lady Highmore, with a knife that she had hidden in her vest. Thia knew that it had been nearly 15 years since any large-scale war where the Maaj had had to face any physical attacks in battle and was probably unaccustomed to switching from magickal to physical defense. Thia thought she had the Maaj at a disadvantage, and after a few well-placed slices, she felt confident.

Ryia faced Lady Nayda, the last Champion to win a Quietus, in combat. This was not a test that any initiate was ever expected to take. Facing the Queen's Champion was considered suicide. Ryia knew her strength, knew when every muscle would hold or give, and knew how to use her magicks to compensate for her weaknesses. She no longer had to be subtle with her magicks, so she called upon all of her powers, both physical and magickal. Her body crackled with protections, as did her sister's. Ryia did not know if she would be able to best her teacher but she had no choice. The air shimmered around them as hits were deflected. Ryia struck with precision and slid from blocking to attacking and back with only one thought...*Thia and I must live.*

Thia was amazed at her prowess as she battled with Lady Highmore. The protections from her sister couldn't deflect every attack, but Thia was able to handle the rest. Thia acted entirely on instinct, blocking magickal attacks as she created and struck with her own. But she was tiring. This was not like fighting other initiates. She now understood why Lady Highmore was the most powerful Maaj in Kratha. As the battle continued, Thia could hear her sister and the Champion fighting, but did not dare to look, lest she give the Maaj an opening. But her moment of distraction took care of that for her. The Maaj struck her with a curse that tossed Thia back into the arena wall. She crumpled to her knees. She was able to maintain her blocking spells, but could not catch her breath. The Maaj did not stop with her attacks. Thia struggled to hold her protections as she struggled to breathe.

Thia knew now that she was no match for the Maaj. She was barely able to keep her blocking protections up and though she had caught her breath, she could not stand under the weight of the magicks being thrown at her. Thia looked for her sister, but couldn't find her. She could still feel her magicks flowing over her continuing their protection, so she knew that she was alive. Thia's thoughts were flicking from spell to spell to find something to save her. All she could do was find the flow of magicks. It was flowing like a river within her. It was not until today that she had ever felt the undercurrent within the river. Once discovered, she could hardly see how she had failed to notice it before. As she pulled on this undercurrent, she could feel the magickal forces around her: in her sister, in the Maaj, even in the air around them. As she explored this new magick, Thia could feel her protections beginning to weaken. She turned her focus completely on the undercurrent that was the Queen's Maaj and pulled. She felt more than saw that she was tearing magicks from Lady Highmore, sapping her and stripping her protections. Thia was slowly able to stand as she continued to pull on the Maaj's undercurrent. It took a while, long moments passed as Thia broke through the Maaj's protections. The Maaj staggered, giving Thia an opening. She spoke a word of power that she had never been taught; it felled her teacher, who had no magicks left to protect herself.

Thia let her protections go and stumbled over to her fallen teacher. The woman had helped Thia to develop her talent and control. The sting of betrayal was harsh but Thia had never forgotten what she had learned as a child. Even those who claimed to love her could never look past her silver hair, not even her own mother. Thia turned to see how Ryia fared in her fight. She was struck by how fluid and beautiful her sister's fighting was, like a dancer. Her face, however, was a mask without emotion.

Ryia made slow headway at tiring her opponent, striking small victories and being struck in return, but she mostly succeeded in fending off attacks. Her magicks had saved her more than once during this fight. When Lady Nayda began to wane, Ryia was still feeling fresh, but she was still wary of her teacher. Ryia launched into a series of fierce and fast attacks that utilized her whole body, flipping, and leaping to keep the Queen's Champion off balance. Ryia felt a boost of energy as her sister fed her strange-feeling magicks. Ryia didn't even know that could happen, but it gave her an extra boost. This distracted her for a second and Lady Nayda struck a long slice along her abdomen. Ryia ignored the flare of pain, increased her speed of attacks, and varied her repetitions to confuse the Champion. When Cindra fell, Ryia was upon her. Sword to her throat, Ryia looked into the Champion's eyes.

"You are beaten. Do you yield?" She knew what the answer would be, but Ryia had learned much from the Queen's Champion, despite her all too apparent hatred.

"I will never allow you to take my place," Lady Nayda spat at her.

Ryia shook her head but plunged the sword into the Queen's Champion neck. After a moment, she looked for Thia to see her standing over the Queen's Maaj body. Ryia went to her sister and took her hand.

"You're bleeding," Ryia told her.

"So are you."

"Are you all right?"

"I'll be fine," she responded, but she winced as she moved. Probably a broken rib, Ryia assessed. They would both survive.

"Me too," Ryia said.

The two stood there silently looking at their teachers, felled by their hands.

This is not a victory, Ryia thought. *This is merely an end for two masters who could not look past their superstitions.*

"We have to leave now," Thia told her.

"Yes, the whole Queendom will be after us," Ryia agreed.

"Yes, and without their Maaj and Champion, they will be looking to kill us." Thia paused and looked at her sister. She pulled her into a painful hug.

"Thank you, Ryia, for keeping your promise." Thia released her and smiled.

Ryia smiled back, "I could never leave you. Look at the trouble you get yourself into."

Withdrawal

Rook Riley

The shakes started in my stomach and spread from the inside out until my teeth chattered so hard I thought they might break, shattering into little sharp shards that would cut and bleed my mouth. Through the small observation deck windows, I could just make out the silent engines of the Autsayer boarding vessel.

The magic, my blood bond to it, should have kept us far from here. It was my damn job.

The floor buckled beneath me, sending me staggering into the bulkhead. Illusion. Damn their heks. I drove forward, sweat seeping through the fabric of my uniform and dripping from my trembling fingertips to dot the floor.

I bit my lip to keep from screaming in frustration, fighting the urge to gnaw and rip through it. My eyes were dry, swollen in their sockets to the point it was hard to blink. Early symptoms of morph exposure. I recognized them easily, but the emergency synthidote was in my quarters, out of play. The captain truly believed in it. I hadn't had the heart to tell him that it wouldn't make much of a difference. Magic addicts went feral pretty quickly and I'd probably tear through his throat before he could fetch it from my quarters.

I staggered forward, holding onto the handrails for support, pulling myself along.

The four years I'd spent drying out in the *Verslaafde*, the prison for morphetzine magic addicts, wasted. My first witnessing since the cure, and I regressed.

Oh, but damn, sobriety could just go fuck itself.

I palmed open the door.

Alarms screamed down body-strewn corridors; the walls awash in blood and gore. With comms wide open, the skittering Autsayer wailed their inhuman prayers to purify their newly conquered offering for their god. It was all I could do to force one foot in front of the other to the cargo bay. I had no intention of playing hero – not that I could. Nothing but chaos and death waited on the other side of the containment field.

And maybe within me too.

Someone, the helmsman maybe, had enough forethought to raise the containment after the Autsayer's first wave boarded, and that's what had spared us so far. Their acolytes lay in scattered piles, mingled with our dead. The size and population of *The Vlees* might work in our favor. If the Autsayer were busy killing in other parts of the ship, that meant they weren't here killing us. Their warriors hadn't breached it yet, but that containment field wouldn't hold forever. They wouldn't be satisfied with the bridge crew when there were more souls to be redeemed. With all the information the heks would get from our dead, finding us would be easy.

But all we had to do was be quick.

Oh, but sweet stars, I wanted a spell, a fix, a freaking blood-magic screw. To just peel off this fucking skin and run screaming into the arms of my Autsayer brothers!

Only some little piece of my brain was still the First Contact Specialist of The Vlees, still me. The me that had dedicated my time at detox to learning everything about the Autsayer. The me that held myself back from licking the undiluted blood of the dead off the carpet to morph myself into oblivion. The me that was still human.

Samika pressed me forward, her face buried in my back, voice vibrating through me, "Hurry, Noa. Go."

Sam. How did I forget she was here?

I stumbled, almost stepping on a dead acolyte, his only weapon, a short-bladed knife, lay bloodied at his side. I placed my finger against my lips to shush her and giggled. "They'll hear you."

Fuck. That's what was wrong! I was breathing it in.

I grabbed a reserve respirator off the wall and strapped it on, not stopping to instruct Sam or Eyman. They were fine for now. Unlike me, years of morph use hadn't bonded it to their systems on a molecular level.

With the sound of my ragged, hampered breaths in my ears, stale, dry air cleared my thoughts, cooled my brain. It was a just a stopgap. What was already in my system would take over unless I got out of here, away from all this temptation. My willpower was shit.

The emergency hatch into the cargo bay was just ahead. We could cut one of the near-planet ships bound for *Kolonie 2* loose and make it to the surface of one of these Abandoned Zone planets. How we got off that rock wouldn't matter. We'd be safe.

"Nobody else is going to die, Sam." Eyman, his voice calm, patronizing, answered. "Look, we're almost there."

I didn't waste time telling them to shut up again.

With Sam prodding me forward, I struggled to keep my balance as I stepped over a gray-skinned Autsayer laying across the entrance to the juniors' quarters.

As if it heard us, the body beneath me thrashed, the head banging into the flooring grate. Dark blood splattered the walls. Its tail, like a third skeletal hand, whipped back and forth, slamming into my leg with enough force to knock me down. I crashed down atop its prone form before I could register the pain.

"No!" the word ripping its way out of my horrified mind as I scrambled backwards on all fours, respirator mouthpiece lost. The heks controlling the dead Autsayer would try to snatch an ear, a finger, any scrap of flesh to use against us. "Don't let it touch you!"

Its eyes were closed. Black entrails leaked onto the floor from a nasty gut shot. But its hand, missing a taloned finger from the third knuckle, opened to reveal a bloody human ear.

"Fuck. They've already gotten the bridge crew," the panicked voice was barely recognizable as my own.

My whole body trembled as I scrubbed my hands on the legs of my pants. Blood magic from the inner makings of the Autsayer. Morph. My body had begged for it and now that sticky shit coated my hands. I wiped the drool away with my sleeve, dying to stick my fingers in my mouth.

"Watch out!" Eyman fired.

A hammer blow of white heat ripped through my thigh where he clipped my leg, missing the dead alien completely. I looked up from the floor to see Sam's horrified expression. She was beautiful when she was scared. Her pink cheeks. Little red mouth. The things I'd like to do to that fucking tight little hole.

I blinked. I can't beat it again.

Balling up my fist, I punched my wounded leg.

Shock. Pain. Focus. It was nothing compared to the thought that the morph had a way into my bloodstream now.

Sam shrieked and the corridor erupted with fresh screams, including mine.

To the left, another dead Autsayer, this one missing its whole hand, struggled to stand. Eyman pumped two more shots into it. Gore and boney fragments of exoskeleton exploded from its chest as it went down again.

Too late. It was too late. They were coming for us.

"Run!" I screamed. "Get to the ships, Sam. Go, Baby, go!"

Sam didn't wait. She was a blur of color moving away from danger. Away from me.

Eyman dropped down to help by slipping his arm under my shoulder and heaving me to my feet. Instinctively, I leaned into him and put weight on the injured leg. Pain blazed and I tottered on the edge of unconsciousness.

My fingers found his side. I could separate each bone from his ribcage because the morph in me wanted to hear the pop.

His voice was a hushed whisper, "Sorry about your leg, Noa, but we've got to move. It's just around the next corner."

Better that he leaves me. Better that I die now than turn into that slobbery mess of morph and violence.

"Shut up," I muttered as I hobbled beside him.

The acrid scent of an acetylene torch cutting into metal drifted into the hallway. They were coming for me.

I hid my smile behind a bloody hand. The joy I felt welling up scared the fuck out me.

Welcome, my brothers.

My office door opened and Sam snatched Eyman's arm, yanking us both into the room. My leg couldn't take it and everything went black.

The morph razored through my body with each thump of my heart. It numbed the ache. But something else coated the brain and dried out the sinuses, leaving my tongue stuck to the roof my mouth.

The chair squeaked. I opened my eyes and found Sam staring down at me where I sat in my desk chair.

"Better now, Noa?" her whisper barely carried over the alarm still screeching throughout the ship.

I shifted my weight and the seat protested again. "How about I shoot you in the leg?" I bristled, my words slurring. "Then we can see how well you handle the pain, sweetheart."

My leg was numb, deadened.

I didn't bother to whisper. The Autsayer would either hear, or they wouldn't. It didn't matter anymore. Either way, we were dead.

Sam twisted the blood-soaked shirt tourniquet around my leg tighter, and sparks lit up my vision.

"Here, let me do it." The chair squealed in protested as Eyman wrenched me around to face his bare chest.

My world blurred around the edges. Sweat beaded up on the back of my neck and I was dizzy. What had they done? There was no chance to warn Sam, who was sitting at my feet looking up at me with concern in her big brown eyes. Leaning over the arm of the chair, I dry heaved.

"Sorry," Sam smoothed my hair away from my eyes. "I didn't cut the synth. I didn't know how strong you'd need it."

No wonder I felt like shit.

I wiped my mouth along the sleeve of my jacket then retched twice more before I could respond. "Beggars can't be choosers."

At least this would counteract the effects for a while. A very short while since I didn't ingest the morphetzine. It was already in my blood screaming out for more. Soon I wouldn't care whether it was the Autsayer's or Sam's.

Over the siren, a low keening wail rose and echoed through the ship's corridors. I imagined the heks rifling through the gris-gris to pick just the right tongue. She'd use it to call for survivors soon.

Sam poked me in the thigh setting off a fresh wave of pain. "I think you mean addicts, not beggars, Noa. Addicts can't be and aren't choosers."

Even now I wanted to kiss her. The way she set her mouth when she was mad. The way she sucked her lip when she was scared. The way her tears of pain would taste.

A shudder ran through me. I steadied myself, gripping the arms of the chair. "Miss High Horse to the end, huh? I did my time, remember? I got clean."

Better I should have overdosed in some back-rim magic den than drag Sam down with me. Her mother already lit candles and cursed my name as a corruptor. And as much as I knew I should leave Sam alone, I just couldn't. Spent all of my pay to get her up here because my mother always said love loves as it will.

"Hey," she hissed. "Wake up. On your feet, Noa."

I blinked and the world went bright again as synthidote conjured the room back into being.

"Huh?"

"Come back to me, Noa. Wake up. We need to get out of here."

"What happened?" I asked. "Why aren't you gone?"

Eyman frowned. "One's still alive, guarding the escape hatch. I don't think we've got a way out of this."

"Shoot the fucking thing. We've got to go." My words sounded odd to me. Distant. Was I thinking clearer than him?

Eyman shook his head, "Can't. Out of ammo. I left it all in that one in the main hall."

The Autsayer were smart. We had to be quick and smarter.

It was only twenty meters. Twenty meters that separated us from freedom. But between us and our chance at freedom stood an untold number of undead religious heks puppets bent on redeeming some unbeliever flesh. If you can see one…

"Even if we make off with another ship, it's useless," Eyman complained. "They'll just run us down."

I was standing now, leaning heavily on Sam. She must have pulled me up. I didn't remember it, I had drifted off in my mind again.

"They never chase an escapee. The heks, their witch, would call it fate. They believe if people escaped it was the will of the god – destiny. Somebody's got to escape and spread the Autsayer's glory."

He looked skeptical. "And everyone else?"

I smiled. "Sacrificed as praise to their god. At least that's what all the scripts say."

Sam managed a weak smile. "So, we run like hell's coming." Controlled panic in the clip of her words. "But you got to stay with me, Noa. You have to get me out of here."

Looking around, I assessed the situation again. As the ship's First Contact Specialist I had my own office. It wasn't much of one, but then again, *The Vlees* wasn't much of a ship, more like a giant refuse barge scuttling barely legal supplies to out-lying colonies than a proper freighter. Other than weapons stowed on an upper deck, there wasn't much of anything handy that would help. And as a convicted felon, I hadn't been issued a weapon.

"Are you sure it's still out there?" she asked.

Was I sure? Who'd spent four years in that joke of a rehab prison studying them? Who'd hacked and downloaded an entire library full of their literature? Who'd even paid a guy to ship in original documents inked on sentient races' flesh?

She crept to the door and cracked it to look out before I realized what she was doing.

"Noa, there's a body in the hall."

"Good."

I hadn't been aboard long enough to grow too attached to the crew. But it wasn't one of them staring blankly back at us, it was another acolyte, eyes closed. If the shaman heard us, we could be gone sooner than later.

"Grab his leg."

She spun to look at me. "What? Why?"

I hobbled forward. "Pull his ass in here. We need what he's got."

"What's he got? A weapon?"

Sam was still looking at me confused, but she and Eyman managed to get him inside without alerting the guard down the hall.

"Sort of," I replied.

Eyman dumped the corpse at my feet. "They're going to kill us, aren't they?"

"Yeah. They'll either tow us back to wherever they've set up temple or they'll sacrifice us and the ship right here."

Sam looked skeptical. "How do they even know we're still alive? Security isn't working. What, can they smell us or something?"

"Yeah," I laughed. "They can. Baby, you're so pure they could smell you a system away." Under my breath, I added, "and probably me too."

I looked up at the drop ceiling. White acoustic tiles covered the electrical necessities of *The Vlees* in some strange attempt to make my space feel more like an office. I'd painted a few of them, but the result had been such an absence of light that I flipped them back over to white. The ones over my bed however, were covered in pieces of mirror I'd cut down from one I'd found in the salvage room.

I'd known we'd make up for lost conjugal visits the first time Sam came aboard and I hadn't want to miss any angle of it. So much effort wasted. We never got a chance to bang away the hurt before the Autsayer attacked.

"What're you thinking?" she asked.

I sighed, hating to deceive her, but needing the distraction. "I was wondering how far this wall went up into the faux ceiling."

Just as I'd hoped, she latched on to the idea.

"You think we could make it to the ships if we went over the wall. Like through the ceiling?"

She was beautiful. The tilt of her head, the flash of

excitement in her dark eyes. Even with the synth fighting the morph numbing my brain, I wanted her. Some things even override self-preservation at the oddest moments.

I nodded. "Yeah. I think it's possible, but I don't know how quietly we could do it. So, just do it fast."

Eyman was a goner, *gutbait*. But if they got their hands on Sam, they'd pass her around until they'd all had her once or fifty times. And then there'd be the redeeming ceremony as they butchered her alive to feast on her knowledge. And maybe preserve parts for later use.

Me? I might be able to talk my way out of it since my soul was as filthy as the best of them. I'd read their texts. I'd followed their ways so closely that they almost felt like my ways. Almost, a strange sister to these monsters.

But I couldn't take the chance with Sam. No matter how well I could speak Autsayer and blend, they would never let *her* go.

She stepped over to my desk and carefully cleared off the paperwork and a manuscript I'd translated in preparation for this run. I watched her glance at its illustrations and then back to my tattooed face. But still, she didn't ask.

"Come on," she goaded Eyman. "Help me move this over there."

I flipped open my knife.

Eyman and Sam lifted on an unspoken three. Moving so carefully as to not make any noise, not to drop it, they set the ends down at the same time against the wall. She clambered onto the desk and popped up a tile. Standing on her toes, she could see into the open space.

"We can do it," she spoke into the darkness. "but it's a long way down on the other side."

"Great." I stretched my wounded leg out straight, the grinding pain bringing me a little smile.

"Yeah, that's a supply closet. Mostly a bunch of useless

crap the captain hangs on to for no good reason. I'd have spaced it as a waste of fuel. He told me that you never could tell when someone's junk might be someone else's trade, 'Course he was about half drunk most of the time."

I opened the desk drawer and took out a pair of nippers.

"Here, I think these will work."

I didn't tell her why I had them and I was thankful she didn't ask. The manuscript curled up on the floor told me more about how the Autsayer disfigured each other and everyone else than I had wanted to know.

Cannibalistic magic-wielding bastards' words compelled me to try it myself.

Something about it had intrigued me and I was suddenly glad for the missed opportunity of banging Sam. She'd have wanted to know about all my scars and why I kept a short-bladed knife in my pocket. I'd had a rehab horror story that she'd have cried to hear all at the ready. But I couldn't tell it now. Not now that it was so real.

The alarms stopped. Over the all-hail Captain Wooten's voice boomed, "All is well crew." The inflections were off, the accent strange. "Come to the bridge and we will drink eat."

Eyman stopped nipping the wires holding the tiles in place in mid-cut and turned to look at me in question. Was he stupid?

I shook my head and said, "It's not him. Their heks witch is using the captain's tongue now. It's how they call the survivors."

His face paled and he nodded. "That's how she was controlling the dead ones?"

"Yeah." I rolled the chair closer to where they were working, Eyman on top of the desk cutting and Sam taking the tiles to stack in the corner. "He can control their newly dead if she's in possession of a body part."

"I thought that was just a story," Sam interrupted.

"No, baby. That's the whole reason I had this job. Having a little morphetzine can make you aware they're close. With the amount I'd taken in over the years, I can feel them."

They went back to clearing a way over the wall that we weren't going to use while I ran the hook of my blade under our Autsayer's eye, severing the optic nerve. I started to do the other eye the same way, but there was only the empty socket. So the heks already had the left eye, but wasn't using it. I glanced at its hands. All fingers intact. This must just be a scout, not meant to fight, but to push as far forward as it could before dying.

The morph from earlier dried on my hands. And now they were covered again with Autsayer blood. It found cracks in my dry skin.

This is the only way.

I glanced up at the love of my life to make sure she wasn't looking at me. The arch of her back was perfect. She was perfect.

I licked my palms and my tongue prickled, setting a fire the saliva glands raced to extinguish. I didn't wipe the drool from my chin. I didn't need the words from the manuscript, I'd memorized them. Or they had simply imprinted in my mind the moment I'd read them. It didn't matter. I mouthed them, the sound barely a whisper.

When the eye resting in my palm twitched, I pressed the blade to my own eye, cutting it free. I should pass out from shock, pain, bloodless. But there was only the rush of morph and I knew. I knew this was right.

The acolyte's eye slipped easily into my orbital cavity. There was a slight pressure and I could see. I could see the bridge.

The hek's cadaver face with the captain's green eyes stared at a collection of body parts, both human and Autsayer, spread out across the control table. When she turned to speak to the warriors gathered around, I could see where a human ear had been freshly stitched to the side of her head with blue thread.

They hadn't started the final crusade yet. There was time. But we had to get that one away from the cargo bay door.

The familiar feeling of heat spread from my tongue into my throat and down into my stomach. Blood ran from my eye, dripping down the arm of the chair.

I had to be faster. I dropped to my knees and sliced open my brother's chest, cracking away bone to get to his heart. As I ate, Sam began screaming. I smiled and wiped my mouth on my jacket.

I screamed too. It was long and piercing and called to my brothers. They would come and meet their death on my blade. All for the glory of the High God.

No, wait. Not yet.

I threw open the office door and loped towards the bay doors, knife in my hand. Hooting and calling a challenge to the one at the door. When the guard saw me, the hek's knew. I saw the recognition in her eyes.

The scout snarled. The confusion of seeing me covered in Autsayer blood must have slowed him a split second, but it was enough. I stabbed the blade through his throat again and again.

I shuddered. Penetration. It was good.

Sam and Eyman followed. Now, it was my turn to push Sam, driving her forward into the cargo bay. Through her shirt, I could feel the thrum of rushing blood. The quickness of her breath as it caught in her throat. The curve of her spine. The fear, it was in the sweat that soaked her clothes. Delicious.

The knife was in my hand. It wouldn't take much to slide the blade between the vertebrae. Watch her fall. Twitch. Drink in her screams and lick the tears of betrayal from her cheeks. A wave of shuddering desire passed through me and I had to stop, bent over at the waist, to catch my breath.

Sam didn't stop or look back, sprinting for the light craft nearest the bay doors. Eyman ran straight to the band of controls on the opposite wall, ignoring the shrieks coming from the other side of the door. I envied him. It was as if they were calling my name, hooking though my tendons and muscles and physically dragging me towards their calls. The pain of not responding ripped into me, but I had to see Sam out of here. I shut my eyes against the vision of waves of warriors cutting their way through the locked cargo doors. But when I saw Sam's nude, destroyed body behind my closed eyes, they snapped open again.

I jabbed the blade through the webbing connecting my thumb to my hand. The fresh spike of pain let me focus again. It wouldn't be long now.

Following Eyman as fast as my dead leg would let me, I headed up the ramp to Sam's escape ship. She stood just inside the door, waiting for me. Her face, that beautiful face, held no emotion. Staring at me, she closed the door.

I dropped to my knees to see her for as long as I could while the partition dropped, sealing them on the other side. Safe from me. Safe from the Autsayer. The hatch doors rumbled, the floor vibrating as their ship readied.

I turned as the door shut behind me and ran to my people.

The Archivist's Lesson

Cynthia Porter

I sat and watched the little spiral of smoke from my incense tail off and go out. The sun had risen higher while I sat contemplating the memorial tablet next to my old teacher's. A lovely pale pink stone carved with beautiful roses twining around the edges. Honoria Alatyr, Head Mage of the Royal School, had lived and died before my birth. I hadn't returned to this city to find her. Like most people I had forgotten her.

The soft crunch of gravel alerted me to the groundskeeper's approach. She walked past me, bowed, then laid a rose on top of my teacher, Alasdair's tablet and one on Honoria's. "It's good to see someone visit here. Your father came sporadically before his last illness, but no one has really spent any time with Honoria since Alasdair died."

"It's a beautiful tablet." I had visited the Memorial Gardens when I'd first returned. Despite burning incense and saying a prayer in Alasdair's memory, I hadn't remembered Honoria's tablet stood next to his. Hidden in plain sight; Head Mage next to Head Mage, mother next to son.

After all she had fought for, Honoria didn't deserve to be forgotten, her memory and work cloaked in shadows.

"Your grandfather, father, and Alasdair put a lot of thought into that tablet. Honoria meant the world to them."

"Alasdair told me stories about his mother, but I didn't know for a long time about the life she left behind to come here." Honoria had left the Collegia that was now my home, turned her back on being an Archivist. So determined to resurrect knowledge our people had forgotten that she'd risked her life to recreate those spells.

The groundskeeper turned to me. "I thought you were going back to the Collegia after your father died. What happened?"

I stood, bowed first to Honoria's tablet, then to Alasdair's. "They left me a riddle to solve, one last lesson to learn. My calling as an Archivist demands I stay, to preserve their knowledge and keep the past from becoming lost again. I owe it to the future, to the young mages who inherited Alasdair's school."

The groundskeeper bowed to me, priest to scholar, not royalty. "Zennaide, may the work go smoothly. May you find your way and walk in peace."

She walked with me to the gates where the carriage waited to take me back to the Mage School.

The short drive gave me enough time to collect my thoughts, remind myself of my goals. Once the carriage came to a stop in front of the main school building, I let myself out and was halfway up the steps when Sosanna appeared in the School doorway.

"Welcome back, Zennaide." The healer looked pleased, like a raven who'd stolen a shiny gem-studded ring.

"Did the books arrive?"

"Indeed they did, as well the letter you were waiting for." Sosanna reached into a pocket and pulled out a slim envelope.

Seeing that familiar seal made my blood race a little faster with anticipation and dread; Mayenna's reply had taken longer than expected. It could have simply been the weather between here and the Collegia, but as Sosanna handed me the envelope I sensed wariness and caution emanating from it.

Without waiting to go indoors, I cracked the seal, pulled out the neatly lettered pages and scanned the contents. After her standard salutation and comments about everyday life, Mayenna got to the point.

You are wise to copy Honoria's journals and leave the originals in safety. Her work, while not outright forbidden, remains controversial and divisive. The Elders remain uneasy at the idea of her research surviving her death.

The letter went on, but this was the warning I'd feared would come. Despite our mandate to protect and preserve knowledge, the Collegia still wanted to suppress what Honoria had sought, without even knowing if she had succeeded!

I folded the pages.

Sosanna wriggled her shoulders like a bird ruffling water droplets through its feathers. "Not the news you wanted to hear?"

"No, however, it was not unexpected." I placed the letter in my pocket.

"Focus on the good news about the blank journals. The crafter only delivered half today, but you won't need the rest for several days and he has promised them by then."

I made a brief head bow of agreement, equal to equal. "I can't wait to get back to work."

I followed her into the great receiving hall and up the stairs towards the private studies of the teachers and scholars.

"Javier is still at the palace, so he won't be underfoot."

The new head of the school had been cheerful about my occupation of his personal study. He was mostly absent these days, consulting with the new king about counselors and future marriage prospects.

None of that meant much to my own heart. I had chosen my path years ago, stepped out of the line of succession with my father's blessing. Even the tragic accidents that claimed my sister and her children hadn't changed our minds. As king, my father had known the types of magic necessary for any heir to successfully ascend the throne. As his daughter, I had always known my gifts lay elsewhere. I had come back to lay my father to rest and to crown my cousin king. I would never rule anything save myself and my destiny.

Perhaps once I might have dreamed of following Alasdair as Head Mage but my skills had led me to the Collegia. Javier had held the school together after Alasdair's murder. He and Sosanna had risked their lives convincing my father to settle on an heir.

Showing me Alasdair's precious books, books I had forgotten about, proved no risk at all for this clever pair. Now Honoria's work, her journals, kept me here, away from the place I had made for myself.

Sosanna touched the lock-panel on the door, and it swung open. I paused inside the doorway as she walked in before me.

It was hard not to expect Alasdair in this room as it had been his study. Javier had changed little. I now knew that Alasdair had changed little from his mother's occupancy, including the built-in bookcase with glass panels and a lock that guarded Honoria's journals. I had been so excited to touch those volumes, to examine them, when Sosanna had first brought me here.

Now I only had eyes for the archway surrounding the window seat; carved with rose vines twining up and around each other, laden with wooden roses and tiny animals tucked into nooks and crannies. I had sat and studied with Alasdair in this window, run my fingers over the wood, and never guessed at the secrets the archway held.

Sosanna stopped near the table we'd set aside as a work space. The new journals were stacked on its surface.

"How long before you could walk in here and not stare at it?"

She chuckled. "Apparently I'm one of the few who isn't in awe of it."

I stepped all the way inside and closed the door securely behind. "How are you not awed by it? Honoria created a Gate, a magical Gate, to travel between here and her farm halfway across the kingdom. No one else has been able to recreate the knowledge our ancestors lost—or destroyed. What she did is a master work—and you aren't awed by it?"

"Not one bit. Not when Alasdair sent us through to safety. Not now." She shrugged. "I think it's because I'm a healer. I am awed by life, not objects."

I walked past her to the arch and placed my hand on the carved wood. Nothing. No hum, no song, no indication of any charge or lingering of power. How had Honoria done it? The Gate hid in plain sight. Unless you knew it was there, unless you had seen it, walked through it, nothing betrayed its presence.

My palms itched. I wanted to reach out, make the gestures that, coupled with focused energy from my gifts, would become the spell that triggered the Gate. Carefully I lifted my hands from the carved wooden roses. Not right now.

I forced myself away from the arch. I wasn't here to study it, not directly. Before Javier and Sosanna had shown me the Gate, my whole focus had been the journals Alasdair had kept under lock and key. I had instantly understood why they perplexed even these powerful young mages. Honoria had written in the scholar's language, something the Collegia Librarians and Archivists studied so they could read, preserve, and translate the oldest texts. It wasn't taught beyond those circles. Some of them kept journals in the scholar's tongue to practice.

It was also a good way to guard secrets.

Honoria started her journals in that tradition when she had lived at the Collegia. She had continued after she'd left to live first as a teaching mage, then as Head of this school. Because of how she wrote, her secrets, including how she had created this Gate, were unknowable to anyone outside someone trained at the Collegia. No mage or student at this school, even if they broke the lock, broke the glass, and took a journal, would be able to understand them.

My type of treasure—old books, knowledge to be preserved.

Sosanna waved a hand in the direction of a small table near Alisdair's old desk. "I stocked all the food and drink you require. I'll bring our evening meal later."

"Thank you."

Sosanna bowed, not in any mode I knew. More like a crane about to dance before a mate, or a rival. "May your work be productive."

I watched until the door closed behind her. After the Gate, and Honoria's journals, Sosanna was a mystery worth solving. I didn't have the time, and this wasn't my place.

I turned my attention to the table where the new blank journals waited. I picked up the one on top, opened it, smoothed the pages to lie flat and set it where it would be on my right as I worked. Then I walked across the room, fetched the little key out of my pocket and opened the cabinet doors wide.

My working journal marked the division between the volumes I'd copied and the ones yet to be worked on. I tipped the finished journal on the left down on its spine, then pulled out both mine and the one on its right. Back at the table, I placed mine to the right of the blank journal, next to my pen and ink. Finally, I opened Honoria's journal. A faint scent of roses wafted from its pages. Roses, always roses, for Honoria.

I couldn't indulge in reading her words now or I would be months making the copies. I did check the date, verifying it followed the previous journal in sequence. Then I smoothed the pages to lie flat and set it to my left. Pulling up the cushioned work stool, I sat.

After many years of invoking it, this spell was simple. I took a deep breath and placed my left hand lightly on the original work. Exhaling, I placed my right hand on the corresponding blank page to my right. Closing my eyes triggered the waiting spell.

Earth, Water, and Spirit rose in a complicated swirl, traveling through me as smoothly as breath. My hands thrummed with power. Minutes passed, then the spell ebbed. I opened my eyes, lifted my hands, and found every dot and flourish perfectly replicated on the formerly blank page.

I took a breath, turned the page of the old journal and the page on the new journal, then repeated the process.

Not terribly romantic or interesting, page after page after page after page, but then a flash of vision: A hand with a pen creating letters across a page. A single ring around the middle finger set with a dark red garnet. A sweep of curtain half-hiding the window seat. Steam rising from the cup of tea next to the inkwell.

I gasped for air as the vision left. These flashes drove me onwards even more than the copies themselves. Seeing what the long ago writers saw, sensing what they felt or touched—this was the magic. These visions were harder on my body than the ones I experienced while sleeping. Asleep, relaxed, visions came as naturally as breathing.

I drew in several deep breaths, pulled my hands together

and chafed them lightly to soothe the tingle from the constant use of the archivist spell. I shifted the stool sideways
towards the space for my journal. It would be nice if I could
inscribe my own words as easily as I created copies, but
originals had to be written. After recording the images and
sensations, along with the journal page they were associated
with, I pushed back from the table.

Time for a break. I rose, crossed the room to the little tea
table where water and food waited for me. I ate and drank
as I paced between the door and the window seat. Stretching
and movement were important for long term work.

I struggled against a sedentary life. I joked with my colleagues back home that I needed to drink ink and paint, but
in reality all I needed was water and minerals to sustain
proper recreation spells.

I cleaned and dried my hands, then I returned to my copy
station and began again. If I was lucky, I might experience
several more visions before I reached the end of this book.

Over the course of my work, I had seen the library where
Honoria had started her studies, the library I now called
home. If I was there, I could walk to the study nook Honoria
had preferred, it was that familiar. I had seen her smooth,
young fingers twirl a rose barely in bloom. Watched those
same fingers move through intricate spellwork or spend
hours writing page after page of spell theory.

I had felt her exasperation and frustration as she argued,
again, before the Collegia Elders, for the validity of her work.
Saw the stack of trunks she'd packed for her journey here,
every volume of her journals tucked beneath her extra cloak
and a layer of her son's toys.

A lengthy gap between entries had occurred between that
vision and the next, when I'd glimpsed the main room of
the Mage School's library. No more fights with others about
her research, Honoria kept her work quiet, and the Collegia
Elders left her alone.

I had also seen my grandfather as a young man, first at the Collegia Library, then here, stealing kisses from Honoria, playing with the little boy who would grow up to be Alasdair, cradling the baby girl Honoria had nursed through a whole sequence of entries. No wonder my father had been enraged by Alasdair's murder. They hadn't just been friends, they had been brothers.

Page after page I continued, pausing for breaks even if I hadn't had a vision. Sometimes they came quickly and close together; other times, widely spaced and rare. I believed it was due to the emotions the writer felt when writing. Strong emotions left traces behind, even when not directly connected to the content. Copying a book that was itself a copy produced no visions. This volume seemed average, but produced a glimpse of Alasdair as a grown man—pacing and shaking his hands in the air as he talked.

I had just finished writing down that scene when there was a knock at the door. Sosanna entered, carrying a pitcher, followed by one of the younger healers carrying a covered tray.

"Put the tray over here," Sosanna set down the pitcher on the low table near the window seat. "Thank you. Please close the door on your way out."

The young healer bowed to me as she passed—student to master.

I stood, weary as if I'd been hiking through the forests near my beloved library.

Sosanna uncovered the tray and arranged the dishes on it. "You did say to interrupt you at meal time."

"Bless you for each and every meal." I crossed the room and dropped into the chair by the tray, my mouth watering in anticipation. "I've been known to get too immersed in my work."

"I looked at the table as I went by. You made good inroads on the edibles and water this afternoon."

"I try keep to strict habits when I'm working." I made a face. "Still, I'm going to have to slow down, take longer breaks, drink more."

The healer looked at me with concern. "This has been a very long project for you. You've been pushing your gifts— even with that break for the new blank journals."

I picked up a roll. "Unfortunately, yes."

"Go as slowly as you need. Javier and I agree that you can stay as long as it takes." She canted her head sideways, bird-like. "In fact, you can choose to take up permanent residence if you like."

I must have looked thunderstruck because she straight-ened, looked me straight in the eyes. "Your gifts as a mage would be a grace to this school, both as Teacher and Archivist."

She bowed her head, deep respect, equal to equal.

I clutched the warm roll in my hand. I had expected to navigate the Court when I'd returned to bury my father. The politics and intrigue that I'd escaped long ago had a fresher tone but still existed. I'd helped to crown my cousin and thought to return to my quiet home and work.

I had not suspected another choice would provide serious temptation: Mage in this new school growing out of my old teacher's work.

"I, I will consider it." The words fell out of my mouth before I knew what I was saying. I couldn't stay here! I had made a life for myself where no one expected me to be any-thing except an Archivist, protecting our people's knowledge from being lost.

Sosanna dropped her head in an entirely different mode, again, one I did not recognize. She looked like a falcon regard-ing a target. Only I was too big to be a mouse beneath her gaze. "I thank you for even considering it."

The following days resumed the pattern I'd followed upon starting this project. I got up and breakfasted with the senior mages and scholars resident at the school. Some I knew from Alasdair's time. Others were from Sosanna's generation, younger, with a different edge to their magecraft. All treated me as a fellow mage, no bows acknowledging my royal bloodlines. Unlike the Collegia Library, their energy felt like a river full of spring snow-melt charging towards the Lakes. For all that I followed a routine, those around me were changing history and writing new pathways.

I shut that energy out when I closed the door to Alasdair's study. Honoria's journals required all my focus. I wanted to finish, be done, leave—but this task, like witnessing my father's passing, could not be hurried.

Sosanna mostly left me to myself, except for sitting down to both lunch and dinner with me. Her Healer's eyes weighed and measured every bite and drop I took in. Even so, my skin grew drier, my joints ached more than they should. In the evenings I began soaking in baths of her concoctions.

My nights grew ever more restless. Visions from my work crept into my dreams. Alasdair and my father playing chess. Honoria overseeing the artisans carving the great arch around the window seat. The many model gate structures Honoria built and her first, fizzling attempts to set the spells on them.

When the morning dawned with only half a book left, I nearly danced my way into the study. I could finish this project and return to the ones left unfinished at home.

Several pages in, a vision came bright and strong, the Gate shimmered before me, before Honoria—then collapsed. Elation and disappointment surged and her hand punched the table next to the inkwell, causing the ink to spill.

When I blinked my way back to the present day, I could see the stain from the ink still a dark shadow on the table next to my ink well.

I recorded, then pushed on, turning the page. The strong, distinctive handwriting wavered across the page, meandered down at an angle instead of Honoria's meticulous straight lines. She had written with her off-hand. I paused. I had to read here. Something was distinctly wrong.

The date was months after her failed attempt at a large Gate.

"I injured my hand and wrist after my last experiment. The Healers tell me it might never fully heal. Alasdair also counseled me to put off my work. He is as stubborn as his father and I both put together! He is right. I cannot manipulate the energies I need unless I am at full strength."

I looked up from the page. How did you finish, Honoria? You don't have much room left. When did the breakthrough come?

This page also produced a vision. Rain beat against the glass window. A bouquet of roses decorated the mantel. A body, tired, weary—difficulty breathing.

I gasped. Honoria was sick. Were we wrong? Did she not finish her work? Had Alasdair, despite what he had told Sosanna and the others, been the one to finally create the Gate?

I began copying, recording, copying. I rushed through a brief break. I had to know! Yet I couldn't read; I had to stay focused on my task.

The last page, my eyes were dry, I placed my shaking hands on the original and blank page. Something felt wrong—no! Finish!

Even as the words unfurled across the blank page I knew, I saw—Alasdair's hand traced words across the page, sure and confident. And yet, he wept as he wrote.

The vision left. I stared down at the last page.

The handwriting half-way down was different. It was not Honoria's.

It was Alasdair's

My old teacher had written, in the Common Tongue: "My

mother, Honoria, hid her last journals before she died. Despite the success of her endeavors, there are too many questions about how others might use her knowledge. If you can find them, consider yourself worthy of being her heir. May you be strong enough to shoulder the responsibility."

I wasn't done. I had to find those journals!

I stood, walked to the bookcase where Honoria's journals were shelved. Well, I had to start somewhere. I looked at the shelf at the top, reached up, and pulled out the first volume.

***

"Put that book down. Stop!" Sosanna's hands were on my shoulders, shaking me. "What happened?"

I blinked, stumbled. Sosanna deftly pushed a chair beneath me before I could fall. She took my chin in her hands and stared into my eyes.

"I've been trying to get your attention since I walked into the study. You weren't responding."

I waved a hand towards my work desk. "Missing. Not finished." My voice rasped as if I hadn't used it in months.

"Stay here." Sosanna marched across the room to my almost untouched pitcher of water, poured a cup, and brought it to me. "Drink this, slowly."

As I did so, she walked to the desk and looked at the still open end of the journal. Alastair's words were easily readable to her.

"Fuss and feathers," she muttered. "You should have told me we had a hunt on our hands before risking yourself." She shut the journal's back cover. "You were using your Sight, focusing on each book when you should simply have used your eyes!"

I held out my hand with the now-empty cup. "More?"

"Yes, more; then some restorative tea, food, and rest."

"But—"

"No. Healer's orders. You are going to rest. In the meantime, I will start organizing the search." She stared thoughtfully at the bookshelf. "You're about finished in here. I'll get this cleaned up then have everyone start in the library."

I decided not to argue. The library was too obvious, but what better place to hide book journals?

***

Three days later we were still searching the school's library.

More precisely, Sosanna's team of students and young mages were searching it while I sat resting, supervised by Sosanna's assistant. I wanted to help, but I still shook when I walked. Climbing ladders was not possible. The searchers brought me any book that looked similar to the journals, or that had text they could not read. The table near me now held several stacks of fascinating books that undoubtedly led down their own paths of discovery. Who here was going to do that research? No one, not even the school's young librarian, had the skills and training of an Archivist. Could I reach out to any of my colleagues here in the city? Would any of those trained have the time to come to the school?

I was increasingly certain Honoria's volumes were not hidden here. It was too obvious; yet we couldn't discount it because two journals could easily be disguised by the sheer volume of books.

Sosanna had summoned Javier from the palace and sent him to look beyond the Gate while she focused on the school. So far, his search had also turned up nothing. I didn't think Honoria and Alasdair would have hidden those journals beyond their easy supervision. They had to be here, somewhere.

Terick, the librarian, entered through a doorway from the warren of special collections. Bits of cobweb floated from his hair.

"Nothing yet. I did find something else to show you if your minder will allow you to walk about for a bit."

"Just don't let her climb any ladders."

I stood and followed Terick. He led me through the first two rooms to where a door stood open.

"We don't store books in here, but I thought I'd take a look just in case." He gestured for me to step ahead of him.

Leaning against the walls of the narrow, vault-like room, were large canvas portraits. I only had eyes for one; Honoria, large as life. She had the same upswept curls as the smaller picture in Alasdair's office; a smile, confident and knowing, played across her face. A mage in the fullness of her power.

"This is amazing, Terick! Why is it in here?"

"We've been rearranging and sorting the school to reflect our current leadership as well as honor our past. Javier and Sosanna want to honor the previous heads of the school in the great hall, so we are storing the portraits here while we complete the renovations." He pointed at the canvas next to Honoria. "See, Alasdair is here, too."

My old teacher looked much as I remembered him. He might have sat for the portrait before I left for the Collegia Library. Next to his mother, I could see the similarities in jaw and cheekbones. However, his eyes, while the same color as Honoria's, were the same as my father's, deep-set, crinkles at the corners. I didn't remember them as being like my father's, but in life they had been so different. Even when I was a child my father's illness had revealed itself in slower movements, a sort of studied consideration. Alasdair had been quick, full of gestures—a fire that came from Honoria.

I looked back at Honoria's portrait, drinking in the visage I rarely glimpsed in my visions. An idea glimmered.

"Terick."

"Yes?"

"Where was this portrait hanging?"

"In one of the studies—oh!" He grabbed my hand and pulled me towards the door. I quickly gained my balance and we hurried through the library.

Along our way, Terick hollered for one of the searchers to bring a ladder to the Adjunct's Study. Despite my recent debility I got ahead of him and beat him to the door. I knocked frantically on the smooth wood.

"What's so urgent?" Sosanna opened the door.

"We need to look behind the painting where Honoria's portrait used to hang!"

She stepped aside and gestured us in.

I looked up at the landscape featuring a heron poised at the edge of a lake that hung above the fireplace. "Terick, are you certain the portrait hung up there?"

"I moved it myself before Sosanna chose this office." He stood in front of the hearth. "If the two of you would please step back near the desk, I'll have this one down before the ladder gets here."

We moved. Sosanna almost pushed her chair under me, forcing me to sit.

Terick made several gestures. I felt the powers of Earth stir, twining with Air. His spell reached upwards, lifted the painting off the wall and gently brought it down to the floor. He steadied it with his hands, leaned it against the wall. Up on the wall I could see a faint tracery of roses.

The ladder made its appearance. Terick steadied it while Sosanna climbed upwards. Her hands deftly manipulated and pressed the perimeter of the roses. I held my breath. A small click and a door swung open.

"Are they in there?" I demanded. "Can you see anything?"

Sosanna's slumping shoulders answered for her. "Empty."

***

After Terick left to resume searching the libraries, Sosanna and I sat staring at the painting that had hung over the fireplace.

"Harbors!" She swore again. "It was such a good hiding place!"

"The little cabinet up there held them at some point, I'm certain of it." I pushed at the carpet with my toes.

"Where did Honoria move them to? Or Alasdair on her behalf?"

I thought of the roses carved on Honoria's memorial tablet, the roses in the Gate arch, the rose embossed on Honoria's later journals, and now the tiny roses carved on the hidden door we had found behind the painting.

"Wherever those journals are, there are roses of some kind marking the place." I sighed, thinking of all the carvings, paintings and tapestries throughout the school.

"Speaking of roses," Sosanna stood. "I found something that might be useful while searching the attics. I had it brought down to Alasdair's study."

We left the painting and walked the short distance down the corridor to the Head Mage's study. A large chest had been brought in and placed next to the one that held my copies. I sank to my knees, my fingers tracing the roses on its top, the glyphs along its edges. "This belonged to Honoria. Where did you find it?"

Sosanna pulled up a stool and sat. "It was near some of Alasdair's things. I started thinking that he might have kept some of her things or she'd hidden it on her own." She patted the trunk. "I looked through it before I had it brought down. I'm sorry, but the missing journals weren't inside."

My heart sank. What had Honoria done with those missing volumes?

"However, I did find another journal—written in the common tongue. I flipped through it—it seems to be

Honoria's journal through her final illness. Maybe you can find the clues we need."

"I'm too drained to make copies of anything right now."

Sosanna took on her intense falcon look. "You can do more than copy. You have visions. There are items in this trunk that Honoria treasured. You have her final writings. You can use them to help trigger a vision and see what she did."

I started to protest, fell silent. I was a Seer, as much as I had harnessed my gifts and focused them on the past, I had known when to come back for my father's final days. Using Honoria's belongings to reach for a vision of her was closer to what I had done all my life.

The chest latches lifted easily, revealing a journal nestled in a folded shawl of pacan wool. It was smaller than Honoria's working journals, and a different color. I picked it up, stroked the cover, and felt the embossed roses.

"I will try."

Sosanna dropped her falcon aura. "Would you like me to bring up something to eat? You look exhausted."

"Thank you. I will read this while I wait."

After Sosanna left the room, I picked up the shawl and draped it around my shoulders. It was soft, warm. Not fancy work; utterly practical, brown with a darker stripe around the outer edge. I had seen it in various flashes of Honoria, draped over a forearm, lying across the window seat or the back of a chair. I had felt its softness wrapped around her, the warmth keeping her company in the dark hours as she wrote page after page detailing her experiments and theories.

Standing, I moved to the chair next to my work table and sat before my legs gave way again.

I pulled Honoria's last journal close to my body, cuddling it as if it was a beloved child's toy. I closed my eyes, just for a moment. Then I would read until Sosanna came back.

The beginning of the dream was difficult to discern. The chair, the snuggling warmth of the shawl, the journal—the journal was on the table, not in my arms. Open, the pen lying next to it and the inkwell in front of it. I knew those words, the last words in the journal; Honoria's last words before dying. In this moment, this place, she still lived. I could feel the rise and fall of her breath, the beating of her heart.

This dream vision was warm, secure.

I found myself sitting on the window seat, looking at Honoria. The mage looked back at me, master and student, with one last lesson between them.

Where did you hide them? Your missing journals?

Honoria turned her head, looked at the open cabinet where her other journals stood. *Where they have always been.*

Not in my time. The last two are lost.

Not Lost. Use your heart, your eyes, your intelligence. If you have come this far, reaching back to ask me, all you have to do is sit in my place and look. If you are worthy of your goal, you will find what you seek.

But...

Honoria raised one hand, it shook slightly, like a leaf in a breeze. *It is not the Master's place to tell you the answer. It is the Student's place to find it.*

Then the mists crowded in, Honoria's face grew dim.

I started awake, my heart racing. A faint aroma of roses lingered around me. The journal had slipped from my grasp and rested in the nest of my lap where the edges of the shawl were tucked around my hands. I lifted it, and with a gentle caress of the cover, set it on the table.

Honoria's chair had stood in this spot. Early in my work I had shifted the table and chair to mirror what I had glimpsed in my visions. The cabinet was off-set in front of me, the glass reflective in the light.

In the dream, the cabinet doors had been open wide, revealing the shelves where Honoria had kept her journals, where they still were kept.

"Oh"—I breathed out the sound. Carefully I pulled the shawl around myself, pushed back the chair. I walked across the room, turned the little key in the lock, and opened the cabinet doors wide. "Honoria, you devious woman." I ran my hands around the frame of the opening, feeling the smooth arch of the wood and the light engraving of rose vines along the inside where no one could see them.

I hummed just a little, bringing up my levels of Spirit. The trigger glowed to my sight and I touched it.

The tiny Gate sprang to life, a glowing arch in front of the journals. This would be an exercise in trust because I could not see through, could not walk through. I would have to reach through blindly and trust there were no traps, no tricks.

It would be smarter to wait for Sosanna, just in case something went wrong. Smarter to write down what I knew first.

Before I could take a step back, I reached through the little Gate, trusting Honoria, trusting Alasdair.

I felt the embossed leather of a book cover, so much the same as the journals I had been working with. One, two— only two. Quickly I ran my hand around the journals, feeling highly polished wood, a small box or cabinet, just big enough for the journals. No joins, locks, hinges. If I were guessing, it was a blind box built into the wall behind the cabinet, but it could be anywhere.

I wrapped my fingers around the journals and pulled them out. I stepped back from the cabinet and bowed, student to master.

I hummed, reaching through Spirit to close the Gate. I would have to show Sosanna and Javier this tiny wonder. For now, I flipped open each journal, checked for Honoria's handwriting, checked the dates. Observed how the second journal was not filled to the end. Honoria's last secrets were at hand.

I would finish the copies, waiting all the while for whatever flashes Honoria and her work still had to reveal. As a dutiful

Archivist, I would escort those copies east, to the Library I had called home. Would I tell anyone except Mayenna about Honoria's treasure? Or would I discreetly place these volumes in a quiet place to await future discovery?

After that? I had spent my time here longing for my Library, for my solitude, for my work. That life did not allow for wonders like Honoria's gates. This place, this school with its library built by Honoria and Alasdair, with its soul tended by Sosanna and her Javier; this place stood at the edge of a new age. This kingdom, no longer my father's, drew on the past but looked to the future.

It was time for Gates to open and to risk the future stepping through.

Lesson learned, Honoria. Lesson learned.

Mastery of the Mind

Nivair H. Gabriel

Warning: This story depicts sexual assault.

Of course, Dara had been bored and loud about it for every minute of the drive here. Now that I needed him to distract us with some antic from all this emotion, he stood still as a stone in the dullest alternate universe.

Papa and I had just finished hugging, and judging by Mom's tear-dampened cheeks, she and I were due for another round. I noticed that everywhere else in the courtyard, students were scurrying, leading or trailing lines of their belongings in orderly hover patterns. They wore suits with ties—even the girls, just like I'd fantasized. They carried and checked black leather-bound notebooks. They moved straight ahead to the stone footsteps of the Public Hall, to the front doorway where they all looked like toys compared to the giant columns. Nobody else was embracing their parents.

Dara broke his silence.

"You think everybody already knows you're the youngest?" he asked.

"*Dara*," said my father. A warning. "Naré, your age is nothing. You have been the most brilliant girl at all of your schools. You will be the most brilliant sorcerer here."

"So, no pressure, huh?" I riffed. Mom and Papa gazed back at me without laughing. A short-haired passerby glanced at me for a second, as if they'd heard us—and I liked that I couldn't discern their gender on first glance. I smiled, but they were already walking away.

"Hey, don't worry, Naré," Dara said. "I bet you could find a guy here to marry you."

"And to kick your ass," I replied.

"Dara," Papa snapped in the tone that still drop-kicked my gut and prickled the hairs on the back of my neck. Dara seemed unaffected. "Enough." Papa turned back to me. "You do not need to meet men. You need to become the best sorcerer you can be."

I wondered what he would do if I saluted. Dara could've gotten away with it.

"Yes, Papa," I said. Mom finally launched herself at me for another hug.

"The men will follow," she whispered. I smirked, and behind her back Papa interpreted it as a smile and returned it. His eyes were redder than I'd ever seen them.

When they walked off this campus, I would be an adult. I would be a sorcerer undertaking practical training at the Academy on the Coast.

When Mom and I let go of each other, a tall white girl with not a hair out of place was shaking my father's hand.

"Very nice to meet you." She caught me gaping, but merely smiled and extended her hand. "Carla. Resident tutor."

I shook—firmly, I hoped. "Naré. Concentration in human sorcery."

"Oh, is that how you say it? We've all been calling you Nair. Like the cream that takes off your hair?"

Dara snorted. Carla looked at my parents, as if expecting them to say, *gosh, that sounds even better. Let's call her Nair from now on.* They did not oblige.

"Yeah, I get that a lot."

"You must be so gifted, to get to start here at your age."

I shrugged. Everyone was focusing on me far too intently. Once again, Dara was useless.

"I'm excited," I said.

"Well, you let me know if you need anything, okay?" Carla didn't wait for my response before peeling off to grab a friend.

I faced my parents.

"We'll see you in a few months," Papa said.

"You'll be great," said Mom.

One more pat on each shoulder, an eyeroll and a stuck-out tongue from Dara, and then I was watching their backs as they walked away.

***

Everyone I knew was hundreds of miles away, far enough into third period that they'd all be glancing at the time and holding back groans of surprise and anguish. I'd been awake for less than an hour, and I was crossing the long courtyard bathed in sunlight. Books and people flew all around me.

I tried to imagine Ness in gym, a senior now, with the rest of our class. She'd be trying to hide a thick paperback somewhere in cerulean shorts and a plain white tee, so she could sneak away after attendance and make it through another few chapters before lunch.

Meanwhile, I ducked under an archway flanked by two stone griffins, and down a spiral staircase. I guess anyone here who couldn't use stairs was expected to know how to float themselves around. At the bottom I found myself in a cavernous chamber, with amphitheatre seating leading still further down to a sort of stage with a podium and a wall of chalkboards.

Filing in behind a group of jubilant boys, I dropped into a seat near the middle. Some of the people entering seemed to know each other, but a lot more of them filled open seats the way strangers in the same place often do—optimizing for maximum distance from the next living person. In the instant before they sat down, I recognized the person I'd locked eyes with yesterday in the courtyard. They were closer to the front, on the other side of the room. Their spiky blond hair now had pink highlights. I breathed in the smell of chalk and musk.

Two sharply dressed men popped through a door on one side of the front platform. The younger man, white and lanky, took a seat in a chair on the far side of the chalkboards. The older man, olive-skinned and bald, stood in front of the podium with his hands clasped. Hisses spread through the room as he waited, and it didn't take long for him to get silence in which to introduce himself.

"I am Professor Roper, and it is my job to teach you mastery of the mind. You are students, and your job is to make mine easy."

A few scattered chuckles.

"Sitting over there is my teaching assistant, John. He will be recording lectures and providing instruction for your practice sessions.

"Now, you all think you know what sorcery is from your personal exploration and your after-school clubs and maybe even your parents, but I think almost none of you have ever experienced sorcery the way it is practiced here."

He paced while he talked, and I watched all of the heads in front of me turn to follow him.

"Most of the population doesn't understand or care what we do. But we steward the universe. It is the most profound responsibility, and to be worthy of it requires more than perfection."

The phrase "more than perfection" is basically meaningless, but I still got goosebumps.

"I like to say that regular people believe in money, warriors believe in strength, and sorcerers believe in the mind. Mastery of the mind is in many ways the foundation of sorcery, especially human sorcery. An element can never deceive you the way a human will. You must possess absolute awareness, total synchronicity of thought, action, purpose, and context."

He snatched the folded pocket square from his jacket, and held it up.

"You can do anything with an object. Right? You can float it"—the fabric rose and hovered in the air—"fly it"—it zoomed over the first row of seats and then back to him—"heat it"—it glowed red, and the air around it blurred with heat—"or cool it." It stopped glowing, and the heat haze turned to mist. The frozen pocket square fell to the floor and shattered into so many crystal pieces.

"You can do anything with an object," he said, "using elemental sorcery. It only takes basic skill. But *living beings* are complex systems. To affect a lifeform requires complex sorcery. And complex sorcery requires the highest level of mastery of the mind.

"A demonstration!" he announced, suddenly louder. "John is going to try to hit me with a curse. And I'm going to try not to let him."

I felt like everyone sat up a little taller as the two men stood and faced each other from opposite ends of the platform.

"Ready when you are," John said.

Roper spread his hands. "Go ahead."

For a moment they were both still and silent. Then John let out a yell, Roper stepped back, and John doubled over and gasped as if he'd just been punched.

"Nice try," Roper said.

Someone whispered in the row behind me: "I didn't see it! Did John do anything?"

"I didn't see it either," someone else whispered back.

John was straightening, and he took another shot—this time I could tell when his eyes narrowed, his fingers tightened, and his posture tensed up. But Roper was smiling, and again it seemed like it was John who got hit with something. He was still breathing heavily.

"Last try. Just for fun," said Roper.

John lifted a hand, and then dropped hard to the ground. Somebody whistled.

"Don't worry, he's fine," said Roper, and John sat up and waved a hand. "Now, what happened?"

Hands shot up—mine, and one from each of the other junior sorcerers who had also been the highest-performing children in their regional schools. Roper gazed out at the crowd, and pointed at me.

"Um," I said. "He didn't close his mind to you. You were able to tell what he was going to do next."

Roper nodded. "Very well put, Ms.—?"

"Naré Vartanian."

"Ms. Vartanian is correct. John—thank you, by the way, John, as always." Back in his chair, John nodded.

I was correct. My parents hadn't put money away for twenty years for nothing. It would have made me happier if I weren't still playing the odd demonstration over in my mind: John tensed in pain, John falling.

"John faced me with an unmastered mind," Roper continued. "He stuck out like a sore thumb in the sorcery web. He might as well have spoken his thoughts aloud to me. Now, he did that on purpose, of course, for this demonstration. But I did it to show you the starting point where you will all find yourselves when you perform your first lab assignment. You'll be amateurs, and we will know what you're doing before you're able to do it.

"Don't be discouraged. It is called mastery of the mind because you can't learn it in an afternoon. If you show up here and in lab, on time, all year, you will have a good chance of almost achieving mastery for a few cumulative seconds. That will be an excellent start. But it's up to you."

He turned to the chalkboard, and equations started to appear. His lecture launched into the theoretical, and I had to start taking notes.

On the way out, the person with the spiky blond hair and I reached the bottom of the stairs first. We exchanged a glance, and I must still have been at least a little bit high from "Ms. Vartanian is correct," because I introduced myself.

"I go by my initials," they said. "SA."

We shook hands. For some reason, it reminded me of home; the last time I saw them, I was with my family.

"Do you, um, do gendered pronouns?" I asked. "I'm she/her."

"They/them."

"Cool. What did you think of the lecture?"

"Honestly?"

I nodded.

"I thought it was a little fucked up."

"I am so glad you said that."

"I mean, it's sorcery. I expected *some* of the lust-for-power, masters-of-the-universe stuff. But that was a lot. Do you think he does that to his TA every year?"

"Now there's a disturbing question."

✳✳✳

After my last day of public school back in June, Ness and I had walked the half mile to the cemetery as usual. It was breezy, sunny, and clear; we both wore tank tops and I had on sandals, while as ever Ness sported her black steel-toed boots and the spiky iron knuckles she calls rings. For most of the way we didn't talk. I listened to the faint hum of a lawn mower, the swishing past of cars, until we were through all the headstones from the 1800s and every other noise faded into the softness of the wind through the trees. I'd taken this little bit of freedom we had for granted, and now that I was fully escaping—I'd never have to go to gym class again—all I could think about was how much I would miss it.

Newer graves, well-kept with fresh flowers, gave way to a short patch of scruff that soon became trees. We stopped just five rows before that, at a stone that read Natasha Lynne Hygone, 1986-2003. Flowers covered it, only barely managing not to obscure her name. There were notes, photographs, art pieces, carefully protected from the weather when necessary: a universe of love that had been her world. Ness was in one of the photographs, smiling cheek to cheek with Nat, sisters in all but genetics.

Ness dropped to her knees and put a palm to the grass for a moment. I sat carefully and did the same, but with my typical awkwardness. I hadn't really known Nat. I'd seen her in the school musical, found myself behind her in line one morning and watched her get patted down at the metal detectors, but we'd never met. What if she didn't want some dumbass nerd who had stolen her best friend visiting her spirit's eternal resting place?

"I miss you every day," said Ness.

For a moment, we listened to birds and wind in trees.

Ness glanced at me. "People used to tell her she was a warrior. She would say everyone is a warrior. Everyone fights. And even if they—if they die it doesn't mean they weren't a warrior."

I half-smiled. "I wish I'd met her," I said.

Ness rooted around in her pocket for her little magic box. When she found it, she pulled out a joint and stuck it between her lips.

"To Nat," she said out of the side of her mouth. She raised a hand with a lighter, and I raised my empty hand in kind.

"To Nat," I echoed.

She breathed in, staring at the forest. Her eyelashes were so long, so dark, so perfectly curved. How did she do that? Why did she ever hang out with me, who wouldn't know mascara from a hole in the ground? I knew Nat had been gorgeous, too, the carefully curated kind—the kind who generally looked right past me and at male basketball players.

Ness caught me staring and grinned.

"Want?" she asked, holding out the joint.

I shook my head. "Nah, I'm good, thanks."

She usually teased me a little about being an obedient daddy's girl, about letting him mold me into a model minority. She had a point. But it was the last time we'd ever hang out after school, and she must have been feeling it more than I'd thought, because she just shrugged and took another long drag.

"Are you scared?" she said after a moment.

"Of course. Yeah. Jesus, I'm going to be a sorcerer. On the Coast. I'm going to be living with...a bunch of other sorcerers."

"You'll learn how to control the world and bend it to your will." She said it like it was an exaggeration, but it wasn't, really. "You won't need a pass to go to the bathroom."

I laughed. "That is a really good point."

"Hey, Naré. Would you try it on me?" She'd never sounded forced-casual like this before, at least not to me. She wouldn't meet my eyes.

"Try what?"

"Sorcery." Once she got that out, she looked right at me. I swallowed.

"Um—"

"I mean, I know it's not legal. But neither is this, right?" She winked at me. What kind of person could pull off winking, for real? Ness made me feel like I was in the kind of high school movie critics called a "cult classic."

She stubbed out the joint on the lid of her box, and pushed it aside to crawl even closer to me. Was it weird that we were together like this, with Nat? If it wasn't weird for her, it shouldn't be weird for me.

"Could you read my mind?" She grinned at me. I never could tell if she was being flirty, or if it was wishful thinking on my part.

"I don't think so. At the most I could probably show you something in *my* mind. But I've never tried…anything with another person."

Ness gently took my hand, and traced a finger through the center of my palm. I shivered, and we watched each other, shared a long slow smile.

That seemed like flirting.

"Try with me," she said in the quietest voice I'd ever heard from her.

"Okay. Um, okay. I'm going to … send you a thought. Like, I'll think of an image or a sentence or something. And then you tell me once you think you have it. Tell me what it is."

She nodded. A breeze blew through the leaves around us. It was a curious sensation, trying to show my thoughts to her instead of conceal them. I tightened my fingers a little around hers, so we were clasping palm to palm. I didn't think that would help, but it sure didn't hurt.

Kiss me, I thought.

She brought her free hand to my cheek, and tilted my head up. I smiled, and then her lips were on mine, and then my tongue found hers and I was tasting ash and I didn't care.

I honestly don't know if it was sorcery or not.

✳✳✳

At the end of our first week, SA and I went to the Cliff for the first time. The Academy's property ended on a bluff over-looking the bay, and every year at the start of term students gathered at the edge to dare each other and conjure shapes in the sky. It was nothing like any high school party either of us had ever attended.

"Hey, it's Carla," I said. My resident tutor had gone full unicorn; her outfit was every vivid shade of the rainbow, and her hair and nails matched her outfit.

SA's jaw dropped. "Who?"

"*Now* you wish you lived on my floor."

"Yeah, no, that's…a *lot*."

Through the hearty crowd, Carla saw me and started to head over. Trailing behind her, I realized with a start, was John.

"Hello hello," she greeted us in singsong. "Who's your friend?"

I introduced SA.

"I'm not finished grading yet, so don't tell anyone," said John, "but both of your labs were very well done." He nodded to SA and me.

"Whew, thank you," I said.

"I'm just glad I finished it," SA chimed in.

Another girl from my floor appeared, and the group grew larger and larger as the sky darkened. SA went off to get another drink and never came back. We were a stone's throw from the dorm and there were plenty of people around, so I started to head back on my own, yawning.

"Hey," said a voice right behind me. I jumped.

"Sorry, I didn't mean to scare you," said John. "I'm headed back the same way."

To Carla's room, I realized. I'd never walked home with anyone who was in charge of my grades.

"Hey, can I ask you something?" I said. "That…demonstration the first day of class looked like it hurt."

He chuckled. "It did."

"So…"

"I agreed to it. Healing is one of my specialties. And Gene and I worked out everything beforehand. As you pointed out in class, I wasn't resisting."

"Well, if he's your thesis advisor, it can't be easy to go against him on anything."

John threw back his head and laughed, like he couldn't believe the things the kids said these days. "You have no idea."

"It just seems like…a lot." Was I so tired, echoing SA was all I could do? "There have got to be ethical guidelines for that sort of thing."

"Oh, there are," John said. "Don't worry. We followed them. Of course."

We'd reached the dorm by that point, and John stopped at the door and waited for me. I was the one with the key—or, in this case, my sorcery signature imprinted in the building's security structure. I waved my hand, sending out a simple command, *open*, and the door obeyed me. John held it and gestured for me to go ahead.

"So, can you hint about any other fun demonstrations you guys have planned for us?" I asked as we headed up the stairs the boring way.

"Hmm." He made a show of scrutinizing me. "I'm not sure I'm at liberty to reveal. Can I trust you not to tell everyone?"

"You absolutely can…but I understand if you prefer not to."

"Ha. I know women. You'll say we're fine, but secretly you'll hold a grudge against me forever."

It was that comment—and the way he said it, smiling into my eyes—that should have sounded some alarm.

"So this is your room, huh?" he asked, and followed me in. This was all happening very fast. My TA was at my desk, probably noticing how messy my notes were, how many mundane books I had mixed in with the sorcery ones. I had posters of musicians, pictures of my friends…a true sorcerer would have Graham's *Principles of Elemental Manipulation* and nothing else.

"Interesting," he muttered.

I glanced at the door, ajar. Was anyone back yet from the Cliff? Was Carla okay with him visiting random girls in her hall?

He started kissing me before I'd even registered that he'd moved, and when I jumped back and tried to put my hands up, he grabbed my wrists and forced them back. I could feel already that if I tried to fight more, I'd lose. I doubted I could hurl any sorcery at him that he wouldn't see coming. My body froze like Roper's pocket square. In the shock of the moment seconds lengthened as my brain raced to catch up, a sick kind of relativity. Why hadn't I expected this? Why *should* I have expected this?

He kept kissing me, pushing forward where I shrank back.

Could I knee him, shove him away? Run? He was so much bigger, so much taller, so much more prepared for a confrontation.

If I screamed? Everyone was at the Cliff. I might get Carla. Which one of us would she believe?

I managed to break off enough to say, "Hey, stop."

"Just a few more minutes," he said, and put his mouth on me again. His hands were still holding my arms, keeping me from moving, reminding me who had the power.

This evening had started with SA and I trying to escape the prep work for our next lab. Where would it end?

Our joking and studying already felt like it had been a week ago or more. My heart hammered, sprinting a marathon. I bet he could feel that. I bet he interpreted it as excitement. How far did he want to take this?

When he broke for air I tried again.

"John, I—"

"Shhh." He kept his grip on my wrists firm. "No one's coming."

I found myself backed into my own door, and then it shut for real. Now the gulf between me and the hallway seemed impossibly huge. Why couldn't I move? Why wouldn't I fight? All my possessions stood around me: my high school diploma, my last birthday card from my parents, the single Lego piece Dara had let me take from his collection. I'd never be able to fall asleep in this room again.

Was it only my fear response that froze me? Was John using sorcery? I felt sick all over again, and my spine turned cold.

Help.

John's hands were under my shirt. To register anything more exact would require me to be much more present in my body than my mind would allow me to be.

LEAVE US ALONE.

For a microsecond I didn't know who it was. *How did*— and then awareness flooded me. An echo of her voice trickled again in my ear. Ness. Fragments shot through my senses: knuckle bruises, skin rubbed raw; the smell of old paperbacks; Nat smiling; me. For a moment, Ness and I were the same person.

I felt her burn through me like solar-powered adrenaline, and John shrieked in pain and flew away from me. It was as if I had turned on antigravity, and was now repelling him at a rate proportional to one over the squared distance between our respective centers of mass.

John tensed as he had in class and I braced for impact, but none came. He fled. I deadbolted the door behind him and listened to my own breathing, *in*-out, *in*-out. Ness was gone.

Slowly, exhaustion sank in. I defied my predictions and fell right to sleep.

***

When I left the dorm the next morning, I almost slammed the door into SA.

"I couldn't find you last night!"

"I couldn't find *you* last night!" I replied. "Are you okay?"

"I'm fine. I got pulled into a spell-off."

I nodded. We started toward the dining hall.

"Naré...are *you* okay?"

"I think you might not want to know this."

"Well, now I *really* want to know it." They stopped, and when I stopped with them they led me away from the buildings, into the shelter of a tree.

"We'll miss breakfast," I warned.

"I can cook," said SA. "What's up?"

"You're going to think I'm stupid. You would have seen this coming. It's like you said—it's fucked up."

They just listened. I got it out eventually, what had happened, in broad strokes. John had gotten me alone and assaulted me. After a time, I had gotten away.

"You're not stupid," they said. "But I think you should tell someone."

"I told you," I said. "Who else do you think I should tell? Carla? Roper? The Dean?"

SA sighed. "You're right," they said. "You're right." They reached out a hand, and I took it.

"You got away," said SA.

"I got away," I repeated. "And I think if I can understand how, you and I could turn it into a spell that anyone could use."

SA smiled, and it wasn't until that transformed their face that I realized how anxious they'd been for me.

"Then that's what we should do," they said.

"Let's have breakfast."

***

The Cliff was the one place on campus I sometimes had cell reception. Go figure. If your friends and loved ones couldn't communicate via sorcery, they weren't worth keeping. I stayed far back from the edge, keeping my gaze toward the observatory building and the rest of campus to be sure I was alone. The dreary Sunday morning helped my cause.

My fingers actually shook as I dialed her number.

"What's up, nerd?" I could hear her chewing gum. She was a starburst in the void. I was already starting to breathe normally, and when I spoke I thought I even sounded casual.

"Not much. I'm learning how to mind control people."

"See, I've always wanted to do that. And yet they reject me."

I laughed, but it faltered a little.

"Naré." She didn't say my name enough. She pronounced it perfectly. "You okay?"

"Thanks to you," I said.

"Thanks to *you*."

I didn't know what to reply that wouldn't sound hollow over a telephone line.

"We're warriors," I said finally. I could almost feel her smile.

"And sorcerers," she said. "That was sorcery, right? We did sorcery. *I* did sorcery."

I laughed. "It's funny you should mention it, because there's something I want to brainstorm with you."

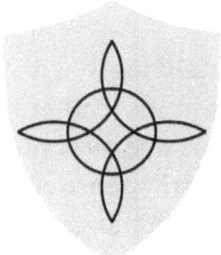

Under the Hunter's Moon

Darian Lindle

The full moon rises into view; vast and strangely crimson against the dark blue of the cold sky. *I should have waited*, he thinks. *I shouldn't have come during the Hunter's Moon.*

Henry whips around, the back of his neck tingling, but sees only his footprints in the newly-fallen snow. He balls his hands into fists and scans the forest. The trees are dark despite the unnatural, wine-colored light of the moon. Snow covers the upper branches of the fir trees and blankets the narrow path beneath his feet.

Turning back toward his purpose, Henry draws his sword from its scabbard.

The cottage he's come so far to find is small and made entirely of white limestone. He'd expected disrepair, spider webs, and a moldy smell. Instead, he finds a tidy hunting cabin where he might enjoy passing a winter. Soft, welcoming light emanates from neat windows snugged on either side of an oaken door. But no snow rests on this thatched roof, nor disturbs the blooming flowers. A pleasant warmth reaches his face. It mingles tantalizingly with the wintery gusts that creep through the gaps in his leather cuirass.

Movement catches his eye, and he halts in the shadow of a tree. A fair-skinned girl with delicate features opens the cottage door and steps into the garden. The light behind her shines through the thin shawl covering her shoulders. She kneels to coax carrots from the ground and stands to snip some herbs; her body lithe and graceful. Henry watches her gather the ill-seasoned bounty in an apron tied at her waist. He blinks, and she's back inside the cottage.

It's too late for doubts, he thinks. Stamping his feet to bring feeling back to his toes, Henry hardens his resolve.

The snow deadens the noise of his approach. With each step, the cold diminishes until he stands on the cottage's front walk in weather warm enough to thaw his frozen fingers.

At his next step, a woman's low and throaty voice tickles his ear.

"There was a daughter, fair and bright
Juniper, Thyme, and Rosemary
She spied a swift and valiant knight
As autumn moon bloomed mulberry
Wounded in heart, she let him in,
the door she barred with silver pin
And cast a spell, though t'was a sin
With juniper, thyme, and rosemary."

Henry's limbs grow heavy. Before he can act, his eyes close and his world is cloaked in darkness.

All I want is to survive my thirteenth birthday with my honor intact.

Summoning my strength, I lift my father's sword with both hands and block the blow aimed at my right shoulder. My teeth rattle with the impact, but I manage to push back and swing an offensive strike before my opponent can come at me again. My swing goes wide, and she comes in close enough to pop an elbow in my gut. The blow distracts me. Before I can recover the end of her blade presses against my chest. I freeze.

"Point!" She laughs. "Do you yield?"

Groaning, I nod, rub my sore ribs, and turn toward the weapons shed.

In the waning light, the training ground looks reddened and angry. It's just a large patch of land cleared of trees and stones with a shelter to one side for posting horses and a shed on the other to keep practice weapons dry. In spring, grass battles to cover the well-trodden ground, but now it's late autumn, and the field is a barren patch of dust and dirt.

"Don't be upset," my sister tells me. "You just need a different weapon. That sword is too big. You'd do better with my short sword or even a hand-and-a-half."

Rose fairly hums with energy. *That's as it should be*, I reason. Her Visitation is finally set. The pre-ordained ritual must take place under a blood moon in autumn when magic paints the world to match a witch's heart. It's called a Hunter's Moon and the next one will be tonight. But I weary of her talk about wishing she could choose her own future. As if it's easier without a Destiny. As if I have so many choices.

"It's father's sword," I say between gritted teeth. She knows this. "It's the one he used during his Trial."

"So what? Use a different sword."

"It's tradition," I say.

"Tradition is just history repeating itself until it becomes a habit."

I only half listen: what will be, will be. I need to focus. At daybreak, I will either be accepted as a page in the king's service, or fail my father. I'm bone tired of failure.

I carry Father's longsword to the shed and slump onto a

bench in the shade. Using a cloth, I wipe the blade with oil. I know the sword is too long for me, but I've been practicing with it for months. I tell myself it won't feel so heavy during the Trial.

As if to point out my hope is in vain, Rose performs a series of graceful calisthenics with her well-balanced short sword. She moves with an ease I envy. She laughs again.

"There is something special about this moon," she says. "I feel this tingly energy everywhere. Do you feel it?"

Despite our differences in temperament, we look alike: light brown hair, fair with freckles, tall for our age. But where I keep my straight hair pulled into a neat braid, Rose lets hers fall freely about her shoulders. In the light of the sunset, her skin glows pink. She looks powerful.

"All I feel is nerves," I say.

Rose frowns at me. I look away and notice her flask on the bench beside me.

"Is that the potion, then?" I ask, unable to keep the longing out of my voice.

Rose shakes her head, picks up the flask, tosses it to me and says, "I brewed this one for you."

"For me?"

"For luck," she adds.

"That's cheating," I say, fingering the clasp.

"You won't do anything you're not capable of doing on your own." It sounds so reasonable when she says it.

Rose is still holding the sword in her left hand. She flicks it in the air and catches it with her right before returning it to its place. It's ridiculous she won't be allowed to try for knighthood; Rose would never embarrass father, but witches can't be warriors. The flask shakes in my hands. My gut churns. Her kindness is unbearable. *Her ritual is tonight. Why isn't she nervous?*

"You drink it," I scoff. "If you have to do what you're told, you'll need luck more than I will."

Her brow furrows. "I just need to go in with a clear mind."

"Well then, you should get along just fine. Your mind is always empty."

Before I can regret my words, Rose lets out a grunt and yanks me off the bench. She turns me around and wrenches my arm behind my back. I lean back into her like I've been taught and stomp on her foot but she knees me in the shin with her other leg and I go down. My face rubs against the ground.

"Gerroff, Ro—" I swallow some dirt and cough.

Rose doesn't get off. Instead, she sits on my back while I squirm beneath her.

"It's not my fault you don't think you're ready," Rose hisses into my ear. "I'd help you if you'd let me."

"Gerroff!" I bark again into the ground.

"What's that?" She teases. "Sorry, I can't hear over the echoing in my empty mind?"

I stop struggling and mutter, "Mmmsorry," into the dirt.

Rose hops from my back and helps me off the ground with the ease of someone whose body always responds the way she wants it to.

"Here." My sister holds out the potion for me like a peace offering. "It may not work, but at least you'll rinse the dirt from your mouth."

I grab the flask from my sister's fingers. It's tempting to throw it in her face but, after this little encounter, I'm reminded I'll need all the luck I can get. The draft tastes of bitter herbs, rosemary, and gin. I know the common herbs for luck: alfalfa, honeysuckle, lemon balm, cinnamon, ginger, orange, sandalwood, dandelion, strawberry leaves. This potion contains none of them.

"Wrong again, Rose." My voice cracks as I speak. "You'll make a terrible witch."

Rose gives me a probing look, but I can still taste the dirt in my mouth, so I turn on my heel and stomp off. I'm halfway down the well-trodden path toward home when I realize I left Father's sword behind. It's dusk now. The edge of the full moon rises crimson in the sky: the Hunter's Moon. Rose will be hurrying off to her ritual.

I sigh, and I head back down the dry, cracked earth of the track I've walked every day of my life.

Then I blink, and step in a cobblestoned rain puddle.

I look about for any sign of the footpath or my sister. Both are gone.

Instead, I'm in a tidy rain-soaked street in a town I don't recognize. A wealthy town at that, for every shop window is paned with glass. *What did Rose do?* The moon flushes the street with ruby light, higher than it was a moment ago.

I look in the window of the apothecary shop on my right, thinking the herbalist inside might be able to help. A middle-aged woman with brown skin and wiry black hair tucked under a turban stares back at me from the pane of glass. I make an awkward curtsy, and she curtsies back. We wave at each other in unison. Reaching up to touch the end of my blonde braid, my fingers rub against her turban instead.

I rush into the shop. Inside, the strong, cloying smells of candles, herbs, and fungi in various stages of use and decay assault my senses. A young woman of fourteen or fifteen years with a dusky complexion stands behind the counter.

"Mama," she says, looking at me. "Did you forget something?"

Henry blinks awake.

Beneath him, a comfortable chair sits close to a blazing fire. Across from him, an ageless, dark-haired woman with skin the color of amber sits perfectly still, her eyes closed. Even without her gaze upon him, he feels watched. *Witchcraft,* his thoughts whisper. He reaches for his sword and finds it missing.

His heart beating fast, Henry pushes a patchwork blanket to the floor and stumbles over it only to be steadied by the girl he'd seen outside the cottage. Up close, he sees she isn't a girl at all, but a young woman. She puts a delicate finger to her lips and leads him to the door.

"You must go," she whispers, her voice so quiet he's only convinced she speaks by the movement of her lips. She reaches for his helm, which hangs beside the door. Her fingers glow in the pink moonlight bleeding through the window.

He grasps her outreached hand. "Isabel?"

The woman covers his mouth with her free hand, which smells of earth and flowers. He pulls it from his lips and brings it together with her other hand at his chest.

Isabel. The girl he'd played with so often when they were children. The girl who'd disappeared during a Hunter's Moon ten years before. The girl he's been searching for since becoming a knight has grown beautiful.

"Henry," she mouths.

"Come with me," he says.

Isabel's soft eyes widen, and her gaze dips to Henry's mouth. She licks her lips but shakes her head slowly. *Sadly,* he thinks.

"Awake, I see," says a throaty, melodious voice behind them.

Isabel's hands disappear from his.

Still seated before the fire, the witch crosses one leg over the other and looks Henry up and down. When she smiles, lines appear at her eyes and mouth, and he realizes that, in fact, she is quite old.

"She says she knows you," the witch states, mildly.

Henry glances at Isabel before nodding.

"She tells me you've had a long journey."

He nods again.

"She assures me you're just a traveler; that your being here is a mere coincidence; that we should aid you on your journey. But I think," she says, leaning forward, "that no knight travels into my domain under a Hunter's Moon without a purpose."

Henry touches the royal seal stamped into the leather at his chest.

"Do many come to see you?"

The witch shrugs. "Some."

"They all come willingly?" Henry asks, catching the tail end of a frown on Isabel's face before she turns away.

The old woman answers. "All who come to me for help do so freely."

"Did a man named Joren come to you?" Henry presses. "His wife was to bear a child."

"Elspeth," Isabel's eyes seek out the witch. "Her time came during the first snowfall."

The witch's hands ball into fists, but she says nothing.

To Henry, Isabel adds, "Some wait too long and come too late."

Henry bristles. "Joren said Elspeth was fine when she crossed this threshold."

"If she'd been fine, she wouldn't have come," Isabel says sadly.

"Women die in childbirth, Knight," the witch's harsh voice chills the air. "That is our battlefield. I can help, but not if I'm called after the battle has been fought." The sorceress rubs the amulet at her neck between two fingers. Her gaze bores into him. "Why have you come to my house?"

Henry means to say, "I'm here to avenge them," but his gaze falls on Isabel. What escapes his lips instead is, "To rescue her."

The witch stands, her eyes aflame.

"You've come for me?" Isabel stares at him.

"Joren recognized you," Henry explains. "He told me you were here."

Isabel nods. "Elspeth died, but it wasn't Thyme's doing. She did all she could."

A terrible thought occurs to him. "If it wasn't hers...was it yours?"

A pained look crosses Isabel's face.

"Enough," the witch Thyme says, stoking the fire. "You're a fool."

Henry stiffens.

"You walked into the north woods with naught but a sword and your wits, such as they are, to rescue this Damsel in Distress from the Rogue Witch." Thyme stands, her presence filling the room. "But you made a mistake for tonight is a Hunter's Moon," she says, "and I am the Hunter."

Touching the amulet at her neck again, she speaks,

"Pass my threshold with ill intent
Forfeit your freedom. Your will is bent
to mine."

To Henry, she adds, "You shall not leave this house again except by my will or your death."

Thyme pulls the amulet loose and throws it into the fire.

First, a bolt of silver falls across the door, shutting them inside. Then, a shock of power slams into Henry and takes his breath away.

"Mama?" the girl asks me again.

I want to run, but where can I go in this strange woman's body?

She cocks her head to the side as if considering me.

"You must be a Traveler," she emphasizes the word, investing it with a meaning I don't understand. Her voice is kind. "Welcome," she says.

The girl's hair is dark and curly, like her mother's, but instead of pulling it into a turban, she wears it plaited neatly away from her face. Her skin is reddish-brown and pimply, and her nose turns up like a button. Her smile, even while looking at a stranger wearing her mother's face, is genuine. I catch a glimpse of myself in the mirrored glass behind the shop counter and see my cold confusion looking out of another woman's eyes. I try to soften my expression, but don't quite succeed.

"This will pass," the girl says. "This confusion. Have you Visited before?"

I shake my head.

"I'm told it's disorienting, the first time."

She crosses to the shop door, pulls a dowel down to secure it, then closes the curtains at the window shutting out the scarlet moonlight. I wonder at the wealth of this shop with its mirrored glass and window panes and curtains. The girl gestures for me to take a seat at a table hidden in a corner behind some shelves full of jars and dried plants. *Hickory. Mint. Cloves.* She puts a pot of tea in front of us both and pours out two cups.

"I'm Nesta," she says. "What's your name, Traveler?"

"Mary."

Nesta gives me a quizzical look. "Well, Mary," she says. "You're Visiting my mother, she's called Juniper."

She hands me a cup. It's warm in my cold hands...*in Juniper's cold hands.*

I smell the tea. *Chamomile. Lemon balm. Skullcap. Sage.* I take a sip.

"Mama says it takes a lot out of a Witch to Visit," Nesta continues.

I swallow my tea too quickly, burning my mouth. "Your mother thinks I'm a witch? Is that why she brought me here?"

"The craft to Visit comes from the Traveler. You came to her."

"But—" I don't even know what to ask.

Nesta pours more tea. "You drank the Alucinaverum," she prompts.

My eyes go wide. Alucinaverum is the potion for Rose's ritual. I never thought to drink it, but now I have a pretty good idea of what it does.

"We thought it was for luck," I say half-heartedly because I'm more and more certain Rose knew exactly what she was doing. "How do I get back to myself?"

Nesta frowns. "I've never needed to know that."

"What am I to do? I can't be your mother."

She snorts. "Tell me what you know of the draft you took."

"My sister made it." I recall the taste of the potion and try to separate out the herbs. "There was mugwort, vervain, dill, something woody and astringent I didn't recognize, rosemary, and… and I thought it was gin, but it must have been juniper."

"You can tell all of that by taste?" Nesta looks impressed. "You have studied the craft."

"Not officially."

"But you took the Alucinaverum; you Visited. If you aren't a True Witch, you've been tricked by one."

I hate her words. Rose and I may fight, but we love each other. The room I'm in feels too small. The walls and shelves are crammed with tokens and potions and the trappings of witchcraft. For the first time in my life they aren't enticing, but sinister.

"Your mother must have done this to me," I spit.

Nesta shakes her head. But I hear Rose's voice in my head; *there's more than one way to cast a spell.*

"Then you did!" I stand and push the tea cup away, spilling tea and leaves onto the table before the cup rolls to the floor with a crash. My heart pounds noisily in my chest.

Nesta looks at the cup on the floor. "That was Mama's favorite." She looks back at me, her eyes flaring with annoyance.

"Oh, sit down, you silly goose."

She stands and grabs a broom from the corner.

"You can't just fly away and leave me here!" I'm looking at her broom. "You have to fix me!"

Nesta laughs. "What I should do is make you clean up the mess you've made."

She lays a cloth on the ground and sweeps the broken tea cup into the fabric, then stores both broom and the shards behind the counter. She flops back down in the chair opposite where I stand.

"You're young, aren't you?" She asks. "What are you, eight? Nine?"

"I'm thirteen today." *That's practically grown.*

"Yet you know nothing of yourself or the craft?"

"I told you, I'm *not* a witch."

"Aren't you?"

"Stop trying to trick me."

"Does this look like an evil lair in the woods? If I had such awesome power would I still have these spots on my face? I know a bit of herb lore. That's one kind of witch, I guess. Anyone can learn about herbs and the body, but I have no magic. There are witches and there are Witches. You're different."

"I'm not!"

"And I will say again, only a True Witch can Travel."

I cover my face with my hands. What Nesta says can't be right and yet, here I am, in her mother's body. I recall all the times I listened to my sister's lessons, aching to be taught. My mother divined my sister's future before we were even born. First-born Rose was chosen, and I was an afterthought. Nothing to be done. If there's one thing I've known my whole life, it's that I've never had any power.

"I won't listen to any more of your lies," I tell her, stepping behind Nesta's chair. The girl turns to look at me, and I use her momentum to grip her right arm and twist it up behind her back. It's the move Rose used on me earlier, whenever it was that I was still me. "Send me home now!"

"Please," Nesta cries out, "That hurts!"

"If I keep lifting it, I'll pull your arm out of the shoulder socket." I raise her forearm a little to emphasize my words.

She cries out again.

"Now, send me home," I command.

"Mama," Nesta whimpers. "Please, help me."

A heaviness presses into the back of my mind. I feel my fingers uncurl from Nesta's wrist. She pulls away and crosses the room rubbing it with her other hand. Fear and anger linger in her eyes.

"I'm here, Nesta." The words come from my mouth. I try to speak, but cannot.

What's happening? I think.

I'm back, says a voice.

I turn, and the woman I inhabit looks back at me from the mirror behind the counter.

That's right, in here, her eyes say. *You shouldn't have hurt my daughter.*

The fire casts Thyme's face in shadow and turns her black hair orange and wild. Flames leap into her eyes. She fills the room with her presence and power.

Isabel grips the back of the chair so hard her knuckles are white. Henry clutches his chest, recovering his breath. His gaze falls on the poker near the hearth. It might serve as a weapon, but he must get past the witch to reach it.

"You must give him a chance, Thyme," Isabel implores. "This isn't his fault."

The witch laughs. "If our roles were reversed, he would—"

"He might," Isabel replies. She looks at Henry, who stops inching toward the fire when she places her hand on his arm.

"He might not."

Her hand is warm, reassuring. Henry clasps his hand over it.

"If he knew your future?" Thyme smirks. "Do you think he'd still have come for you?"

"What is it?" Henry asks.

Isabel bites her lip and squeezes his arm. "When I was a girl, I came to Thyme to ask her for a spell... a love spell." Her eyes focus on the ground. "I'd hoped it would show me my future husband. But I saw more than that." She closes her eyes and shakes her head. "I saw what would've happened if I had stayed. Disappearing was for the best, for...everyone. Thyme allowed me to live with her. She trained me. She saved me."

"From whom?" Henry's voice catches in his throat.

"They would have discovered the truth eventually, and tried to kill me."

"You're a witch, too."

She shook her head. "But I will bear a witch child."

Henry frowns and drops her hand.

"See," Thyme spits. "He isn't worthy."

Without knowing how it came to be there, Henry sees his scabbard in the witch's hand. Thyme draws his sword from it and points it at his heart.

"Nesta, fetch me the Silva Rerum." The words pass through my lips.

The pressure in my head grows; it feels like a tight band encircling my skull. I long to massage my temples, but I don't control Juniper's hands anymore. My fear spikes. Being in another's body was uncomfortable but being trapped in their mind is terrifying.

Well, if you'd been reasonable then I wouldn't need to be here, says Juniper's voice in my head. *Now you'll just have to deal with it.*

There's been a mistake, I think.

There are no mistakes under a Hunter's Moon, my dear.

Nesta returns from another room with an old book. Its pages are wrapped in leather with long, tapering straps that hang well below the pages. Someone's tied the ends of the straps into a large knot so the book can be hung from a post, a horse, or a belt. I recognize it. It's my sister's commonplace book, the one passed down from True Witch to True Witch. Rose received it the day she was born. She'll write her own spells in it, one day. Nesta handles the book with great care, placing it on the counter. She opens it and flips to a list in the front, scanning the words there with her finger.

"I don't see the name Mary," she says.

Of course not, I hiss. *I'm not the sister with Magic.* I'm almost amused remembering how often I've longed for this kind of adventure. How Rose wants to fight battles by our father's side instead of brewing potions. How we both feel cheated by her destiny.

Try Rosemary, I think. Juniper repeats my suggestion aloud.

"There is a Rosemary several hundred years ago." Nesta turns the commonplace book around so Juniper and I can read it. Her finger points to the word Juniper.

"This is Mama," Nesta says.

Her finger travels up a list of herbs several inches until it stops at Rosemary, which someone crossed out to read Rose Mary.

That's you, Juniper's voice says.

Juniper points to the word above Rose Mary; it's Thyme.

But who is Thyme? I wonder. *That's not my mother.*

Witchpower doesn't pass from mother to child. We are reborn. Aloud she says, "Nesta, put a pint of water on the fire."

The girl nods at us, pulls a bucket of water from behind

the counter, and steps to the hearth. She ladles the water into a three-legged pot and then places it over the glowing coals. She adds a pinch of dust from a jar on the mantle to the flames, causing them to roar higher.

How? How are you reborn? I wonder.

We choose our future, she says, as though that explains anything.

Juniper turns the pages of the Silva Rerum until they fall open on a page with "Alucinaverum" written at the top in a curving script.

She reads, "Add one ounce each of dried eyebright and mugwort. Twist a sprig of vervain with one of dill and boil until the liquid reduces by half." Juniper flips back to the front of the book and the list of names. "Next we'll add rosemary. And then some thyme, I think."

Nesta pauses. "But Thyme came before. I thought that was forbidden?"

Her mother shrugs. Nesta nods and adds the ingredients as directed. An astringent, herbaceous smell fills the room.

Juniper flips back to the spell and chants.

"Eyebright for clear sight into moments unseen.
Mugwort to ensure safe return to what's been.
Entwine fresh Vervain for protection from pain
With a new sprig of Dill impose Visitor's will."

She looks away from the book and gazes into the fire. *Now, we get to the good part,* she thinks. I feel her smile. Panic flares in me as I realize Juniper is improvising the spell.

"Rosemary for remembrance: Find truth beyond fear. Protect and purify."

Nesta pulls a spring of rosemary from a potted plant in the window of the shop. When she places it in the boiling water, I catch its woody, healthy scent and feel a burst of power. I force Juniper's hands to grab the commonplace book.

"What does this mean? Why isn't she following the spell-book?" I say aloud.

Startled, Nesta throws the thyme she's gathered into the pot. My arms lose their strength as Juniper chastises me. *Quiet.* She continues her chant out loud.

"Thyme for temerity: Safe passage to the next life. Or the one before."

The pain in my head subsides, and I'm suddenly weary. Only Juniper's will keeps the body we share on its feet.

"Flush with power under the Hunter's Moon.
Stir thrice and twice more with a silver spoon."

Nesta holds out a silver ladle. Juniper takes it and stirs the potion three times to the left, then twice to the right.

"Now, distill and cool it, Nesta."

The young apothecary pours the potion into a flask through cheesecloth, catching the wet herbs. The tincture that remains is amber colored and aromatic. She stoppers it and plunges it into the bucket of water to cool it. After a moment, she withdraws the flask and wipes it dry on her apron, then hands the potion to her mother.

What will this do to me? I ask.

In lieu of an answer, Juniper drinks the potion. It's slightly bitter. I taste each herb individually. The addition of thyme instead of juniper berries changes the flavor, but it's similar enough to the Alucinaverum my sister brewed that I recognize the taste.

Go find the answers you seek, Juniper thinks and closes our eyes.

Henry thinks of five ways to disarm the witch, but none that won't endanger Isabel. Before he makes a choice, Thyme swings the sword. Henry steps back reflexively, then watches in horror as Isabel steps in front of him, blocking the sword's path with the palm of her raised hand.

Thyme checks her swing with what must be magic because Isabel's hand remains intact. Nonetheless, he regrets the blood that drips down her palm.

Thyme growls. "He won't be yours. I won't allow it."

"My only power is choosing," Isabel replies, cradling her injured hand. "And I made my choice long ago."

"Not with him," the witch sneers.

Henry looks between them, wrinkling his brow.

"I owe you a great debt," Isabel says. "But whom I choose is not up to you."

"I am flame and rage," Thyme howls. "I am hearth and home. I am night and sky. I do what needs to be done. I am the one who will make your future, I can unmake it as well."

Then something passes through the witch's face, a softening, a confusion. When she focuses on Isabel again, she exclaims.

"Mother!"

I stare at my mum. She looks so young and so sad. Blood drips from her hand onto the floor. The same blood clings to the sword I'm holding in my hands.

Not my hands, I think. *Thin, calloused, woman's hands.*

"Did I hurt you?" I cry.

Mother drops her wounded hand to her side.

The man behind her leaps toward the hearth and grabs a poker. He moves in front of my mother and brandishes it at me. My heart constricts. It's my Father.

With the witch distracted, Henry grabs the poker and pulls Isabel behind him. Witch-mother or not, he will protect her from Thyme.

"Henry, stop," Isabel yells. She leans around him, reaching both hands out to Thyme, who looks the same but seems smaller somehow, younger.

"Visitor, welcome," Isabel says.

Henry looks between Isabel and the witch. Something passes between them that he doesn't understand. He doesn't like it.

"Mother," the witch implores, "It's me."

Isabel's voice shakes, "I'm afraid I haven't had any children, yet."

"I—where am I?" The witch blinks heavily and takes in the room as if for the first time.

"Isabel?" Henry asks.

She squeezes his arm as if he should understand why the witch threatening them with his sword suddenly requires his patience.

"Don't be afraid," Isabel coos at the witch. "You're Visiting my mistress."

The sorceress nods and says, "Thyme." She looks between Isabel and Henry. "But how are you both here?" As she asks she steps toward them and tilts the tip of the sword toward the floor.

One step closer, he thinks.

"Your father and I only met again this evening."

His thoughts catch on Isabel's words.

"Her father?" he asks, afraid he understands all too well what she means.

"I told you my future is to have a witch child." Isabel smiles weakly. "With you."

Henry thinks about the girl he'd befriended all those years ago. On a whim, she'd asked a witch her future, ran away and changed their lives. He thinks of his training and its discipline and hardships. He remembers the battles he's fought, often winning only by a hair's breadth. So much of life is luck; any moment could go one way or another. One thing he knows, *the future isn't written*.

I'm staring at my mother when my father strikes. I don't expect it and barely get the sword up in time to keep the poker away from my head. Another inch and I'd have had it in my eye. Fear threatens to freeze me in my tracks until I realize I know the feel of the sword in Thyme's hands. I've practiced with it for months. Father slides the poker down the blade to put pressure on the hilt, probably hoping to force it from my grip. If I don't do something, it will work.

My lessons never taught me how to fight like this. My father is stronger, as always, but his longsword finally feels right in this taller, borrowed body.

What would Rose do? I think.

Blinding pain brings stars to his eyes. The damned witch had kneed him in the groin.

Henry can't maintain his attack and falls back, doubling over in pain. When his vision returns, he stares up the edge of his own blade at the witch. He feels it prick the tender skin of his throat. The agony in his loins continues to plague him, but all his attention is on the spell caster.

"Point," she says, trembling. "Yield."

"Never," he answers through gritted teeth.

The witch's lower lip pulls into a pout, the childlike expression incongruous on her mature face.

"But I bested you," she says. "Those are the rules of dueling just as you taught them to me."

"This isn't a proper duel, witch."

"It is, and I've won." A smile creeps onto her face. "I've beat you with your own sword. I passed my Trial after all."

"Will someone tell me what the hell is going on?" Father says from his position on the floor.

"If you'll stop attacking her, perhaps we can find out," my mother says.

He presses his lips together, then nods. "I yield. For now." He holds one hand up in surrender. The other still protects his sensitive parts.

I bested my father!

I look around me and see items I recognize: a patchwork blanket on a chair by the hearth that swaddled me as a child, and Rose's Silva Rerum hanging by its leather straps on a hook by the table. I note the door is barred with silver.

"Why is the door barred?" I ask.

"Thyme cast a spell on it." Mother nods sadly at Father. "On him."

"Can you undo it?" I ask.

My mother frowns and approaches the door. She reaches to touch the silver and pulls her hand back quickly, sucking her finger into her mouth as if it burns.

"I guess that means no," Father says.

"Magic is *Intention*. Thyme created this spell to keep you here. I suppose she intended to keep me in as well."

"So, we are well and truly trapped, then." My father says. "Until I die." He looks at me, and I don't like the darkness I see in his eyes. "Or she does."

"To counter a True Witch's spell takes a deep connection to Magic," my mother says, looking at me.

Silver conducts energy, including magic. Any spell cast in silver will be amplified and its energy more easily directed. I am not a witch. My mother made this clear from birth. But she also said she never expected to have twins.

I walk to the door and touch the silver bar. Moonlight streams through the windows and coats my hands in its red glow. The silver feels cold and docile under my fingers. I lift it from its place and toss it to the floor.

"I hope you'll remember this when I'm seven and accidentally set the weapons shed on fire," I say, feeling my blush rise in Thyme's cheeks.

"Thyme hasn't decided on me yet," my mother says, glancing at Father. "On us. Not for certain. She could always make another choice."

"You mean, this person, our daughter, doesn't have to be a witch?" Father asks.

I laugh.

I thought I knew what it meant to have a Destiny. When your mother sees the future, it's easy to think your choices don't matter. Perhaps nothing changes, and everything is predetermined. Or, maybe, this is why Rose sent me on this journey. She needs me to help her shape the way things will be for both us from now on. Maybe Destiny is just the consequence of choosing my future for myself.

I step forward and put my hands over their hearts. To my surprise, my father doesn't flinch away, just tilts his head and considers my hands. "Mother. Father," I say. "I choose you both."

For a moment, the crimson light of the Hunter's Moon fills the cottage, then just as suddenly, it recedes.

"What's your name?" My mother asks me, a little breathless.

Names have power. Share a name, share the power? Maybe we can both be what we want after all. *Leave it to Rose.*

"Rose Mary," I say with a smile.

Then, I close my eyes with *Intention.*

Henry's gaze rests on the hand pressed gently on his chest. His daughter's hand. Warmth floods through him. Warmth and... love? *Rosemary,* she's called herself. He meets Isabel's eyes and smiles. She smiles back and clasps his hand.

"Well," the witch scoffs.

Henry jerks his head up to see the look of innocent pride has left the witch's face. Rosemary is gone.

Thyme has returned.

Her eyes are cold and angry as her fingers curl against his tunic. Henry doesn't step away from the witch's touch, just meets her gaze and waits.

"Our daughter chose us with your hands, Thyme," Isabel soothes. "It's done."

Thyme sighs and gestures for them to sit. "I suppose I have to welcome you to the family." She grunts at Henry.

Isabel squeezes his hand and tugs him back to the chair by the fire. Despite everything, it seems he will still follow wherever she leads.

The next thing I see is my sister's face.

"Rose?" I say, sitting up.

I'm in the Visitation chamber, lying on a dais. The daylight that fills the room tells me it's mid-morning. The Hunter's Moon is long set.

"You were gone so long, I feared—" Rose says as she hugs me. She is dressed as a page, her hair pulled into a braid. I find I'm wearing her clothes, my hair wild and free.

"I passed your Trial! I'm a knight," my sister laughs.

A slow smile spreads across my face. "I'm a Witch."

"I knew you would be," she replies and hugs me again. I hug her back.

In the back of my mind, I hear a throaty voice singing.

"There were two daughters, fair and bright
Juniper, Thyme, and Rosemary
One born a witch; t'other a knight
As autumn moon bloomed mulberry
They ope'd the door and played a trick
For ne'er is Rose without a prick,
Bespelled the truth and made it stick
With juniper, thyme, and rosemary."

What the Future Holds

Kallyn Hunter

Someone was waiting for her.

The hot spot in the woods pulled her towards it like blood in an artery. She could feel the tug. Short, eager pulses that stretched from navel to big toe. Insistent. Excited. It tugged again, harder this time and Oriel moved to a trot.

There was always the possibility that someone would come with an offering. The empty pit in her gut reminded her that the woods were hungry. Three weeks had passed since the last substantial offering had been given and their appetite made them impatient.

Oriel cut a path through the murmuring trees. She heard their questions whispered to her in the part of herself that had become part of them. Who trod on their roots now? Indecision. Fear. The woods tasted it, and Oriel tasted it, too. She spat into the brittle snow, but the taste stuck in her throat.

The spot she headed towards was an old one. They came and went over time, vanishing and recreating themselves in an ever-changing pattern that Oriel kept careful track of.

Once, hundreds had spread throughout the forest, yet the same people who were drawn to the spots in the woods were always eating away at the edges. The last time she had counted, there were forty-six, but it had been forty-eight only a month before. Last year had seen sixty-three in total, but the woods were shrinking at an alarming rate and so when the spots disappeared, some vanished for good.

Oriel reached into her pack and pulled out a weathered composition book. Her records revealed many interesting patterns; spots lasted for an average of eighty-seven offerings; the spots about to vanish were prone to rot; the ones that were newly-sprung were prone to fire. But what was more interesting was the type of *people* they drew. Some spots drew the desperate, others drew the heartbroken. Number seventeen, the spot she headed for now, drew those who hungered.

In another lifetime, it was the same spot Oriel had chosen.

The woods pulled her to a clearing that wasn't supposed to be there. Acres of land stood bare and sectioned. A paved street, lined with newly-installed streetlights, made a simple loop before disappearing back the way it came. Developers had beat the ancient trees back. The few that remained had been curated.

Oriel gaped at the sight and hesitated at the edge, stopping where wild grass turned to sod. The tug shifted to a push and she felt it against her back. *Go, go,* they urged and Oriel carefully stepped into the clearing. The tether between her and the woods loosened to allow it.

The whispers were left behind as she walked into the clearing. Alone, she stepped across the newly fallen snow to a sign that had been erected under one quietly humming streetlight.

It read: *Hammerstein Builders. 17 lots available. Rural acreage.*

They had certainly succeeded there. Oriel looked around the clearing in shock. The people who lived outside the woods had always been chipping inward, but this was the first time they had built so brazenly inside.

She knew she should be horrified. The world was out-growing the legacy of the woods they built into. The time for bent knees and averted eyes had long passed. Though she bargained for what she had now, the offerings used to come to her as freely as they came to the forest. The food and wines had been given with revere and awe, not just for the woods, but for her.

Some had called her a goddess, others called her a witch, but at some point, while the woods were cut for lumber, she had become superstition.

An abandoned excavator stood silent watch over the new clearing. Against one rubber tread lay a bundle of sage. A paltry offering and in the wound of the clearing, the woods hadn't noticed it. Oriel picked up the bundle all the same and stored it in her pack.

At the end of the street stood the fiberboard skeleton of a lone house. Wind crept through the quiet clearing and the new wood groaned and flexed, stirring the plastic tarp that covered the windows. The front door gaped like a toothless mouth and Oriel slipped inside. Something sensed her as tiny feet skittered across the floor and out the back door that opened to the woods. Through the shadows of the exposed pillars and pipes, the house appeared empty.

The woods whispered at her through the portal, a quiet encouragement.

On instinct, her fingers moved to the hilt of her dagger. Archaic by today's standards, but a small comfort all the same. Danger always lurked in the futures. Over the years, she had avoided so many deaths. But as the ones outside the trees reached deeper—had someone finally come to deal with the witch in the woods? Without the ancient trunks and canopy around her, she felt exposed and vulnerable.

Near the back of the house, she heard a quiet shuffle. Oriel froze and the woods fell silent. Carefully, she crept towards the sound, steps light as air. A plastic tarp hung from the rafters, obscuring the back corner of the house. In one quick jerk, she grabbed the tarp and yanked it down, dagger poised.

Someone shrieked.

"Please don't hurt me!"

A girl was huddled between two exposed water pipes, hands thrown up to protect herself. Not a danger at all. Oriel relaxed and slid her dagger back into her belt.

The intruder was young. She existed in that angry in-between world, no longer a child, and not yet an adult. Thin in a shriveled way, as if she had lost weight very quickly. Illness perhaps, or a sudden streak of very bad luck. She was rank with neglect; even from a distance, Oriel could smell her.

Oriel looked into her and saw her futures thrown out like a net. The threads of fate overlapped, merged, and broke away again; but what startled her the most was how *many* there were. In all of them, one thing remained constant: the girl was a fighter. The struggle was ahead of her—it would be a long journey, longer in some futures than in others. So much could go wrong. So much *would* go wrong, but the girl would always fight.

She had so much life to live. Oriel saw it, and through her the woods saw it too. They wanted her. She would be a feast.

The girl stumbled to her feet. She wore a coat that was far too large. It covered her to her knees, but she still shivered, ill-equipped for the frigid night. She wiped her nose with one dirty sleeve, gaze flickering between Oriel and the door.

"What are you here for?" Oriel asked.

The girl didn't run, but she edged towards the door. "Didn't have a place to go," the girl said, though it sounded almost like a question.

"Are you here to go into the woods?" Oriel asked.

The girl looked uncomfortable, hands slipping into the sleeves of her coat. She balled her fists around the cuffs to conserve warmth in her un-gloved hands. "I don't know," she said at last. "I haven't made up my mind yet."

"What's your name?" Oriel asked and flipped to the page in her notebook that held a list of names.

"Etta Boone," the girl said.

"Etta Boone," Oriel repeated, pulled the cap from her pen and scrawled the name at the end of her list.

Seeing the futures gave her insight into the past, and she could see Etta's behind her. There was a long line of mistakes that had led the girl to where she was. Some of her own doing, undoubtedly, and the rest were others inflicting their mistakes on her. Oriel saw her past like a single, snarled thread. Something in the weave felt so familiar.

The girl straightened and seemed to come to some internal agreement. Oriel watched as she readied herself to make one final mistake. Her futures began to narrow. This was not the fighter that Oriel saw in so many futures. This was a girl about to give up.

"I'm ready," the girl said.

"No you aren't." Oriel was surprised by her own words. The futures were so vast, but something lurked in Etta's. Something Oriel could not allow. The woods could not have this one. The whispers of yes, yes, were muted across the clearing and for the first time, Oriel was able to ignore them.

Oriel would think back on the moment often in the days and years to come, but looking down at her notebook now, she realized she had already drawn a line through Etta's name.

"It's a bad decision for you," Oriel said, and outside of the skeletal house, the woods hissed as if caught in a sudden wind. Etta jumped at the sharpness of her voice, but Oriel wasn't finished. "There's nothing for you here. Go back where you came from."

The reprimand from the woods was swift and more painful than she expected. Even inside the wound of the clearing, Oriel felt their fury like a punch in the stomach. She braced herself against the plywood wall, feeling ill.

The girl didn't seem to notice. Something inside of her crumbled as tears spilled onto her cheeks. She looked shattered. It was a long moment before Oriel saw the fighter again. With ice in her eyes, the girl steeled herself and wiped the tears from her face like she was angry at them. She wrapped the coat tightly around herself and wordlessly, resigned, she walked out the door.

Later, once the sickness had passed and morning dawned pale and brittle, Oriel crawled back under the canopy of the trees.

***

Rotten teeth winked at her from gaps in the woman's mouth. Oriel slid the bottle into the Ida's waiting hands and accepted a parcel in return. It was heavier than she expected.

Inside was a pack of batteries, a new lighter, and a notebook. It wasn't the black and white composition book she had been expecting. Instead, she pulled out something shorter and thicker with an aged leather cover. Oriel looked at Ida curiously. "What is this?" she asked.

The old woman opened the bottle of whiskey and took a sip. "I thought you might like it," she said. "Someone just threw it away."

Oriel opened the book and flipped through the yellowed pages. Some of them were stained at the corners and they smelled old and slightly sweet. "It's beautiful," she said as her fingers dragged down the textured spine. "Thank you."

Ida cackled and said, "That pretty thing will cost extra. I get another question."

Oriel looked at the old woman, amused.

"All right, then. What is your question?"

"Saturday, who will win in the race at the kennels? I have the money to bet and I want it to be a good one," Ida said.

Oriel sighed. She slipped the new notebook into her bag and pulled out the old. Ida watched her curiously as she started writing in the corner of a page already covered in scribbles and calculations.

Oriel narrowed down the possibilities, jotting down the turning points that could lead the future in so many directions. Ida waited patiently, but it was a long moment before Oriel spoke. "If it rains, bet on Could Be Worse. If a dog named Monte is racing, bet on Salazar, but if Salazar gets in a fight beforehand, bet on Small Bev."

Ida repeated the conditions back to her as the tug clawed its way to the forefront of her attention. "Good luck, Ida," Oriel said hastily. "I have to go."

The old woman took another drink and raised the bottle to her. "Good hunting!" Ida said, not realizing how close to the truth she was.

Oriel flipped through her old notebook, seeking out a specific page. She flipped to her numbers and updated her tally. Winter had remained the busiest season for the past twenty years, yet this was a slower winter than most. The woods urged her on, hasty in their hunger. This time, they were confident.

They brought her to an old man who sat against the curved trunk of a tree. Oriel heard him before she saw him nestled against a cushion of snow. Every breath was a labored wheeze. His chest rose and fell, as if automatic functions suddenly required thought. His eyes were dull in the gaunt hollows of his face.

Number thirty-two had always drawn people of a certain disposition. The rhythm of his life was coming to an end earlier than he had expected. The man had come with a purpose and the woods smelled it on him.

He looked up as Oriel approached and didn't seem surprised to see her. "My grandmother used to say a lady lived in the woods. Said she could see the future," the man said, though he paused every few words to draw another phlegm-rattled breath. "Tell me, is there any chance I'll make it through this?"

Oriel knelt down and looked into him. The threads of his future were sparse. There was one morning, three weeks out where he could get into an accident on the way to his treatment, but at least he died quickly. More saw him fading away—at his home, in his bed, at the hospital, fading everywhere. There was always a possibility, but Oriel could read the odds and they weren't good.

"There is always a chance," she said.

The man wheezed and Oriel realized it was a laugh. She read the story in the lines of his face. He had a wife that had taken care of him through the year that had felt like a lifetime. When everything had started to go wrong, she had been with him—ballast in the storm his life had become.

Their two children had left the house years ago. One, a lawyer, the other in school for art. Only his daughter had made it to see him. He held so many regrets, but at least he could end it on his terms. He was so proud of them both.

"What is your name?" Oriel asked and opened her notebook.

"Marvin Lawrence," the man said.

Oriel went to the end of her list and saw Etta Boone's scored name. Below it, on the last line of the notebook, she added him to the list. It felt like mercy.

"Would you like to go into the woods, Marvin?" Oriel asked.

"Yes."

Oriel saw glimpses of what lay that way. His family would be devastated. His son would slip into an even deeper depression. He would drop out of school to wander, lost in regret.

His daughter would bury herself in her work, a distraction from the pain of loss. His wife would live another decade, a widow to cancer.

The man closed his eyes and coughed with a thick, wet noise. It hurt to listen to. Above them, the woods whispered, branches swaying gently. It could be a breeze if they didn't move in unison.

"What are your terms?" Oriel asked.

The man wiped his mouth with a handkerchief from his pocket. "I wish my family happiness. May they be better without the weight of me. May they prosper," he said. "I will go into the woods for that."

The man's words were eaten by the woods and they murmured their agreement. The voices crescendoed, swelling from a whisper to a chorus that sang to him, calling for him to join.

The woods accepted his terms.

Oriel felt the threads of fate shift. The world would be a kinder place to his wife, now. There were paths that could lead her to love again. The path to success grew less perilous for both of his children. His daughter would achieve great things through her tireless work. His son would take time to find himself and be better for it. It would never be easy, as life never is, but fate had shifted in their favor. They would learn to be happy again.

Oriel pulled the dagger from her belt. She offered the black blade to him and asked, "Would you like to do it yourself, or would you like my help?"

The man looked at her and drew a steadying breath. "I will do it," he said. Oriel expected him to take the knife, but he reached into his pocket and pulled out a small pistol.

Oriel looked away as he lifted it to his temple and squeezed the trigger. A loud crack ricocheted through the trees, playing again and again before fading into silence.

Then, the woods spoke, and she heard the man's voice answer. Roots grew over his fallen body, through clothes and skin to hold him close to the trunk in a gentle embrace. Oriel made a final note in her ledger before she picked up the gun he had left behind.

Her work was done.

***

The woods were quiet for a time. Meals so substantial were rare these days. Though there had been so little left, the old man's remaining life had been meat after so much bread and water. Even gristle was better than nothing.

Everyone's terms were different, and the terms had changed as much as the people making them. Blood had diluted to wine and liquor. Flowers and herbs came from ones who remembered some of the old ways. Traditional offerings, but not preferred.

The rings inside the trunks of the trees would show years—decades that were thick with the blood of war and superstition. Sacrifices had been made, armies had been slaughtered. Men had given their terms and the woods had greedily accepted, drinking in life after life.

Now, smaller favors were asked and sometimes granted. Terms became trivial, but the woods still craved the taste of life given to them fresh. When someone left a new cut of meat or the body of an animal, the woods were quick to take Oriel to it. They rarely denied offerings that were still warm.

Oriel picked up one of the bottles of liquor the woods hadn't accepted. The label was peeling and a faded orange sticker read $6.99. The gold-leafed letters were appealing so she twisted the cap open and took a sip. Too sweet, too artificial, burning her nose and throat like a kerosene peach. She poured the rest onto the knotted roots of the nearest tree. Nothing stirred to retrieve it and she couldn't blame them.

As winter faded from the brittle cold of the solstice to the wet, heavy snow of spring, Oriel didn't help any new voices join the chorus of the woods. She tended to the hot spots, as always, gathering the herbs to burn and the liquor to re-sell. Since Ida first wandered across her path, every transient and addict in the area had heard rumors of the woman in the woods who would trade unopened bottles for pennies and favors.

Oriel grunted as pain suddenly laced down her leg. The tug was sharp, harboring no argument. Every call was followed with pain now. The woods had not forgotten her transgression and they didn't allow her to forget either. It pulled again and she followed as quickly as she could. A heavy snow had fallen the night before, snapping limbs from trees. It was a nightmare to trudge through, but the woods drove her on.

There, amongst the wreckage of spring, Oriel saw Etta Boone again.

The girl wore a thick coat and boots that were far too large. The extra space had been padded tightly with bundles of socks to keep her feet in place. Warm clothes and a few steady meals had changed her. She walked tall, with a kindling confidence that hadn't existed in her before.

"Have you returned to go into the woods?" Oriel asked, though she could see the girl had no plans to. Oriel glanced behind Etta to the chain-link fence that had been erected as soon as the ground was soft enough. It was a poor barrier between the woods and the world outside. "You're already part of the way there."

"No," Etta said. "You said there was nothing for me here. You lied."

The woods echoed the girl and under the quiet whispers of *liar, liar, liar*, Oriel shivered. So few futures brought Etta Boone to her again, yet here she was, defying Oriel's expectation. A girl of potential, either great or terrible. The woods could feel it.

"Oh?" Oriel asked, careful of what she said. Her tether had gotten so short since the last time, but the woods seemed just as eager to hear what Etta Boone had to say. Around them, the bare branches trembled and snow plopped wetly to the ground.

"Some people say the woods can give you gifts if you ask it right," Etta said. "Ms. Jane got her little boy Stuart that way. Everyone knows she couldn't have kids after the last time. She said she asked the woods."

"The woods don't give anything without taking something first. Either your Ms. Jane paid a price, or she stole that child," Oriel said and leaned down until she was eye-level. "So. What would you give, Etta Boone? The forest takes many forms of payment. Fortunately for someone like you, payment never involves cash."

The girl's face flushed red, but Oriel could see her thinking. What could she offer?

The tether snapped tight, pulling her to her duty. Oriel pursed her lips to stop the grunt of pain. "So, are you here to offer?"

Etta bit her lip and searched through her many pockets as if looking for something she could give. The woods knew a waste of time when they saw it—there was only one thing they wanted from the girl and she had already said no.

"Get out of here, girl," Oriel said. "There is nothing for you here. Not unless you wish to pay a price."

***

So many futures led Etta Boone to her again that Oriel began to anticipate the day. She had been foolish to dangle the possibility out for her. Instead of scaring the girl off, she had only tempted her. The power of the woods was bait in a trap she hadn't meant to lay.

But fate seemed to take less likely paths where Etta Boone was concerned. Oriel saw other futures where she steered the girl away for good. Maybe her gamble would pay off.

Snow had turned to runoff, and the gray sky spat at her as an insult on top of the days of rain that had preceded. Through the patter of water against the ground and budding leaves, a lone bird chirped. Everything felt wet, but underneath, the world was waking up.

The woods woke as well, eager and hungry. With a giddy sort of confidence, they steered her towards number seventeen once more.

The house at the end of the road had gained intestines of pink insulation and windowed eyes. More structures stood in varying stages of completion and men tracked mud through them as they worked. There were no fences here, nothing to stop the woods from bumping right up against the new subdivision.

The men were installing a garage door when Etta Boone slipped around the construction site and into the trees. If any of the workers saw, none moved to stop her.

Oriel cut through the trees and found the girl with a coat bundled under her arms. It squirmed and forced Etta to readjust her grip, uttering a quiet swear. Oriel's eyes narrowed. Etta kept a tight hold as the coat bulged and hissed.

"Have you brought payment?" Oriel asked.

Etta bit her lip and Oriel was reminded that she was just a child. So much life to live—or to give. Nervously, the girl unwrapped her coat enough to expose the head of a thrashing cat. Long, gray fur was too clean and the neck too fat to be a stray. It yowled loudly and hissed it's hatred and fear at them as one paw clawed free. Etta held the squirming creature out to Oriel.

Oriel looked at the cat, a frown on her face. "Well?" she asked.

"Well, what?" Etta asked. "You said I had to pay a price—here it is." The girl held out the cat in offering. Her hands shook and it squirmed a little closer to freedom.

Frowning, Oriel looked at the creature. The woods were disappointed; it wasn't what they wanted, but they allowed Oriel to continue.

"And what are your terms, Etta Boone?" Oriel asked.

Etta looked uncertain, as if she hadn't thought that far. A streak of good luck hadn't left her without needs. She wanted so much. "I want to have power," she said at last.

Oriel scoffed, but dread coiled in her stomach. The darkness in Etta's future became a little clearer. "Those are broad terms," she said and the woods whispered, sensing it too. Seeing the possibilities through Oriel, they only wanted her more.

Etta looked up at the trees, hearing them for the first time. Fear leaked into her eyes. Good. She should be afraid. "The woods reject your offering."

The woods would give her power—whatever manner of power she wished—but the life of one cat wouldn't be enough. There was only one thing the woods would accept for a request like that, and Etta Boone had gotten away once before.

"What else would you give?" Oriel asked. "The woods are still willing to negotiate."

Etta's grip loosened and the cat squirmed free. The gray blur darted through the trees, disappearing towards the distant sounds of construction.

"Would you like to go into the woods?" Oriel asked.

The woods around them creaked in a non-existent wind and Oriel felt their agitation like ants under her skin. Etta looked around her, behind her, searching for something that wasn't there. The whispers grew louder, demanding an answer. Etta's lips were pale with fear.

"You better decide, Etta," Oriel said. "I could even help." She slid the dagger from her belt and let it hang at her side. Etta spared it a quick glance and her eyes were wider when they looked back at Oriel, but she didn't run.

"Or maybe you want to go quickly," Oriel said and acted before she could dread the consequences. The woods could not have her. She dropped the dagger, letting it fall, blade first into the earth. She reached into her pocket, grabbing the pistol the old man had left behind. She pulled it from her coat as something wet slid through her bare toes and glided over her foot in warning. *Don't, do not dare,* they whispered.

Oriel leveled the gun at the girl and Etta's eyes went blank with terror as she pulled back the hammer with a quiet click. "What will it be, Etta? Would you like to go into the woods?" Oriel asked. Her hand started to shake as the woods tightened their grip, constricting her like a snake. Sharp pain laced up her leg as something cut through the skin of her ankle and burrowed in. Oriel felt her body shudder as she fought for control.

The woods wouldn't allow her to scare this one away again. The feast of Etta Boone was so close. What could be done with someone like her?

Oriel's limbs froze, joints locking as her throat started to close. Her finger twitched, involuntary. With a shock of horror and flood of relief, she saw the future where Etta died by her own hand pass to just another possibility.

"Go!" Oriel shouted, her voice emerging as a broken croak.

Etta Boone ran. The woods hissed as she passed. They wailed for her to come back, for her to join them, *join them.* But it was too late. The girl was gone, and instead, they rounded on Oriel and whispers turned to screams of rage.

***

More voices joined the woods around her. More offerings were left. Though she continued to serve them, the woods had not been kind to her. Her leash had been shortened and honed to a razor wire that cut every time it pulled her to her duty. A constant reminder of the one who had made her act so rashly.

Oriel was left with nothing but time to think. Too often, her thoughts drifted back the one who had gotten away.

In the heart of the forest, lit by candles and flashlights tethered haphazardly between roots, Oriel opened her new notebook. She cleared her mind and let the fates reveal themselves. As the futures spread, the whispering of the woods faded, if only for a moment. The boundless possibilities were easy to get lost in it—how often had she caught herself seeking and longing for futures that may never come? The future was so vast, so complex—she should have known what a futile task it was when she had declared her own terms so many years ago. How could one like her comprehend all that the future holds?

But she read the threads as best as she could. She marked the turning points and probabilities that could lead Etta Boone back to the woods. The futures were immense, but she tracked them, filling pages with tallies and calculations with the many possibilities of Etta Boone.

In all the futures Oriel saw, in all the branches of possibilities, there were few where Etta returned to the woods again. The odds were in Oriel's favor. She tried to forget how the girl always seemed to defy the odds.

Even the possibility of her return haunted Oriel because in the futures where Etta came back, it was always for the same reason.

If Etta Boone came back, she would go into the woods.

With a sigh of frustration, Oriel shut the book with a snap. Driving herself mad over the possibilities would do her not good. She had learned that in the past, trying to track her own. How many years had she spent looking for the future that held her freedom? So few futures led her out of the woods—but as the people cut deeper, the possibilities had grown. The woods were disappearing, and doing so rapidly. With a thrill of defiance, she wondered what would happen to her when the last tree was cut.

The tug pulled her from her frustrated thoughts. She left the heart of the woods behind to follow it, but once she realized where she was being led, dread snaked through her veins. Number seventeen was calling her once more.

When Oriel saw the woman who waited, she didn't recognize her at first. Her hair was cut short, shaved half a finger from the skin. Her face had filled out from the gaunt, starved youth, and she was property tall instead of lanky. Dressed in clothes that fit, fed and healthy, Etta Boone had grown up.

Etta seemed to be expecting her and Oriel felt the threads of fate grow taught. She read the story on Etta's face. The girl had seen a hard struggle. Had fought tooth and nail against those who called her weak and stupid. Etta Boone had built her own part of the world from nothing, and she was not going to lose it now. Etta was here for power, and this time, she knew how to ask for it properly.

Etta was quiet as she stepped through the undergrowth. It was summer now. The night was warm, but a chill rustled through the trees. The breeze whispered with the woods, but it didn't mute their excitement.

Oriel saw the possibilities narrow towards the dreaded future. The woods were a vice, holding her to her duty. She opened her mouth to scream at her to run, but the only words that emerged were, "Have you come to go into the woods?"

"Yes," Etta said.

Oriel's hopes vanished. The future came as it would and Oriel would see Etta Boone become just like her. Another wraith to walk the woods.

"And what are your terms?" Oriel asked and watched the woman's futures disappear, spiraling towards ruin until only one remained. Power was what Etta wanted, and power she would have. Such great and terrible power. Oriel saw the future in nightmare flashes—broken buildings and sidewalks, streets reclaimed by trees and moss, bones picked clean with roots sprouting from empty rib cages. The woods would grant her power, and use Etta just as they had used her.

With Etta Boone, they would take back so much of what they had lost.

Any hope in a future of freedom disappeared. Oriel felt the tears hot on her cheeks, but the woods held her to her duty, leaving her mute and powerless to stop the future she had helped create. Etta would give her terms, and the woods would grant it to the ruin of them all.

The woman was quiet for a long moment. She had spent years thinking of the answer to such a complicated question, surely. Etta had sought her out for one reason. Oriel saw it, and through her, the woods saw it too. There were no futures but this one. For all her meddling, all her pain, Oriel had failed. The dark future of Etta Boone had arrived.

But Etta hesitated. The weight of Etta's gaze was heavy as the woman studied her, taking in her appearance that hadn't changed over the years. Oriel saw the questions lurking behind her eyes and knew she wouldn't be able to answer them.

Finally, Etta smiled and gave a small laugh. She kicked her foot against the ground, scattering pine needles with the toe of her boot. "No. You know? This is too good to be true. Nothing comes without a fight, and this is too easy." Etta met Oriel's eyes. She seemed resigned as she said, "I think I've made a mistake." Oriel couldn't answer, but she watched the woman war with herself.

"Yeah," she said at last. "This is a mistake."

Oriel let out a breath as the threads of fate snapped. The woods around them shivered in fury even as Oriel was flooded with relief. Their protests were loud in Oriel's ears as they shrieked in anger and disbelief. Oriel had seen it. Etta Boone, the girl of potential, was finally theirs!

Oriel didn't hear their protests. Instead, she watched as Etta Boone walked away and new possibilities grew out from her like roots.

Storm's Daughters

Kristen Blount

Aylynn and Della rode into a large, prosperous town built along a river that fostered sizable baking and garment industries. Medford generally was happy to see visitors as new customers for their wares. Today, as the Sworn pair entered the yard of their favorite inn, they noticed that the town seemed quiet and nervous.

"Hello," said Della at the countertop. "Anyone home?"

"One minute, be right there." The rosy-cheeked, grey-haired innwife came out of the kitchen, wiping her hands on her apron. "Scholar Della, what a lovely surprise and what impeccable timing!"

"Stella, good to see you! We need a couple of rooms and some time in your bathhouse, but I'm not sure I like the sound of the rest of that."

Stella agreed to see them to their favorite rooms, talking all the way about the goings-on in Medford. Things were not entirely well, it seemed. As the town grew, they had recently instituted a larger, more formal council.

"If it isn't broke, not sure why we needed to fix it... the trademasters and big farm owners seemed to be doing just fine to me, but nobody asked me." Della continued to make encouraging noises toward the innwife while Aylynn claimed the first bath. "Now, we have this new Head Councilman, Mr. High-and-Mighty Conrad Himself. He considers town life to be far superior to any other choice. Not sure where he thinks his food comes from, and he does enjoy his supper. You need to ask some questions. He now owns parts of an awful lot of businesses, but he doesn't seem to do much himself."

"I shall indeed ask some questions."

Two days later, three exhausted women met to discuss what they had learned. Stella proved a valuable member of the team, with an ear firmly to the ground as an inveterate gossip. Aylynn visited with her contacts in the local constable's office with the excuse of seeing and evaluating drills with an expert eye. Given her quiet nature, she knew how to listen to what was said and not said. For her part, Della went right to the source as a Goddess-sworn Scholar. She could ask questions of anyone and expect to receive respectful, honest answers.

"Stella, you first."

"Five Lords, gossip was strangely hard to get started, but everyone has pretty much the same story. Town isn't the same, and it all started when Master Conrad came to town. Seems he went to that Abbey of yours."

Della smiled slightly. "And you, My Sister Staff?"

"No one wants to talk to us. Not even shop-talk ever came around to anything more than a heated discussion on favorite take-downs. It was almost painful—how much they didn't want to talk. I did notice that most of the equipment, while clean and well-tended, is beginning to show its age. Many men in older, worn-about-the-edges boots and belts. Everyone seems to be doing more with less."

"Well, they have to talk to me, and I have a notion to take a look at Medford's ledgers."

The next day, Della and Aylynn donned their official Abbey uniforms. Stella had worked her back channels so the square was full of local folks. The Sworn Sisters stepped onto the platform, held their internal hands, and raised the outer hands in salute.

"By the Goddess and her five Lords: We ask. We listen. We find. We decide." They chanted together. Della then said, "We have asked, and we have listened. We have heard you not say that Medford has changed, but we have listened to your fear at those changes. We have heard you not say that the new town council seems to do little but reap great reward, but we have listened to your confusion how your prosperous town doesn't benefit all its citizens."

Aylynn spoke in turn, "Today, we find. By our Abbey oaths and as our Father's Daughters: I am sealing town hall and all its business office. I personally shall hold the doors. Scholar Della has work to do." She continued, "I will be in place by the doors, the Scholar shall be within, but if you have testimony that the Abbey needs to hear, please present yourself to Stella. She will make a list of names, and we will talk to everyone on the list tomorrow."

As the sun sank below the sills of the large windows, Della rested her elbows on the desk and her head in her hands. "Goddess, help us all. How could this get so bad so fast? It's only been two years since we were last here."

Aylynn stuck her head into the office, "How are you doing, love? You look like you spent the day with a shovel not a bunch of ledgers."

"It would have at least have been honest labor, and there's nothing honest here. These books are so cooked that I'm surprised we can't see steam rising from them."

"Oh, my Lords. Stella has a list of people now willing to talk to you that stretches almost all the way down the steps."

"I will hear them, but we have more than enough to Decide. What do we do? Does the thieving council and its new leader pay it all back? That doesn't answer to the unfairness and fear they have sowed."

They spent the next two days taking testimony from town folks, farmers, well-to-do shop keepers, and stable hands. Once again, everyone gathered in the town square. Aylynn stood next to Della, both in uniform but not holding hands. Della held the town's ledgers in her arms, and Aylynn had her metal-capped oak staff across her chest.

"We decide. By Hecata and all her Consorts, we offer Abbey's Choice."

Aylynn turned to the council, which was lined up at the edge of the square. "Your Choice: Labor or Leave. You have taken two years' worth of wealth and worth from your fellow townspeople. You have elevated your own station, while denigrating theirs, forgetting that all work is meaningful and necessary. You may spend two years working a farm or in a trade, or you may leave town with what you currently have on your person. The local constables are locking your houses as we speak. If you accept labor, you may keep your house. You will also keep the same work hours as everyone else and report directly to the guild masters. Choose wisely."

***

Della turned to Aylynn as they rode out of Medford. "How are you holding up? We haven't had to offer Abbey's Choice in a long time."

"Fine. It was a good, fair choice. But?"

They rode in silence for awhile. "But what? You can't just let it dangle."

"I'm trying to find the right words. The two previous times

we offered judgment with staff in hand, I've always felt the approval of our Fathers. Did you feel that today? I felt three nervous women and a bunch of angry townspeople. I was also pleased that only the new Councilmember, that Conrad person, took to the road. It's supposed to be harder to play these sorts of games in Metarra. Medford will recover, but we will have to pass the word to other Abbey-sworn to be on guard."

"Hmmm. Do you think the Abbey will listen?" Della wondered.

"What do you mean?"

"This seems to be all part of a bigger picture to me. Few students were in residence when we left the Abbey this spring, and they aren't studying to be judges like us. We still see a fair number of incoming musicians and healers, but how many circuit riders are there right now? I spent some time looking into the records. Fewer of us are dealing with more unrest. It had been two years since anyone had visited Medford. I can't help but wonder what would have happened if that situation had been left to fester longer. Conrad had a least a little Abbey training himself, though obviously he's not sworn to Goddess or Consorts. I hate seeing a Cousin go bad."

They rode, each woman chewing on her unhappy thoughts.

"How do you feel about going to see Gran, instead of heading back to the Abbey? If she thinks a message should be sent about Conrad, we can do it that way." asked Aylynn seemingly out of the blue.

"Yes. I think that's an excellent idea," agreed Della.

***

The leaves shone gold and copper in the late autumn sunshine as the sound of horses' hooves traveling at a gentle walking pace reached Berta. She was resting in front of her cottage on a bench polished by weather and use. Resting meant she held a bowl of peas in her lap and had a basket of knitting snugged up beside her. She shelled two last peas, tucked the bowl into the corner of the bench, and dumped the shells into the bucket by her feet. She glanced up to find the horses stopped by the stone wall separating her yard from the road, but the girls, her girls, were still sitting atop their mounts.

The older woman took a minute to appreciate the picture they made. The one tall, cinnamon-skinned with hair to rival the trees behind her. She made an odd (but perfect) match with her Sworn Sister, Della, who had skin like cream and raven-black curls barely contained in a long braid.

Berta stood in her gate, loving these two down to their toes, suspecting a hard road was just beginning even if they'd already been on the road for weeks at this point.

"You two are here early. Is there any trouble I should know about?"

"Oh, Gran," said Della. "We're exhausted and thought to some rest with you a bit. I don't know what's going on, but it's not good. Can we stay for a night or two, take advantage of clean beds and your home cooking?"

"You know you're always welcome. Come in and get settled. We can rest tonight and talk in the morning."

Eventually, the horses were unladen and allowed the freedom of a small pasture. After a tasty meal of butter-fried trout and fresh peas, Berta, Aylynn, and Della settled in front of the fire to enjoy the first apple pie of the season.

Della stretched her long legs toward the fire. "As always, Gran, you feed us royally. That was the best pie since we were here last year! Maybe even better."

Aylynn nodded. "Your food really is the best."

Berta looked at these seemingly mis-matched Sworn Sisters, and loved that they could still call her Gran. She had tucked these two tight into her heart when they all still lived at the Abbey. "Be honest," she chided herself, "you needed them as much as, if not more than, they needed you. It gave you something good to love to offset the daily headaches of being Abbess and to remind you why it all mattered."

She chuckled as she remembered the night when the two had decided to sneak into the kitchen after curfew for a treat and found her wrist deep in the beginnings of bread. There was still nothing as therapeutic as kneading dough for working out resentments and crankiness. The two novices, with hair in braids and socks slouched around ankles, had slipped giggling down the back stairway to stare in horror at The Abbess, Herself standing at the butcher's block countertop. They all agreed that names didn't belong in an after-hours kitchen, and Gran further agreed to teach them to make bread if they'd tell her all about their worries and wonders. "Best deal I've ever struck," she thought.

Now, though, Scholar Della and Staff Aylynn spent the majority of their time away from the Abbey, settling disputes and cleaning up unusual messes. Not all Sworn pairs did this kind of work. The Spells and Songs, being enchanters and entertainers, also traveled, but less frequently and often with more of a strict itinerary since towns and cities could request them. Other Abbey-trained professions like healers, teachers, and architects tended to find a home and settle in where they were most needed and appreciated. Her late-night kitchen daughters thrived on the road.

"Did I tell you I have an apprentice for the year? She goes up to the Abbey soon. You'll meet her in the morning."

Della asked, "Is she a Cousin, then?"

Berta nodded. "Most probably a Daughter of Summer, just turned sixteen. She's not sure, but I am. She'll take her tests and aptitudes like all novices, but she gravitates to sunshine and is always busy. She's excellent help in the forge, since sunshine and heat go together nicely."

Aylynn mopped up the last of her crust and cream. "I'm glad there's a new class headed to the capital. The Abbey echoed strangely as we left with everyone out on the roads in one fashion or another. We were just saying how there doesn't seem to be as many Cousins coming in these days."

"Fewer cousins is worrisome," Berta said. "Baneith is winter-born, and he won't encourage much that is new or different. Things change. They must. He also has been overly fond of his own comforts. As long as his life isn't affected, he's not interested. I bet he has no idea what you have been seeing."

Della frowned, "I'm Winter's Daughter, but I don't mind change. Lords know, I see enough of it on the roads."

"Yes, dear, but you are sworn to one of Spring's Daughters, and she keeps you from getting too fussy."

As the light just barely began to seep into the room the next morning, Della woke warm beside Aylynn and her brain started turning over all the many tasks ahead. Instead of disturbing her partner, she dropped a quick kiss and went downstairs to talk more with Gran.

Berta was already sitting at the kitchen table with her neighbor and close friend, Kate. They had their heads down, deep in some planning process. Della decided that she'd rather not know, and helped herself to a cup of tea and a warm scone.

"Morning, Cousin Kate," she said as she sat next to Berta. "How are you?"

"Bright Day, Cousin Della," Kate smiled. "I stopped by for our weekly chat, but didn't realize you and Della were visiting. We tried to stay quiet and not wake you, sorry. Berta and I have been keeping an eye on some disturbing trends. What have my favorite Goddess-sworn Pair been seeing?"

The entire Medford misadventure spilled out over the pot of tea.

"So, we are seeing more of what you have noticed. I'm

not sure exactly what to call it," Della mused. "Help me out, Aylynn," who was making her way down the stairs.

"Did you leave any tea? I'll brew a new pot. The best word I have for it is stagnation. We keep seeing the same stories, the same sadnesses, and people seem to default—even more than usual, mind you—to 'but this is the way it's always been.'"

"Except," said Della, "It hasn't. People used to help each other more, build new things more often, or devise their own solutions. Stagnation. Yes, that's right. They seem to be waiting for us, or some other Pair, to come solve their problems for them. The helping hands are slower to extend, too."

Della continued, "At the Abbey, I was able to access the histories Berta suggested I read when we were here last year. They support her idea of someone meddling with the Consorts' access to Metarra. One tome told of an ancient abbot who tried to control the interactions between divine and mundane about 125 years ago, but no one realized it until after his death. He was a strong magician and sealed the Chapel doors with an interlocking set of spells. It seemed really impressive on one level. You don't think Abbot Baneith has tried to interfere at that level, do you?"

Berta made a noncommittal humming sound. "I've never been best pleased that Baneith succeeded me. He was inflexible when we were students together, and I'm sure he's not improved much with age. It's not entirely my choice, you know, to live so apart from the Abbey. I do love the freedom having my own forge it grants me. If he could reinstate those spells, he'd do it in a heartbeat."

Later that day, Berta took a break from her forge and checked on her girls who were in the open area of the back yard going through slow hand to hand routines. She wasn't sure how they were going to take the idea she and Kate had concocted.

"Sisters, come meet a new Cousin."

"Tami," she called into the back of the forge, "Meet Della, winter-born and sworn Scholar, and this is her Sister Aylynn, Spring's daughter, sworn Staff and wind-witch."

Tami stepped over from where she'd been laying tools along a workbench. Berta was glad to see that she confidently came to meet the Abbey-trained circuit judges. As Aylynn had noted the night before, the Abbey had far fewer members these days and not everyone had seen—let alone met—a Goddess-sworn Pair.

Tami reached out an open palm and shook both women's hands with a small curtsy. "Please to meet you. I am Kittamy, but call me Tami." With large brown eyes and honey toned curls, she had probably fought to be taken seriously for years.

"What do you like best about being in the forge?" asked Della.

"I can tell you that I'm not particularly fond of shoeing horses. I want to do harder, more complicated work. Last night, I even dreamt of a sword!"

Berta's head, crowned in silver braids, came up sharply. "What do you mean you dreamt of a sword? Literally?"

Tami looked around, "Huh. We were, the four of us, here in the forge along with your friend Kate. It took all of us to create this fancy sword made of lightning. It was a great dream!"

"Hmmm. My Father seems to be reaching out to those around me, since I've been hesitant about even thinking of a sword. I have the spells for it, but it's been a long time since I've used them. If Baneith is wandering paths he shouldn't, you might need more than that staff."

Aylynn started shaking her head. "Oh, no. Absolutely not. There are excellent, historical and social, reasons that we don't carry swords. I like my staff. I can do a fair amount of damage, but it's not seen as an immediate threat in towns and villages."

"More stupid, they," muttered Della. A bit louder, she said,

"You are deadly with it, and you know it."

"I am. I am trained to be, but the threat of death isn't what you see when you look at my staff. People see a sword and think, 'Fight.' People see my staff and think Abbey justice, or so I dearly believe."

Berta took a look at the mulish set of of Aylynn's shoulders and sighed deeply. "You might not have much of a choice."

"What does that mean? I have a choice. You taught us that. There's always a choice. Not making a choice may sometimes be the worst choice, but I chose my staff! My rank and title is Goddess-Sworn Staff, not Sword. I made that decision with your blessing and the Consort of Spring being fully aware!"

"You know these trends you've been seeing?"

"Yes … and the threat of a sword won't make them better. It will only make people more afraid. Plus, I don't know how to use one!"

"If we are going to fix it, and not just one town's problems, but all of it, all over Metarra, you are going to need an edge. Figuratively and literally."

"No." Aylynn promptly left the forge, with Della looking after her worriedly.

Tami looked at her Forgemistress, and she said quietly, "I thought it was just a dream. I am so tired of horseshoes."

"Hush, now."

Della found Aylynn sitting on the bench where they had met Berta the previous day. She sat down quietly beside Aylynn, and tried to appreciate the sun on her face and the breeze in her hair. Her Sworn sister seethed, seemingly oblivious to the bright fall afternoon.

"Would it be that bad?" Della asked eventually.

"I don't know how."

"Ignorance is easily cured. You could learn. You are already deadly with your hands, your staff, and many other things that most people don't consider to be weapons. Why balk at another tool?"

"*You* could learn. *You* are the smart one who knows all the histories. I like being your strong arm and staying mostly overlooked."

Della looked at her hard. "Sister, self-pity is not attractive. You are so much more than muscle and force."

"You know what they say about those who live by the sword..."

"Lords and Lady, you can pull arguments out of thin air! Must be your wind-witch tendencies. You will not be overtaken by the glamour of the blade! As you balance my stuffy Winter tendencies, I can guarantee you shall not become a flighty, society-drunk dueler. Have you ever known Berta to steer us wrong?"

"You know she hasn't," Aylynn muttered, coming around a bit. "But she and Cousin Kate have A Plan. That scares the pants right off of me."

"Now that you mention it, it's terrifying. Are you at least willing to hear what they have to say?"

After an evening full of contentious conversations, Della and Aylynn set out the next morning each lost in her own thoughts. It took most of that day and the next to reach a small manor by the sea.

"Lords and Their Lady," Della exclaimed. "There's so much!"

"Have you never seen the water?" Aylynn asked.

"Never. One of the other Pairs has always taken this road, while we've been riding between The Abbey and Gran's cottage." She slid slowly from her horse, and held the reins lightly in one hand, completely mesmerized by the moving water that spanned the horizon. "Leave me here, please. I need to just, just watch for a bit."

"Take your time, love," said Aylynn. "The sea takes a lifetime to learn. You won't manage it this morning or even this season. I grew up just south of here, and I'd forgotten that you'd never been to the coast."

The pair eventually made their way to the house, where they were met by an entirely too efficient staff who quickly divested them of horses and possessions. They were escorted into a training studio behind the formal gardens and terraces. An older man stood in the center of the room and bowed precisely to the two Sworn Sisters.

"I am Master Tomas, current and sole possessor of the title Abbey Sword. I am willing to train you, Staff Aylynn. Are you willing to be trained?"

"I am working on it."

"Indeed. We shall work on it together."

The next few weeks were spent in the hardest physical training of Aylynn's career. They started by reviewing the basics, footwork and hand to hand combat. They worked with short sticks and Aylynn's favorite, her quarterstaff. They worked indoors, in the gardens, upon the hillside, and even along the beach. Her legs ached excruciatingly after practicing footwork in the sand.

As hard as they worked during the days, they argued in the evenings. Aylynn wanted to know why she had never heard of the Abbey Sword and why one was needed. Tomas challenged every preconceived notion about the application of force and Abbey-wrought justice Aylynn held. Della often joined the debates for the sheer joy of argument's sake. She would take whichever side interested her on any given night, adding historical and philosophical asides. Della looked at her time at the manor as one her most delightful vacations, spending days on the beach and nights in heated conversations. Aylynn looked at her bruises and slightly wobbly brain as the hard-earned wages of each day, but found herself becoming stronger and faster.

One day, still pondering a particularly fierce verbal battle, Aylynn walked into the studio. Master Tomas again stood in the room's precise center. In front of him, three swords rested on a stand, one of wood, one of metal without an edge, and one clearly sharpened steel.

"Now," he said. "We begin. Are you fully willing?"

Aylynn looked him square in the eyes, and said, "I am fully willing. By my Father and by my Abbey-sworn oaths, I am willing to be your successor. I agree to be an Abbey-sworn Sword."

"Good."

When another month had passed, Della answered a rare invitation to meet Aylynn and the Swordmaster at the studio where she watched a bout of epic proportions. They passed the offensive lead back and forth, in a conversation of steel that asked and answered each other's strengths and weaknesses. In the end, Aylynn executed a perfect parry and thrust that carried just inside Tomas' tiring defense to score the final point.

"And so, Sword Aylynn!"

"Not so! I have so much I don't know, still."

"I cannot teach you how to honor your sword. You know that in your heart already. The sword in your hand you may keep, but it is not your sword. You must return to Berta for a particular blade forged for your hand alone. You have earned your place as an adopted daughter of the Lord of Swords. Welcome to our small family!"

That evening they celebrated with a grand feast in the manor's formal dining hall, just the three of them. They laughed and shared stories of the road, for Tomas had spent his younger days following the Abbey's circuit. As he wished the women good-night, he asked to be remembered to Berta.

"I don't see my half-sister much since we both left the Abbey when Baneith came to power, but I do miss her. Tell her that I would welcome a visit, but I don't travel far anymore. I am honored she sent her favorite students to me."

The trip back to Berta's passed much more pleasantly, as the women continued to discuss all they had learned with Tomas. They arrived back at Gran's cottage late in the afternoon, in time for hot baths before dinner. It was getting quickly colder as the last of the leaves fell from the trees, and the hot water eased their traveling aches.

Five women met in the forge the next morning, Aylynn and Della, Berta as Forgemistress, Tami her apprentice, and Cousin Kate. Berta brought a piece of sky-iron she found in the hills years before. It sat on her large anvil, an odd dull grey in the early light, strangely heavy for a hunk of metal not much larger than her twinned fists. She asked Aylynn for the sword she'd earned with Master Tomas.

Lady Berta turned to other women with a deadly serious face.

"You are each here as your Father's Daughter. Winter and Spring, Summer and Fall. I am Daughter and Priestess of the Lord of Storm and Swords. Are you ready and willing? This working will place us all at odds with the current Abbot and his policies."

They answered in turn, "Yes, Forgemistress."

She looked at the Abbey-trained Pair. "Do you swear again to the Goddess and the Five Lords to serve this land, first and last, by your blood and by your magic, with your hand's work and heart's truth?"

"We do."

She looked at Cousin Kate, "Do you promise, in this your season, to invoke Fall's might and bring only blessings to this working?"

"I do."

Berta turned to Tami and said, "Do you trust me to recognize you as Summer's Daughter and to bring you safely through this ritual? We need you to bring your Father's blessings. Are you willing?"

"I trust you, and I am willing."

Berta stepped into the circle traced in mixed metals on her forge's floor, and into the center of the star within the circle.

Della raised her arms and intoned, "Lord of Ice and Order, lend us your aid. We ask for a blade as everlasting as the green upon your pines, that it might bring justice into our land through the cold winter nights.

Aylynn reached for her Sister's hand, "Lord of Wind and Change, lend us your aid. We ask for a blade as supple as the willow, that it might bring compassion into our land through the bright spring mornings."

Aylynn held her free hand to Tami, who took it gladly, and said firmly, "Lord of Sun and Striving, lend us your aid. We ask for a blade as mighty as the oak, that it might bring abundance into our land through the golden summer days."

Kate joined the ring, "Lord of Fields and Fire, lend us your aid. We ask for a blade as lovely as a maple crowned in glorious red, that it might bring fairness into our land through the crisp evenings of autumn."

Berta closed the circled, praying, "Lastly, Lord of Storms and Swords, look favorably upon this forge and me, your Daughter and its Mistress, as we craft a sword to bring all and only good things into this land."

All together they finished the invocation, "Mother Hecata, hear our prayers and help us to do your bidding. Selah. Selah. Selah."

After they left the circle in reverse order, Kate raised a magical shield. Berta set to work with hammer and anvil, with prayer and spell. The other three women took turns keeping the fire hot and tools to hand. As the sun sank toward the horizon, Berta took the last few strokes against the blade newly forged before her. She called everyone back into the working circle.

She turned to Aylynn, "Quench it."

Just beyond the anvil, a large trough stood filled with seawater and sacred woods steeping in its murky depths. As Aylynn grasped the blade by its tang, Berta cried, "Sky iron. Blessed Steel. Sacred Wood. Ocean water. Lord of Storms and Swords, be with us here!"

Aylynn slowly lowered the new blade as wind whipped through the forge. The fire flared, then extinguished. In the darkness, the women could see a light emanating from within the water. Aylynn released the metal and stepped quickly back as the sword rose of its own accord and began spinning in place. Lightning appeared from seemingly nowhere, a blaze of electricity that set everyone's hair on end. It raced along the blade, which turned from a dulled pewter to a bluish steel.

A voice filled with rolling thunder and pelting rain spoke, "Go forth, Sworn Sword, Spring and Storm's Daughter, and serve justice. It is time to open doors and hearts."

The wind abruptly subsided, the fire flicked softly amongst the once-again glowing coals, and everyone sat down hard. As all eyes turned in her direction, Aylynn joined her Cousins on the floor, cross-legged and straight-backed with her new sword resting across her knees. The sword had an odd indigo sheen, and occasional sparks still fell at slow intervals to the earth.

She looked at her first and best beloved teacher, "Gran, Reckoning is going to need a practical hilt and wrapping. And, a good sharp edge. We have work to do."

Witnessed

Jessica Aelwood

St. Malo's cold nose on the road-burned side of my neck jerks me back from the ass-end of consciousness. A groan, like tires on wet gravel, crawls out of my throat as I get my arms under me. One worried bronze eye is fixed on my face when I manage to turn my head, my neck grinding in protest. I get a hand off the ground and reach out to drag it over his ears. "Good boy," I tell him. I'm smearing my own sticky blood through his fur.

It ain't over.

I can hear the guy's footsteps behind me. His hipster loafers are scuffed to shit. Turns out the Witnesses don't give a rat's ass about shoes. Don't give a rat's ass about much, until you fuck up and they get the idea to intervene.

My baseball bat is close, but I have to reach slow or he'll be on me again. His head tick-tick-ticks to one side, watching my fingers spider-crawl across the road. Malo stands between us, low thunder rolling through his chest. "Don't," I warn him, but he knows better. He won't budge unless the host does.

I pull the bat over, leaning my weight on it. My left hand is bloodier than the right. I clench my fingers until it starts to drip. Good thing the mark is simple. Good thing it doesn't matter if it's crude. I drag my palm across the street beneath me, matching the shape of the token dangling from my neck: hard right angles on the diagonal, verticals top and bottom. Supposed to be a slammed door, I guess. Always looked like trees to me, or an antlered head.

I can feel the Witness watching me, fascinated, too fresh to know he should stop me.

I circle the mark, closing it, and the asphalt drinks down my blood. The rune burns light-sucking black in its place, and now the Witness is pissed. Malo barks as the host lunges—fast, sure, but so am I when I might die—and then jumps out of the way as I spring up, wheeling the bat up for momentum.

I clip him upside the jaw, and it's not *quite* the crack of metal on bone—too drowned in faraway cicada screams. But he staggers, and I get behind him before he can recover, major-leaguing him across the back of the neck and sending him sprawling forward. He hits the pavement and I follow, kneeling on his back and laying the bat across his shoulders, shoving his face down on my mark.

My vision darkens two shades and my ears are full of kettle-whine, but I hold. He's strong, but not strong enough, not with his Witness getting pushed out. He's a fresh take, still mostly a person—the iron of my token wasn't enough. He needed blood, and Atlanta's own memory of when she burned to send it screeching out of him.

The Witness can't touch me without the shield of his blood and bones, and the black fog of it spins and disperses with nowhere to hide. By the time it's gone, he's unconscious under me.

I use my bat to lever myself to my feet. City noise starts to creep back in. Malo pushes his head into my free hand, and

I rub over his ears again. I'm sure grateful for his company. The Witnesses don't bother with dogs. Pure souls are useless to them.

The guy's wallet is in his back pocket, and I fish it out, opening it as I roll him over with the toe of a boot. College ID, couple hundred bucks cash—which I pocket—a handful of loyalty cards.

No sign of the Eye.

My weekend in the city might have been wasted. I know there are people down here using the mark of the Eye to call the Witnesses—people intentionally doing business with them, in exchange for what, I don't know. I've been wrecking up their calling card wherever I find it, but so far it's only been on buildings. I'm starting to think someone is giving them unwilling sacrifices.

I bend over to lift the guy's shirt, checking front and back— nothing. But something glass rattles in another pocket, and I pull out three little vials of clear liquid: GHB. My doubt about this guy dissolves.

Sometimes the Witnesses pick people for a reason.

***

I'm in no shape to carry him, so I drag him into an alley and limp the two blocks to the parking garage where I left my truck. It's late enough that no one's around to watch when I get back and haul him into the bed. I drag myself into the cab, and Malo takes the passenger side so he can backseat drive with his good right eye.

I drop the asshole off in front of a police station on the way out of town, wallet and GHB wiped off and shoved back into his pants. They've already got his description. By the time he comes to, he'll be under lock and key for attacking two women before I got to him.

The August sun is touching the sky as I get out of Atlanta and head for home. Would have been nice to get some sleep.

I keep myself awake with a string of cigarettes—my radio doesn't work, so I chat up Malo between drags. He's a good listener.

It's an hour and a quarter north, doing five over on the highway, before we pass through the first gateway of trees into Chattahoochee National Forest. Oma's house—mine now, still getting used to the idea—is another ten minutes up at the end of a dirt road, a crow-call from the closest neighbor. I park and kick my door open, stumbling out of my truck, stiff all over.

Malo follows me out of the cab, and two other dogs charge down the driveway to swap howdies. Bulletface crashes into my calves and I fall to his level, his tongue plugging my nose before I can push him off. Old Bobo's too busy getting the weekend's story from Malo to bother with me, so I only have to pry myself away from eighty wiggling pounds of bull terrier before staggering up to the house.

I have some work to do before I can take a bath. Shouldering the stubborn door open, I lean my bat against the wall inside. I move across the living room into the kitchen to drag thirty pounds of Alpo out of the pantry and fill the troughs on the back porch. I think I'm feeding eight or nine, now, plus a couple of coywolves coming down from the hill. As long as they play nice, they're welcome. They know stuff.

When that's taken care of, I put on a pot of coffee and start freshening Oma's runes.

She had them over all the windows and doors, for protection, and there's about a dozen more littering the house, for luck and good cooking and keeping company in line. I'm glad she taught me before she left. Glad someone taught me something.

Coffee's done right about when the downstairs runes are, so I pour myself a mug, dumping in almost a quarter cup of honey and a sprig of lavender from the bush under the kitchen window. My boots drag on the way upstairs, and I kick them off, shedding my jeans on the way into the bathroom and discovering just how bruised I am on the hip that hit the street.

I set my coffee down on the counter. There's a mason jar full of Oma's greenish cure-all salve on the shelves over the toilet—the recipe was buried in her library. It's pot marigold, plantain leaves, echinacea, comfrey, and peppermint in aloe vera gel. She made it in her blender. I pop the lid off and take a glob of it, using it to paint her healing mark on the bottom of the bathtub, and then start the hot water.

While it runs, I face the mirror and peel off my shirt, groaning. The fabric is stuck in my road burns, opening them again as it comes off. Under all the dirt, my skin is a patchwork of piss-yellow pus and bright red scrapes. My bra is riddled with holes on one side. Next time I'm gonna have to wear a jacket or something.

With all my bruises and abrasions uncovered, I step into my steaming bath. It stings like hell at first, but once I'm sunk down up to my chin it starts to feel better. I turn the faucet off with a foot and take a long drink of my coffee, then sit my mug down on the edge of the tub so I can dip my hair under. Oma never told me that witches spend most of their time filthy and cut up, but—I guess I do it a little different anyway.

When I surface again, raking wet hair out of my face, someone is knocking on my front door.

I hear Bulletface scrambling over the wood floor, barking his head off. I let him, sinking back down to my nose, groping for my coffee. I'm not dressed for company.

There's a merciful pause. Then the knocking starts again, Bulletface howls, and Bobo's shrill bay joins him. Malo doesn't bark, and I think they're the only three around right now. I sip my coffee. They'll get the idea. My busted doorbell clink-clunks against its casing, and the dogs bellow. Finally, a minute later, they shut up. Whoever it was gave up, I guess.

"Hello?"

Fuck. Found the back door open.

I haul myself out of the tub. "Coming!" I holler. All my towels are in the dryer still, so I yank my tank top back on and fight wet legs into my jeans at the top of the stairs. The dogs are all hovering in the doorway to the kitchen, Bulletface still boffing under his breath at the door.

I march past them, ready to pass out some fresh hell, but the woman on my back porch—well...

She's tall, and I've got this thing for tall girls, and—she's got a mile of stick-straight, crow-black hair draped down her shoulder blades, and eyes the color of rain-fed moss.

I lose the nerve to yell at her. St. Malo follows me to the door, his head low on his shoulders like he wants to growl, and I shoot him a look. Bulletface and Bobo stay back, but the Malinois sits right behind my heels as I reach the door, whining low.

"What?" is still all I'm generous enough to say.

"I'm sorry to bother you," she says smoothly. Not from around here, and not upset by my rudeness. "But I'm told you're the one to talk to about—strange things happening."

"Nah. You're looking for my Oma, and she's three years dead."

She purses her lips, turning to look over her shoulder. I lean out the door to follow her gaze across the tree-ringed field between me and the Gilmer place to the east: the sprawling old mansion is packed to the rafters with ghosts.

I hold my breath for a second, then let out a sigh. "You just move in?" I ask. It's been on the market a year and a half, but it went under contract a few weeks ago. She turns to face me again, nodding. I drop my head, looking at Malo, who flicks his ears back against his neck. "I'll be over at five," I tell her. I need to finish my bath and get some sleep, first.

***

The field is loud with insects when I cross it. The ground is damp with afternoon rain, and there's a green carpet at my feet, but the grass brushing my hips is crackly yellow. Grew, starved, died. I could just about swim through this humidity, but Georgia grass'll drink 'til we all drown.

There's a gardener working outside when I get to the mansion, yanking down the kudzu in sheets. It'll be back. He glances down from his ladder, pausing long enough to give me a little salute. People know who Oma was. I nod to him, then step up onto the porch to ring the doorbell. Sounds like church bells screaming.

Place like this, I'm not surprised a new resident is attracting attention. I'll go in, bang some pots and pans, tell the ghosts to fuck off, and she'll be fine.

She answers the door herself. I'm a little more presentable this time, and I earn a smile from her before she stands aside for me. "Come in," she says. "I didn't ask your name before."

"Maxine Sadler," I provide. I tilt my head back to take in the ceiling, two stories above me. The entry hall takes up the whole height of the house—must need a ladder to dust that chandelier. The silvery marble floor practically glows with fresh polish all the way up the stairs, and gleaming cherry-wood railings line the balcony. Despite the sunlight streaming in through the white lace on the huge front windows, the air inside is cool as spring water and just as sweet.

I stand in this cathedral of dead rich men and wait to hear their legacy whisper, or brush up against me. But it's still. There's nothing here but dust and white sheets on the furniture left behind. The ghosts are gone.

Which means something pushed them out.

"I'm Violet Blackburn," says the woman behind me, closing the front door. "Can I get you anything to drink, Maxine?"

"Max. I'd take a bourbon." This calls for it.

She gestures me into what someone, a hundred years ago,

called the drawing room. There's boxes of books along one wall, a couple of shelves still on their sides—but the wet bar's stocked. She gets out two glasses and a bottle of Jim Beam, pouring as I ask, "So the place is haunted?"

She turns, handing me a glass and taking a sip from hers. "Something like that," she says. She swallows, sitting down on the edge of a big desk across from the bay window. I wait while she takes a steadying breath. "My fiancé went missing a week ago."

I look out the window as the gardener works his way around the front of the house, then toss back my bourbon. "You need the cops, not a witch," I tell her.

"They're looking for him," she says. "But I—I wanted to talk to someone who might understand—this."

She gets up, opening a drawer in the desk and taking out a piece of paper. She moves away from it as soon as she sets it down, folding her free arm across her chest and turning her back on it. I move over in her place to look, and the Eye looks back.

I cross to the wet bar, refilling my glass.

"He had something with that symbol on it, a—a metal disc, four or five inches across," she tells me. "I know he was involved in something, and I know the cops…" She trails off helplessly.

"Nah, you were right. Cops can't help with this."

"I'll pay you," she says. "Any information you have, any-thing that can help—if you could use this to find him—"

"I'll try," I tell her. Then again, like it'll help somehow, "I'll try."

✳✳✳

She tells me he was headed for Atlanta when he disap-peared, but the cops found his car parked just inside the trees, on one of the dirt tracks that goes into the forest. I'll have to go at night to avoid whatever's left of the search parties.

It's approaching midnight when I grab my bat and throw open the back door. Bulletface charges out ahead of me, tearing a wide circle out into the field and scaring up some sleep-slow birds. Old Bobo trots out after him, disappearing into the grass, and Malo hangs at my heels, worried. There are two others—an old lab I've only seen a couple times and the big pitt I call Sixteeth—eating on the porch. They pull away from the troughs after a minute and bring up the rear.

We cross into the trees in minutes, but it's a long walk before we really hit the *woods*.

Chattahoochee at night has a language all its own: frogs sing chorus under the soprano of bats chirping. An owl mourns somewhere off in the canopy. The underbrush is alive with critters running through it, little rustles weaving frantic around dog-feet.

It's a little luck, and a little magic, that Malo knows what we're looking for. He moves out ahead, shooting a glance back at me occasionally, but I let him lead. I trust his nose, and his instincts, and the other dogs defer to me. Even Bulletface pulls back next to me after a while, the pack huddling up.

The forest is well and truly dark around us, the moon just a glow between leaves, when things start to get quiet and I know we're close. The wilds don't shut up for no reason.

Everybody knows Chattahoochee has *things* in it. Not everybody calls them Witnesses, but in places like this, something's always watching. Sometimes kids get the bright idea to come looking for it, but I'm here for a grown-ass man who's dumb enough to call them down, and the air is taut with eyes.

The bat's only good against hosts, though. You can't hit the breath of darkness that whispers *bless your heart* like a curse, or the tornado siren that wails on a cloudless day. We're never alone down here. There's only so much I can do.

Malo slows down, then stops. The pack and I come to a halt right behind him, and then he settles on his haunches, one ear flicking back to me, his gaze unwavering ahead. I don't see what he's seeing, but I can feel it. And then I can hear it, that slow, prickly drag through the brush. It's not just a guy, or a thing wearing a guy's body. It's scraping under branches, shaking leaves seven or eight feet up. My knuckles crack as I tighten my grip.

But the dogs aren't worried. I sling the bat up to rest on my shoulder and stand my ground.

The thing that emerges between trunks ahead of me is sort of flesh and blood, and it's sort of not. I know him from stories. In the boring ones, he used to be a soldier, and now he's looking for a head blown off by cannon-fire. But that aberrant head is intact. Melancholy eyes gleam creek-jade over a skinny snout under a wild tangle of lichen and hair. I've heard he's a charnel ghost, carrion-eater, but the corpse he's dragging is untouched by teeth.

Ol' Green Eyes stops ten feet in front of Malo and pulls the body around in front of him, presenting it to us.

I step around the dogs to meet him, never looking away. You don't look away from things like him. "Did you kill him?" I ask. But I already know.

Green Eyes sways his head back and forth, reaching down a spindly root-hand and pulling back the guy's shirt. The Eye is carved into his chest, a foot and a half across, his blood stuck black to the edges. He tried to call the Witnesses, and they answered.

Something's wrong, though. I've seen the Witnesses kill, but when their hosts are burned out they usually fall apart. He was stupid, but he was still human when he died.

"Were there more?" I ask. "Did he have friends?"

Green Eyes' head sways again. He was alone. It doesn't make sense, but—none of this makes sense. At least dead guys can't invite trouble in.

The cops can't see this. If they try to investigate, they're liable to open more doors. Green Eyes knew that, so he hid the body—hid the cracked window. I get it. "Thanks," I say, "but I need you to do more. I need you to get rid of this." Because I can't. I'm only human. They can't arrest a phantom for disposing of a body.

Green Eyes' hands worry over each other, those dog-sad eyes scraping across the body to a space between the trees. He's scared of the Witnesses, too.

I lift my warding token off over my head. The thin moonlight catches on its edge as it turns, and I step forward to offer it to him. His head twitches to one side and he freezes, eying my bat. I lower it, then drop it in the brush. He flinches. Then he stretches out an impossibly long arm to accept the gift. "Stay safe," I tell him. "And don't let anybody find him."

His hand retracts, clutching the iron of my token to his chest. Then he wraps his fingers around a handful of the guy's shirt and starts to drag him back into the woods.

"Wait."

He stops. His profile appears behind the snarl of his hair as he glances back at me.

"He had something he used to call them," I say. "A metal disc. Nobody's gonna dig it up, are they? It's not where some idiot's gonna stumble across it again?"

His head shifts, moonlight drifting across one of those eyes. He doesn't know, or he thinks I won't like the answer. I'm not sure which, but that's all he offers me before he turns away again, and disappears into the trees with a fool's body leaving a trail through the underbrush behind him.

I do what a witch is supposed to. I wait until the woods give me permission, the orchestra pit of Chattahoochee waking up around me, before I take my leave.

***

Common courtesy would tell me not to go knocking on her door with bad news at dead time, but I never did have much of that.

Malo whines as I take the stairs up her front porch two at a time. The others went home already. I look down at him, his one eye as sad as both of Green Eyes', and pause. "It's okay," I tell him. "I just have to let her know that he's not coming back."

He sits down at the foot of the stairs, ears falling back against his neck.

"Go home if you don't like it," I say.

He lingers for a minute, glancing across the field at Oma's house. Then he turns and starts to slink away. I'm still watching when he shoots me a baleful glance behind. I get that the house casts a dark shadow, and I get that she was involved with a guy who called the Witnesses, but I'm not gonna deny her the truth just because my dog doesn't like her.

When he disappears into the grass, I step up to the door and send the church bells singing on the other side. I think Violet must have been up already, because the door opens inside of thirty seconds. I'm expecting her face to fall when she sees me. It doesn't. "Max," she says. "Did you—"

"You should sit down," I tell her.

She swallows, withdrawing from the door to let me in. I close it behind me and follow her into the drawing room, flipping on the lights as she sits, perching on the edge of an antique chaise she must have uncovered sometime after I left last night. "What did you find?" she asks.

I fold my arms over my chest. I've never had to do this before, and I'm not good at dancing around shit, so I spit it out: "He's dead."

It rolls over her slow. She takes a shuddering breath, then gets up and goes to the wet bar, pouring a pair of bourbons with shaking hands. She's gonna spill, so I move over to pick them up, ushering her back to the chaise and then handing her a glass. She fires it back like a pro, so I give her the other one.

"I knew this—was possible," she says quietly. "Likely, even. What was he—what was he thinking?"

"Dunno," I tell her. That's not the answer she's looking for. I let out a breath between my teeth. "He invited something dark in," I say. "I don't know why. Power, maybe. Some people go looking for them, sometimes they come knocking. They don't usually kill anybody outright, but I've never seen—" I stop myself. She doesn't need the details. "They use people as doors," I go on after a second. "And I guess some people—get ripped off the hinges."

I'm kind of babbling, so I stop. There's nothing I can say to make her feel better, anyway.

She sips from the second glass of bourbon, staring into it helplessly. She looks so alone that I sit down next to her, hoping that the six inches between our knees is respectful enough. She glances at me, mossy eyes traveling up my neck in a way that makes my skin prickle. Then her head jerks up. "The disc," she says. "Did you get it?"

"No. It's somewh—"

"You have to get it back. I need to—I need to see it."

"No fucking way," I tell her. "That thing is dangerous, and now it's lost somewhere in Chattahoochee where no one's ever going to see it again." I try to say it with authority, but it's hard when I don't know if it's true.

"We can't take that chance," she says. She sets her glass down and stands. "What if someone finds it? What if someone else—?"

"I'm not bringing it to you!"

"Then find it and destroy it," she says. I open my mouth to refuse, but she reaches out, winding her long fingers around my wrists. "Please," she breathes.

I don't know how I'm gonna do that, but something in the back of my mind whispers that I should have done it to begin with. Someone *will* find it if I don't. He was still human, I remind myself. I don't like thinking it, but there was probably someone else involved, someone that loosened the pins a little, or maybe a lot. And if that someone helps the Witnesses start ripping more doors off their hinges—this is only gonna get uglier.

And I don't know how to say no to those fingers.

"Fine."

She sinks onto the chaise next to me again, the six inches gone. "Thank you," she says. Then, quietly, "He hadn't been with me for a long time."

"His mind was probably all but gone," I tell her. "I'm sorry."

She leans closer, breathing, "I'm not talking about his mind."

I get hot through the air conditioner. "Oh."

One of her hands slides up my arm, her fingertips grazing across the still-fresh skin of my shoulders. "He couldn't help me," she whispers. "But you can." I'm frozen until her mouth meets mine, as spicy and soft as it looks like it should be.

"You don't want this," I should tell her. She's in shock, and come dawn she'll be in mourning. I'm the last thing she needs to wake up next to. I should say that.

But I don't. And she's pretty convincing.

***

I dream that I'm biting into a peach. It's perfect—fresh and tart and wet. And after I've sucked the last of the flesh from the pit, I look down and the juice has stained my hands, my wrists, my teeth and my tongue life-blood red.

My eyes fly open.

I sort myself out of the sheets, careful not to disturb Violet on the other side of her bed. It's barely dawn. I hope she sleeps for another few hours. I should be long gone by the time she wakes up, let her deal with her loss.

My clothes mark a trail up the stairs. I go slow to keep the house from creaking as I work backward, dressing on my way out and pulling on my boots only as I ease the front door closed behind me.

It must have rained in the last few hours, because the field is damp again. Over the bowed grass, I can see the shape of St. Malo lying on Oma's porch. He pushes up to a sitting position when I get close, ears back.

I tromp up the steps to him, reaching out to rub him. He ducks his head away from my hand, whining softly. Guilt spills over me, and my hackles rise. "Fine," I mutter. I move into the house to grab the Alpo. Bulletface and Sixteeth are lying on the cool kitchen floor, and they don't seem too happy with me, either. "What?" I bark. "I didn't do anything wrong."

They won't even look at me.

I drop the Alpo and storm out of the kitchen, stripping off my clothes again, gathering them in a bunch and flinging them through the doorway into the laundry room. Then I stomp up the stairs to shower. The hot water stings even though my road burns are closed, and my hair feels stifling plastered against my face, but I scrub her off me. I shouldn't have to. The dogs have never been this upset about my questionable decisions before.

They're not wrong, though. I took advantage of the poor girl's grief.

I stay in the shower until the water goes cold, then shut it off, slicking my hair out of my face. Malo's waiting for me when I step out, lying on the bath mat. He doesn't look mad, just—worried.

"Yeah, I know," I say. "Won't happen again." His tail

thumps against the floor, once. "Still gonna help me find that thing?" I ask.

He gets up, pushing his head into my hand. Never did get the towels hung up. I close the lid of the toilet and sit down on it, still dripping, to rub his ears.

"Thanks, kid," I sigh.

I stand after a few minutes, trudging into my bedroom for clean clothes. I should try and get a little more sleep if I'm going to go looking for a Witness relic tonight, but I know I won't be able to. Best use of my time now is to try and figure out how to destroy it—not the metal, but the power. Magic doesn't have a melting point.

Dressed again, I head into the cramped library, tying my wet hair back so it won't drip on Oma's books. She's gotta have something. It's her own spiky handwriting I tug down off the shelves, making a pile on the broken rocker and sitting down on the floor to read. Malo sits at my back, keeping watch.

I keep hoping to find the Eye buried somewhere in Oma's runes, but of course I don't. She always told me that Sadler witches don't fuck with what's beyond us. But I find *something*, and I realize I'm not gonna make it back into Chattahoochee tonight. I'll be spending the next day or so making. But after that, I might just make it through this, and the Eye might not be a problem anymore.

***

I don't take my bat this time. Can't hit storm-wracked air.

Seven dogs come: the old lab brings a friend, a springy ghost-eyed husky I've never met. We start out right after sunset, because I don't know how long it's gonna take to get where we're going.

The Gilmer mansion is lit up when we pass it. I don't look, but Violet's eyes rake trails up my neck from the windows.

I've tried not to wonder, the past two days, if there's any chance that could work. She's got other shit to deal with before she decides if I was a mistake.

Chattahoochee swallows us up quick this time. The moon's dimmer tonight, waning. Can't wait for better timing, though, not if I have a chance at ending this.

We still have to delve deep before the chorus quiets down. Malo stops. He circles once, scenting the air. He's lost the trail now that we've crossed into silence. The other dogs are getting nervous without his confidence. Then, just at the edge of my vision, I make out the leggy silhouette of a coywolf. It turns, the amber gleam of its eyes catching. Then it takes off.

Malo follows. More coywolves join as we go. I count five of them, plus seven dogs and one junkyard witch. I don't know whether a pack of thirteen is bad luck for us, or for *them*.

I've never been to the place the feral guide leads us.

The trees part around a flat of exposed stone, kudzu tangled at its edges. In the middle is a pool of rainwater three feet across and god knows how deep. The fingernail moon's reflection in the surface is cracked by branches arcing overhead, and everything is still. The coywolves assemble along the edges, barely visible as darker patches of shadow marked by eye-glow.

I can just about hear Oma singing through my bones. Magic calls to magic. This is it.

The new symbol sits heavy in my pocket, and my left hand is bandaged from where I bled for it. I used what I had. The bars are nails, the closing circle a pair of old horse shoes, all welded together in my garage, iron and rust stained red. It's wrapped in a silk scarf from Oma's closet, because even though I made it and fed it, I can feel it when it touches my skin. It's a neutralizer, and it's permanent.

The plan is to bind it to the Eye and bury them far away, in a grave I'll never have to walk over again.

I can feel the Witnesses watching me from that pool. The pack hangs back, but I don't have that luxury. I catch the gleam of creek-jade eyes as I step onto the rock, and a spindly arm reaches from the trees. My warding token dangles from a root-finger. Ol' Green Eyes don't talk, but the sentiment vibrates through the soles of my feet: *you need this more than I do now.*

I loop it on over my head and then go to kneel at the edge of the pool. I draw the neutralizer out of my pocket, my fingers grazing its edge as I set it down by the water. I can't see past the glassy surface in the dark. Taking a breath, I dip my hand in—

—and am sucked down headfirst.

Water roars around me, tearing at my hair and clothes, trying to rip the ward from my neck. I clamp the iron down against my chest. Through the current I can see the disc, somehow buried partway in the rock. I try to swim for it, and gravity slams me to the bottom of the pool, knocking the breath out of me in an explosion of bubbles. I don't have enough air to pry the disc free, but the Witnesses aren't going to give me another chance. I can hear the insect scream of them even down here.

The bandage on my left hand comes loose and is torn away by the current as I get my fingers around the relic. My knuckles open against the stone, blood sloughing away from my hands in a dark cloud. I'm yanking as hard as I can, bracing my boots against the bedrock, but it won't budge. The earth itself is trying to consume it.

I'm running out of oxygen. The noise of the water and the screaming of the things beyond starts to dull in my ears, and my vision darkens. I can't leave without it. I pull harder.

The world is black, and I drift.

I hear the clicking of claws on stone. Malo rests his head on my shoulder, nudging my neck with his nose.

The disc loosens under my fingers and I wrench it free, kicking for the surface. I drag in a ragged breath as my head hits air, and then I'm falling back against rock. My hair and clothes are dry, but my head still spins in the grip of the vortex and I'm shivering.

Doesn't matter. The disc is in my hand, the Eye throbbing against my unbandaged palm. I pull myself up on my knees and set it against the stone, reaching for the neutralizer.

Malo puts his muzzle under my wrist, stopping me.

I look up. Twelve pairs of eyes and one extra look back. The clearing is still. The pool ripples faintly with the passage of my arm. The Witnesses are quiet.

It's not calling them. I look down, and the Eye looks back. Even an idiot doesn't carve a summons into his own chest. No one carves anything into their own chest unless—

Unless they think it's going to save their life.

Oma told me all the time that I was too stubborn. My problem, she said, every time I ranted or argued or ignored a warning, is that I decide I'm right and then it don't matter who or what tells me I'm wrong. My mind is a blunt instrument: effective, but rigid.

Past the edge of the trees, I look at Green Eyes. "It's a seal." I meant it as a question, but I don't really need to ask. He inclines his head, then turns and disappears into the woods.

"This is perfect," I tell the pack. I thought it was power on the wrong side, but I can take it back and give it to Violet for protection while I fix the rest of this. Her fiancé wasn't trying to call the Witnesses, he was trying to guard against them, and someone killed him for it. They're still out there, which means she's in danger—he couldn't help her, she said, but I could. She needed someone who knew what they were doing—

Malo's eye searches mine, stopping my thoughts.

Oh.

I get to my feet and kick my neutralizer into the pool. The water of the gateway swirls around it, evaporating. I have to tug my boots loose of the kudzu as it rushes in to take the stone back. It leaves the disc free, and I pick it up, turning it over as moon-gleam glides along its edge. The coywolves scatter as the pack and I start back the way we came.

I'm finally starting to understand.

***

I wait for morning to go knocking, this time. Some things are better done in daylight.

She opens the door smiling. Malo sits down on the doormat to wait for me and I head inside. She closes the door between me and the dog, then leads me into the drawing room. "Is it done?" she asks.

"It's safe," I tell her. I didn't know how this was gonna go, so I didn't bring it with me. It probably would have helped, but I'll need it later.

"So it's gone."

She's standing just beyond the edges of a shaft of sunlight spearing through the window, and her eyes pick up the light like moons. "No," I sigh. "It's just—safe." I turn and open the window, leaning against the sill. The kudzu has already started to climb over it again, locking the house down, trying to figure out what it can take back.

"I thought you were going to destroy it," she says behind me. I can hear something like thunder in her throat, and I wonder how long it's been since Violet Blackburn was a person.

"Plan changed," I tell her.

For a second I think I should have brought my bat, but— not all fights can be won like that. I turn around, and she's right on top of me, but I don't think she can touch me. Not now.

"Why are you doing this?" she pleads. "I thought you wanted to help me."

"Yeah," I say. "So did I."

I yank my token from my neck. She's not fast enough. My palm locks over her forehead, and I feel the iron of the ward sink into the bone—what used to be bone. Mercifully, she doesn't scream. Her Witness pours out, whipping my hair into a tangled mess as it tries to find a way into me. For the first time, I can hear words in its whine. It whispers the secrets of power inches away from my ears, maybe the same ones it used to tempt this husk.

What used to be Violet Blackburn is dissolving without it to hold her up. In seconds, she's nothing but a little heap of black dust. The last gusting breaths of the Witness spread her across the floor of the drawing room as they sweep out the window. I shut it before I leave.

St. Malo walks across the field with me, my fingers in his mane. Back at the house, I fill up the troughs with fresh Alpo and make sure there's clean water in all the bowls. "Watch the house," I tell the dogs. The coywolf sleeping under the porch steps opens one eye to acknowledge me. Nice to have them here, but Oma knew better than I did. Nothing's getting past her runes.

Malo hops into the passenger seat of the truck, and I slide my bat into his footwell. The Eye is wrapped up in the glove box already. I broke a lot of seals in Atlanta. I've got fixing to do.

Counterclockwise

Kate Larking

"Please, Mother. Allow me." I reached across the ornate metal table and gripped the teapot's handle. Heavy! My embroidered lace gloves caused the porcelain to slip in my grip, but I held fast. I managed a smooth pour, refilling the Queen's teacup.

"Thank you, my Freya."

I smiled, put down the teapot, and resumed sitting, trying to ignore the odd stretch aching in my forearm. It wasn't often I spoke to the Queen in such privacy, without servants even, and I would do anything to extend our time together.

A knock sounded against the interior wrought-iron gates of the greenhouse.

"Ah, yes, here they are." She stirred a spoonful of rose-infused sugar into her tea. "Our Magician, have you met them?"

The gate creaked open—an antiquated sound my mother loved yet simply grated on my ears. Over the rim of my gilded teacup, I caught a glimpse of a violet capelet through the vivid red bark of the paperback cherry trees. I stilled and watched the Magician stride into the room, head held high.

When my mother said she had summoned the Magician, surely she didn't mean this young creature, flaxen hair falling in waves to their shoulders, their skin taut with a fresh glow, and youthful hands with relaxed fingers at their sides.

Our old Magician withered away last fall. I expected the familiar grey frizzled hair, age-spotted skin, and bony hands of a well-trained, well-aged master like every Magician I had seen visiting every Spoke Kingdom on my father's diplomatic tours. I had thought that the age lines gouged into their flesh and white hair so thin you could see their blotchy scalp was the reason they identified as genderless in their unmagicked state.

But this. This Magician barely appeared my age—fine, I'd give them a few years over my eighteen, but certainly not the forty-some years over mine that the other Spoke Kingdoms possessed. Lean body and ambiguous palace apparel spoke definitively to no gender. The only thing announcing their status? The tell-tale violet capelet.

They mustn't deserve it, so young; our Magician was clearly a halfwit weed.

The mixture of disgust and curiosity churned inside me. It was akin to the Commoner Question: could our citizens possess a sense of pride when, say, working in pig shit every day? But I suppose that was an unfair comparison. Magicians weren't commoners. Because commoners wouldn't be allowed into this castle, especially among the exquisite orchid plants and cherry trees my mother bred in this stained glass greenhouse.

"Majesty," the Magician bowed, fist over heart to my mother, their unbound hair slinking over their shoulders.

"Ah, yes, perfect timing. Magician, this is my daughter, Princess Elestria den Vonwerth of our Seventh Spoke Kingdom." Mother needlessly gestured to me with an upturned hand. She was always about full and proper introductions for our family.

"Highness," the Magician bowed to me, their eyes, more vibrant than my emerald ring, stared into my own, unphased by my royalty.

"Mother, I don't see why you deigned to interrupt our perfectly lovely tea before I leave for Dial with this—"

"Elestria, you will be accompanied by our Magician to Prince Tallom's debut ball."

My mouth snapped closed. Replies, retorts raced through my head faster than I could grab the individual words to speak them. And my mother simply raised her cup of tea to her lips and took a delicate, silent sip.

Even the Magician seemed to pause. They ought to. Magicians were meant to be secret tools, working behind the scenes of a Spoke, pursing their lips before finding words I couldn't scavenge, "In what capacity, Majesty?"

"I have arranged for a pseudonym." She lifted the packet of papers I had been intently curious about this whole tea. I had thought it to be for me—an inheritance? Instructions? New responsibilities for learning the intricacies of ruling the kingdom? My mother continued, "You will pose as a high noble. This information should be sufficient." She extended the packet to the Magician.

"Of course, Majesty." The Magician took them and tucked the packet under their arm without opening it.

"Mother, this is hardly appropriate. This is the Crown Prince's debut! Such overblown theatrics of disguising a *Magician* as a noble is surely unwarranted—"

The queen raised her hand sharply, cutting through my words. "Magician, leave us."

The Magician bowed and exited in the same confident manner they had strode into this private, royal retreat.

I leaned forward, holding the decorative tendrils of hair that artfully draped from my tiara out of the cream flourish atop my berry tart. "Mother, this is hardly appropriate. If you insist upon a concierge, send me with a real lord, not an entirely too young, surely duplicitous, Realm-hopping—"

"Enough, my Feyra. While I am pleased to have raised such a proud and willful heir, there is little gained left in hiding any more from you."

"Hiding?"

"That Magician—who you look upon with such disdain— they are the only major asset our Spoke Kingdom has left."

"Asset? Don't be ridiculous, Mother. They are hardly an asset, being barely in the infancy of their power, certainly barebones trained. The only way that Magician could have obtained Master status is through deceiving their instructors."

"That young Magician was all we could afford, my Feyra. Even then, the Dial's academy owed me a personal debt and, still, this was all they could offer us. Do you understand?"

I frowned, leaning back against the ornate wire of my garden chair. "We should easily be able to afford—"

"*Should*, my Freya. We are not able. We are poor."

I shook my head and lifted my teacup. "Mother, we drink from finest porcelain, adorned with gold. We cannot possibly—"

"There is as much in our vaults as there is flesh on that teacup's bone. We coast on old perceptions of wealth, curried favours that are drying up, and the respect of our people. One wrong move and the cracks will show to the other Spokes and we will be liable to takeover."

My mouth moved, trying to shape words but there was nothing to convey. We weren't poor! My dresses were all the newest styles. The military and guard were sharply dressed and weapons were well polished. Our food—the tarts before us, the duck with ten accompaniments yestereve—we lived luxuriously.

The Queen sipped the last of her tea, turning the cup as she replaced it on its matching saucer. She stood, smoothing her dress in the same regal movement I had envied from toddlerdom, trying to perfect under my own hands. "Until that Magician ages to the point of other Magicians in the other Spoke Kingdoms, we cannot let on that our financial resources are failing. Our hope lies in you, my Freya. A political marriage proposal to another Spoke will expose us. Only a Dial marriage will suffice to ensure that our people survive, ensure that you can continue to live as we have been able to afford you until now. Use that Magician to do whatever they must to ensure your success."

She turned and strode away, passing her vanilla planifolia orchids facing straight ahead, not raising her nose to adore their ripe scent.

All I could do was stare at her teacup, a thread-fine crack showing under the lingering under the print of my mother's burgundy lipstain.

***

"You are unusually quiet, Highness."

I frowned, glaring at my lady-in-waiting in the mirror to where she tended my hair. But once I saw the ridges in my face, I tried to smooth it, make myself as impassive as possible. I would not have Great-Grandmother's horrific frown lines that scarred her official portrait from her fiftieth year of rule. "It's nothing, Charla. The queen has assigned me a companion for our journey to the Dial."

Charla twitched the brush, still deep in the strands of my hair.

I pulled away from her. "Honestly! How many times must I tell you to move smoothly to—"

"Avoid breaking the ends, of course, Highness. I am sorry. I will pay better attention." She reached up to start again.

I huffed, leaning back in my chair once more.

Weeks I had been meticulously overseeing all the preparations for the Crown Prince's debut ball, not the least of which had been my own beauty routine. Weeks of massaging warm almond oil into my hair, bathing in lily and rose water, and drinking teas to keep my complexion from drying in the chill of winter.

"A companion, Highness? Did she say who?"

There was no way I would admit that that... *child* was our kingdom's *Magician*. "A high noble. She insisted I have an escort."

"I see." Each brush stroke, Charla's tiny silver locket thumped against her breastbone. "Do you know who is accompanying us? I could see if I could find any information on them for you..."

It dawned on me that I did not have knowledge of the Magician's pseudonym. I rolled my eyes. "Enough about that, Charla. I am tired and we journey far tomorrow. Is it further than you have ever travelled?"

She replaced the brush on the vanity and deftly plaited my oiled locks. "Living near the border, I have travelled to Sixth Spoke before. But never beyond that, and certainly not the Dial."

I sighed. Perhaps we were as poor as mother had made it seem. I bet other Spoke princesses had worldly ladies-in-waiting.

***

The heels of my boots clacked against the marble floors, the sound sharp and satisfying in the hall despite my skirt's muffling tulle layers. Charla trotted behind me, the front of her gown pinched up to avoid tripping while her short stride struggled to keep up.

The violet-uniformed guards pushed open the double doors ahead of my arrival, and I strode into the Hall of Realms without pause.

Carved wood stretched around us before the Realm gate. The gate rippled with magic, teal and aquamarine shining bright against the pale oak and pine carvings. Our Spoke honoured the element of wood, and this room was our core.

I glanced up. A twisting tree nymph, cradling a bouquet of lilies and ivy, blinked emerald eyes at me before blending back into the carved foliage.

A young noble stood next to the portal, sandy hair, now slick and pulled back into a low ponytail with a black ribbon, arms crossed over a navy waistcoat. And who was this now? If my mother expected me to have yet another companion—especially an eligible-for-marriage noble accompanying me at all times, she ought to kiss her wishes of me securing a profitable marriage farewell.

A guard leaned into my ear. "Lord Merrith of Outer Seventh Rim." Meanwhile, the noble stood straighter and gazed at me.

I halted.

Those eyes, as bright as the Realm-gate behind them, told me what I needed to know.

Of course, I had known that Magicians could change their appearance with glamour. Not their age, nor their voices, but features twisted in the light and shadows cooperated to deceive the eye.

The Magician turned to me and bowed, deeper than the one the ranked Magician had given me yesterday, a testament to the Magician's noble ruse for this event. Yet it carried the same genuine reverence. There was no posturing, nor an exaggeration to feign loyalty like almost all of the visiting nobles did, eager to be found in new or better favour.

I tsked.

Charla's muted steps caught up to me. Despite breathing heavily, she whispered into my ear, "Does the Queen want everyone to think you are betrothed? He's gorgeous!"

✳✳✳

The sweet smell of Dial-style roasted pork permeated the welcoming gala. I suppose that was the point, given how the hog was propped on a table under the enormous magelight chandelier. Chefs worked on either side of the beast to carve the best, most mouth-watering cuts for the noble guests.

I scanned the crowd over the rim of my champagne glass.

Dial nobility was easy to pick out; most of them were middle-aged or older, reminiscing in groups with others of whitening locks. They wore more gold than it ought to be possible to walk under the weight of. In contrast, the young Spoke nobles wore rich and vibrant dress, styled to be just under the measure of gold-swathed ostentatious, vying for a political marriage.

My stomach clenched. I fought it, my face impassive. I channeled the pain into my pinching fingers on the champagne glass stem, relying on its quality to ensure I didn't shatter it. I had to do this.

"Ah, a moment, Highness," the Magician's now irritatingly familiar tenor said.

I held still, ignoring them.

The Magician's hand reached into my hair. Pressing a tugging pin back into place, I nearly winced before remembering the rich pigments of my makeup and how it liked to transfer itself within wrinkles. Even so, as they dropped their hand away, my scalp felt immensely less irritated than before Charla began this updo three hours ago.

"There. Fixed. Would you like to visit the buffet, Highness?" The Magician, dressed in a slick navy suit with silver edging, extended a hand toward a crowd of other Spoke princesses oohing and aahing over the complex flavours.

"Pig doesn't interest me." I sighed. This was going to be a dreary evening. I had no interested in mingling with my competition. Better to let them bloat themselves on brined meat and out of their best apparel for the debut ball tomorrow.

"Then perhaps some of the desserts, Princess Elestria?"

I turned to a *still* high-voiced Prince Phiroth of Sixth Spoke. At least he managed to move out of his childhood smocks and into something more befitting the occasion. If one ignored his voice and baby-fat face, you could at least admire how hard his tailor had worked to make him appear slimmer in the black suit with ruby-encrusted shoulder decals.

Prince Phiroth continued, lifting his own plate of sweets. "The truffles are excellent."

"I am content with my beverage for now." I took another sip of champagne.

"Of course. Princess, I came over to ask, would you do me the honour of your first dance tomorrow evening?" He smiled, but then frowned, as if just now noticing the Magician. "Who is this?"

I ignored the first question, which honestly turned my stomach moreso than it already was with my nerves, and gladly offered up the Magician as a decoy. "Second Prince Phiroth of Sixth Spoke, this gentleman is Lord Merrith of Outer Seventh Rim." I knew full well that the desert of our Outer Seventh Rim was entirely unoccupiable land, but no one outside of our Spoke would know.

"The Outer Rim! It isn't often that those tasked with protecting the Rims are able to venture inland, let alone the Dial."

The Magician bowed. "It is a kindness that our Queen graciously afforded me for my service, Highness."

"Hmm. So a gift, not a prospective intra-Spoke match?" He raised his eyebrow. Well both eyebrows, and awkwardly.

If my lady-in-waiting's comments hadn't already tipped me to know how attractive of a gentleman the Magician made, I would have sputtered champagne all down my dress. "Alas, Lord Merrith here already has a delightful husband." Acknowledge the lord as unavailable, but don't acknowledge my lofty ambitions for marriage. That is what I had decided. I'd need to continue to ride our wealth's illusion until a match was made.

The Magician bowed to me. "I shall pass on your compliment, Highness, thank you."

Yes, yes, pass it on to your fictitious husband I just manufactured. I scanned the room again. A person in a gold-embossed tailed jacket and snug black trousers idly paced alone, away from murmuring gluttonous crowds.

The tigerlily embroidered on the label over her heart gave her away; Princess Pienia of Dial, debuted before her Crown Prince brother but made ineligible to rule due to her bastard nature. No lingering Spoke nobles nibbled at her ringless-finger status, and the gold-laden Lords of Dial walked as though she wasn't even there.

"So, Princess, would you?"

I blinked and stepped back, turning toward Phiroth again. What was this about?

"The dance." The Magician's voice breathed, their words somehow drifting to my ears alone. How they had wafted their voice over the din of the hall and the space between us, I didn't know, but I was thankful for the reminder.

"Alas, Phiroth, perhaps you ought to sniff for truffles somewhere else." I tapped the rim of his plate before I strode away, toward the Princess Pienia.

The Magician bowed and followed after me. "Was that wise?"

"It's as I said; pigs don't interest me."

***

I shoved open the doors to my room, heedless of the Magician trailing me. "A bath, Charla! Ready a bath!"

Charla hopped up from the pressing she had been doing on my debut ballgown. "Of course, Highness!" She rushed to the bathing room and turned on the golden tap.

In the meantime I started pull the most vexing of her pins from my hair.

"Oh, my! Sir—my lord. You must go."

I blinked and turned. Sure enough, Charla was shooing the Magician from the room. I suppose they *were* technically an unattached noble to Charla's perspective right now. I sighed to the ceiling and stalled my pin-removal until Charla had closed them out of the room.

Charla turned to me, blushing furiously at my indecency before the young lord. "Why so suddenly, Highness?"

"The ballroom became as sweaty and sticky as the boar they roasted." Forget the pins. The ones that vexed me most were out now. I began to pull at the lacing over my left shoulder.

Charla surged forward to take over for me. "How was it otherwise?"

I let her. "I had the most wonderful conversation with Princess Pienia." I adored the Princess more than I ought to.

"Princess Pienia? The bastard?" Charla frowned, moving onto the laces at my other shoulder. "I don't understand, Highness. You had conversations with her... about her brother?"

"No, not him, but about everything and anything else, Charla. But she said so much by saying so little."

"I thought your mother emphasized that this ball was to focus marriage prospects. I mean, for a long time, Prince Phiroth has expressed a genuine interest—"

"Oh, how horrific, Charla. Have you even met that pig?"

Charla pursed her lips.

"He is grotesque. Absolutely not."

Charla remained quiet, helping me strip out of my gown with a competence and expediency she didn't usually employ at home. I rolled my eyes. I bet other ladies-in-waiting maintained a consistent quality standard of work.

I slipped into the mint-green enamel tub and sunk down the slick surface to my neck. Warm water speckled with floating rose petals sloshed over the rim. The splash dampened the hem of Charla's skirts as she hurried to save my underthings from the rippling wave spreading over the floor, en route to the gold-painted floor drain. She crept out of the room with the slip bundled up against her neck.

The warmth of the bath leached the film of sweat from against my skin, soothing me. The conversations... we dallied between fashion and essential oils, but the layer under our topics! Princess Pienia twisted her sapphire pendant in her fingers, her subtext critiquing the crowd, critical on the structure of the Dial and the Spokes. She wielded the conversation to skirt wide around her powerlessness, ruled out of line for the throne but not disinherited, disenfranchised but a piece still in play on the chessboard.

I imagined her subtle actions over and over again. I was not mistaken. She was a brilliant woman—

A cord of black silk—the cord I had meticulously selected for my ballgown—fell through my vision, and cinched.

I gasped—well, I tried! I clawed at my neck, fingernails digging into my skin. Get under. Get under and pull free!

I stood, pressing my feet flat into the bottom of the tub. Whoever held pulled tighter, arching me back, over the back edge of the tub. I dropped a hand to the bath's lip. Lily oil, impossibly slippery over the enamel, prevented my purchase.

"Hurry up and die!"

Charla.

I flicked my eyes to the side. Charla's eyes bulged as she yanked tighter, again.

My heartbeat pounded inside of me, cinched under the cord. My feet slid forward on the enamel, losing their leverage as the oils softened my skin.

The cord cut in harder, deeper. How was that possible, still?

I flailed, catching Charla's cheek and raking my fingers over her face.

Blood smeared on my fingertips, I flung an arm behind me again, trying to scratch at my assailant, but my hands only caught sleeves.

Someone…

Help.

My vision flashed emerald, bright and deep like the portal, the nymph's eyes… the Magician's eyes.

My heart stopped pounding. Was this death?

A halted scream.

The cord loosened, its work done.

My body slammed into the bath water. My head submerged. Lily and rose clotted my nostrils and throat, filling my lungs. What would they do with my body now? Send me home to my now-heirless mother?

An arm looped around my naked waist and hauled me from the water.

I gasped and sputtered into coughs. The burning of breath, the pain as oil seeped into my wounds... Too real. Too... alive?

A familiar voice, quiet against my heaving gasps. "Highness, please open your eyes."

I did. The Magician's calm and steady gaze stared back into mine, green as dazzling emerald death.

I asked why. At least, I tried. But my voice wouldn't come. "You are safe now."

So I looked.

A tree—black cherry if I wasn't mistaken by the smooth, dark bark and deep sweet scent—twisted and twined about most of the room, growing back into itself. The main trunk grew from the bath, the vines half into the tub water and half reaching into the floor drain.

A major branch pierced Charla's torso from left shoulder to right hip, the flowering branch in full bloom, petals painted with blood.

The second major branch curled back around, passing along her open mouth and pinning her speechless against the wall of the bathroom. Her nostrils flared for desperate breath, her wide-eyed gaze flicking between the cord dangling from the limp fingers of her right hand and the Magician.

How...

The Magician reached out and pulled a pin out of my hair. "I gave you a pin, Highness. My own design." They turned the pin to me, a rose gold cherry blossom eroding under the weight of spent magic. The Magician dropped it. It didn't make it to the floor, spreading into ashen dust in the air.

The Magician lifted me, grunting under my weight. I suppose they were a slight creature. I couldn't lift a person, could I? They sat me on the cherry tree limb that impaled Charla.

She screamed as the tree branch sagged, her left leg limply kicking, spreading diluted blood with her heel.

"None of that," the Magician scolded, crouching in front of her.

And the scream was gone.

I swallowed, twice, three times against the burning in my neck and throat. "Why?"

The Magician glanced at me, then curled their hand in the air.

The branch pulled back from the wall, releasing Charla's head. Blood spilled over her bottom lip, staining her chin.

"My lord, how improp"—she sputtered more blood at the Magician—"improper. A nobleman in a lady's bath—"

"Indeed. Improper." The Magician replied, tone bored. "Why did you do this? Who do you work for?"

"I'll take that to the grave."

"Such theatrics aren't necessary." The Magician waved their hand again, the branch pinning her head against the wall once more.

Charla screamed, and tried to reach up with her compromised arms.

I glared. I suppose it would be as comfortable as being choked.

The Magician plucked the locket from Charla's neck.

Charla screamed louder, harder.

The Magician rolled their eyes. With a wave of the hand, even with the locket still dangling from their hand, the cherry tree responded. A fresh sprig grew out of the smooth new bark, pinching Charla's nostrils down.

Charla ceased screaming, saving the little air she had left.

I pointed to the locket. What were they doing?

The Magician flicked open the locket. "Usually these types

of amulets are activated by blood." They pressed the open side against Charla's bloodied chin.

"Char! Is it done?"

Phiroth. My eyes bulged, my body trembled, rage turning my body to ice. I gasped once, twice. I had no words. Nothing. Just as I was paralyzed against my mother, the situation stilled me.

The Magician glanced at me, and lifted the locket as though requesting if they could speak.

I nodded.

"It... it's done," the Magician replied in a hauntingly familiar voice, choked with emotion. Tears trickled from Charla's angry eyes, hearing her voice used against her.

"Are you okay?"

"I... yes. No? I don't know." The Magician watched me as they said it, eyes neutral despite the panic dripping into their feigned voice. Did our Magician know new magical arts?

"Char, I know this is hard." Phiroth's voice was full of soft and supportive emotion. *"But you are saving your kingdom."*

My lady-in-waiting closed her eyes.

The Magician continued in Charla's voice. Not any words, but a distressed whine.

Well put, Magician.

"If she would have married me, you and your people would have had a chance to survive under ours. We went over the figures the spies gave us. Your kingdom needs this. You did the right thing. Her pride is what killed her, refusing to see reason."

My mother gave me this pride. Bred it into my bones until it was inseparable from me. And she gave me all I needed to know, but I wasn't wary enough. Perhaps she had heard of Sixth's ambition. Or perhaps she hadn't, and just knew it was a possibility if our finances were revealed through a marriage match.

I didn't want to hear anymore. I shook my head.

"Get out of there now. Come to me, Char, and—"

The Magician closed the locket. A tiny snap and Phiroth's voice was gone.

I closed my eyes. The tree muffled the echoes in the room. I heard only my breath, and the Magician's, and the drip, drip of Charla's blood from the flowering tree branch.

Charla no longer breathed.

"I thought magic couldn't replicate voices." I wondered in the scratchy tone I was left with. Husky and breathy, it would seem like a flirtatious tone if not for the raw pain and the tang of blood in the rose-and-lily scented air.

The Magician choked out a laugh. "True, Highness, however that was not magic; it was merely theatre." They sighed, clothes rustling as they stood.

This was a setback, and an awakening. I would fight for our kingdom's sovereignty. I would prove to Charla's corpse and whatever others worked with her that I would fight through anything, death or pig shit, to preserve our place in the world.

I could see my mother in my mind. *Use that Magician to do whatever they must to ensure your success.*

I opened my eyes, tilted my head up. The Magician stood wiping blood off their hands with their silver pocket square. Gone was the masquerade of their lordly glamour. Instead, there stood the intense lean youth I had met among my mother's orchids and cherry trees.

"How bloody are your hands?" I wondered.

The Magician's eyebrows raised, still scrubbing their hands. "Death is a close friend of mine, Highness, since my training in the Dial's Academy. I won it all, over the bodies of my cohort, yet the Magician's Court graded me a failure—too obstinate." They flicked their pocket square and the blood smeared on the fabric vanished. As they tucked it back into their pocket, they added, "I have the Queen to thank for interrupting my execution."

"I, for one, know my mother to be partial to obstinacy." I held out my hand to the Magician.

The Magician smirked and helped me stand.

✳✳✳

Glamour tickled the skin of my neck. Not like rough pinching and crawling fingers over my muscles like wrestling children did, but like how I would lightly draw lace samples over the back of my hand, letting the reception of my quivering skin guide my wardrobe decisions.

The Magician had led me unseen in the evening-lit hallways. It was a long, winding walk to where the ballroom, but that didn't stop the noises of the party from drifting in the air of the whole palace.

The Dial's Magicians took the conversation from the amulet as evidence, and addressed the bloody scene of the bathroom of my suite. Explaining the tree took time, but they kindly didn't chop it down. The Dial humbly requested we keep the assassination attempt quiet. I understood their concerns, especially with the ball so near.

The physician had advised me against overexertion—such as confronting Phiroth at his arrestbut I refused to miss out on showing him how alive I was while his life ended in shackles. Also such as attending the ball—but I had a duty to perform for my Spoke.

The Magician stopped at the guarded doorway and cleared their throat. The herald, reviewing a list of names, jumped to attention. "Highness," the herald bowed to me, then less-so to Lord Merrith next to me. "I'm afraid it is too close to the Crown Prince's debut procession to announce you properly."

Of course it was. That was my intent, being this late. I gestured to the Magician to speak in lieu of me.

Princess Pienia rounded the corner, tugging on her left gauntlet. Her suit, a purple so dark and rich it shimmered in

221

the magelight. Her formal rapier's hilt guard bore enameled tiger lily petals.

I froze. The Princess was also this late for her brother's debut?

The Princess drew to a stop seeing us, but smiled and edged closer. She bowed before me—a sword-wielder's bow. "Beautiful Elestria, you are gorgeous this evening."

I smiled and curtsied. "And you, Highness." My voice irritated me with how thin and weak it sounded.

"I must say, it is a daring play to bring a Magician to the Dial court."

"My mother insisted."

"And she did disclose that a Magician was accompanying you. I just didn't expect one so..."

"Young, yes." All the things I had said and thought already flooded my mind. But there was no reason to say it now, to challenge their skill. I touched the magic pin they had replaced in my hair. I could feel the wood nymph's tiny fingers against my temples, offering me peace and strength.

Pienia strode right up to the Magician. "I hadn't imagined you to be a Magician, Lord Merrith." She curled her gloved fingers under their chin. "Drop the glamours you are maintaining."

I stilled. I mean, of course a member of Dial royalty could command a Magician—any Magician. They were bred to be of the Dial first, then of the Spokes. But I couldn't help curling a hand over the glamour draped over my bruises.

The Magician was unphased. "Including those covering Princess Elestria's injuries sustained?"

Pienia glanced at me, her gaze lingering on my neck. To the Magician, she said, "Drop your own."

The glamour blinked away. The Magician's features resettled into those I had met them with, the smooth silk suit of their lordly suit untouched.

Pienia grinned. "Ah, so young and yet so powerful. You are a marvel, Seventh Spoke Magician." She dropped her hand from their face. "And now drop Elestria's glamour."

I jerked back but that didn't stop the lacy magic from slinking off my neck. I closed my eyes and kept my hand over my bruising. I knew what it looked like. I very much matched the red bananas I had for breakfast, but with mottled skin and bloody bruising.

Silk-covered fingers brushed the ringlets the draped beside my cheeks.

I opened my eyes.

Pienia's nose held a petal's breadth away from mine, her breath scented of vanilla and peppermint. "Perhaps you could call it love at second sight."

"Second sight?" My words cracked under the faint weight of my voice.

"Well, it was after first sight." Pienia tucked a curl behind my ear. "I wasn't completely sure if you received my messages yestereve. You listened and watched me as some have, but you did not blindly fall into the superficial conversation I set. And when I heard from my father that a Spoke heir had been nearly killed, but requested leave to confront the murderer herself, I knew it was you. Seeing you standing here, bloodied and bruised, defiant..." Her hand hovered near my face. She grinned, bright with enthusiasm and excitement, and asked, "May I kiss you?"

I blinked. Not many noblewomen preferred the ladies outright. Most would take mistresses to work out those feelings on the side of their heterosexual marriages. It felt forced at first to interact with such a lady, hearing my mother's voice in the back of my head, pleading to secure a Dial marriage.

She hadn't specified what type of Dial marriage.

I took up her other hand in mine and pressed the backs of her fingers against my bare collarbone. "Only if you do me the honour of your first dance at this evening's ball."

Pienia didn't wait. She leaned in and brushed her lips against mine, inviting me to take the lead. A concession to the wounded perhaps? But her lips trembled, yearning. I gripped her waist and pulled her against me. Her rapier pommel dug into my torso alongside my corset's boning. I pressed my tongue between her lips, tasting the tender vanilla that laced her breath.

The erotic tingle like lace stung me, all over.

The Nine Trials of Ullah Du

Edith Hope Bishop

In the deep swamp of the world, beneath a wide ochre moon and tangles of hanging moss, beneath the wandering eyes of Sister Screech Owl and the closed eyes of Old Man Heron, a chorus of spotted frogs bellowed in the mud behind a small wooden home. The home perched precariously on the knees of the oldest cypress, just above the dark water, and inside the home, wriggling in a snug little bed, was a sleepy and belligerent child of seven.

"No," said the child.

"Yes," said her mother.

"I'm not tired."

"It's time nonetheless."

"I want a story."

"I know."

"Tell me your fiercest battle against the wicked Ullah Du! Tell how you almost lost everything and died."

"I told that one last night, Little Fish."

"But I want the battle of Ullah Du, Mama! Tell it now or I'll never sleep. Not til I'm dead!"

"Hmmm. Try again."

The child frowned and squirmed under her cotton sheet. Her bed, built of lemon wood and woven reeds, was fragrant and soft. She stuck out her bottom lip but complied. "Mama, please tell the story of Ullah Du. Please."

Her mother kissed the child's forehead and dimmed the oil lamp that lit the room. The orange moon hung quiet outside the window. Sister Owl cackled like a drunken woman who'd lost her hat.

Inside the home, in a dusty corner, the mother's staff leaned against the wall like a cane. It gleamed, a dull shine in the darkening night.

"Close your eyes, Little Fish. And I'll begin."

The child closed her eyes. "Start at the very beginning, Mama. Tell it right."

Her mother began.

***

Long ago, before the Great Rain, I left my home in the North. I carried with me the staff of my mothers and the will of my people. I knew only ambition, and anger, and a fierce desire to prove myself.

In the first year, I battled thieves. In the second, I schemed against a tyrant. In the third and fourth years, I fought in the San Sullahban wars. There, I saw death, I felt loss, and I learned, at great cost, that not all magic can be controlled. Not all ghosts are wicked. Not all gifts are kind. I left the wars with an injured body and a tired spirit, uncertain where I belonged. I despaired that the world was not at all how I'd imagined, and feared my journey would come to nothing but a dead end. I longed for new challenges and motivations, but there were none left to me.

That was when I met Ullah Du, at a crossroads south of my childhood and north of here.

She came to me in a dream, uncertain in her shape, gentle and soft, tall and dark, like the late shadow of a sapling. She spoke in a voice low as the ebbing tide. "Soldier, do you know me?" she asked.

"No," I said. "Not that I recall."

"I know you," she said. "You're strong and brave, but not yet wise."

This was true enough, so I nodded.

"You can learn," she continued. "You have that right. Do you wish to learn?"

"Yes," I said, though asleep. "I wish that."

Ullah Du's voice softened and purred. "Good. I can grant you the answer to any question, the key to any door, or the light to any path."

That's when I knew her to be a witch. What kind, I wasn't sure. Lucky or cruel. Gentle or wild. "Who are you?" I asked.

"I am Ullah Du," she said, "and I've followed you here. I've seen you fight, and I've watched you fall. I believe you have the bones to survive my trials."

I had no reason to trust her, but I was curious, and I was asleep, so I thought I might go on.

"What are your trials? What's required?" I asked.

"My nine enchantments must be outlived or unspun. If you survive, you may choose your prize."

"The answer to any question, the key to any door, or the light to any path?" I asked.

"Yes," said Ullah Du, and I saw her move closer, but only just.

I had nothing to lose. Maybe this was all a dream. I might wake and find myself still hurt and confused. At least in that moment, I had a clear choice: accept or reject her challenge. Yes or no.

"Very well," I said. "I agree. I accept your challenge."

"Good," said Ullah Du. "Wake up."

She was gone, and I was left half asleep, drowning in a warm bath of thought, lost in a dark and starless night. I could feel little more than the heaviness of my limbs and the sluggish, vague worry that I'd been cursed.

I pulled myself awake, and sucked in a breath. I stood and found I was soaked to the bone in my own sweat. My travel clothing was heavy and saturated, my hair streamed. I waded on dry land. This was her work.

Sleep still called to me, pulling me down and back to darkness, back to rest, back to sweet oblivion. I stood at the crossroads, soaking, exhausted, delirious, and confused. What was I to do? I was afraid that if I fell back asleep, I might never wake.

In battle, we'd been forced to stay alert far longer than was safe. Some warriors used spells to drive sleep away. Some used herbs. Some went mad. Others fell to illness and death simply from sleep deprivation. I learned to safeguard what limited energy I had, to take rest sitting, standing, or even on the march.

I left the crossroads and continued south. Despite my fatigue, I resolved to keep moving. The South was unknown to me, but I'd heard tales of kind folk and abundant wilds, and I didn't belong in the places I'd been. Better to shuffle on.

I was careful not to demand too much of my body or mind, aware that they might break under the new burden of my exhaustion. I walked slowly. I closed my eyes for three steps, then opened them for three. I focused on my breathing. I made no effort at speed. I did not shake myself awake. The way out is through, I told myself. The way out is rest.

At midday, I sat beneath a dying oak and ate. I found a soft hollow of grass and curled into myself. "I'll sleep now," I said aloud to no one. "I'll rest and rise again."

I did. This exhaustion, and this ritual, went on for many miles and days. Perhaps weeks. I lost count, but I remained plodding and persistent. Even when my frustration flared, I returned, doggedly, to patience.

Then, one grey morning, I woke up refreshed.

Ullah Du stood over me, tall again but now in a pale green robe. She handed me a bowl of hot soup.

"The first test is done," she said. "Eat. At nightfall, the second test will begin."

I drank the soup. It was a rich stew, full of vegetables I didn't recognize. I didn't ask any questions. Witches only answer sideways. I might as well wait and see.

That night, I came to a village and took a room. At dawn, I was violently ill.

I couldn't keep anything down. I could barely stand. The woman who rented me the room was kind enough to bring me clean towels and bowls. She checked on me every hour. I didn't want to stay; I wanted to run, but I knew I wouldn't get far.

The illness was painful, but the embarrassment was worse. I was reduced to the weakest version of myself, humiliated by my inability to control my body's most basic functions. I hid in my room and let no one enter. I was supposed to be a fighter, but I groveled and retched like a poisoned dog.

After three days of agony, I lay in bed, unable to rise. The landlady came into my room and placed a cool hand on my forehead. "Can I help you?" she said.

I hated the idea of a stranger spending time with me in my condition, but my throat burned. The sides of my mouth were blistered and cracked. I could barely lift my head to signal no or yes, so I reached for her hand and gripped it in thanks.

The woman brought a damp towel and laid it on my forehead. She tipped a cup of water and poured a few drops in my mouth. She wiped my chin.

I sank further into illness. She sat with me through the afternoon and visited me at night. By midday the following day, I could sit up again. Finding my voice, hoarse as the wind through dry bracken, I asked her name so that I might send her gifts of thanks one day. She smiled and transformed into Ullah Du. She stood in dark green robes, now vague again as the figure in a clouded mirror.

"You've done well," she said. "You've passed Sleep and Illness."

"You helped me," I said.

Ullah Du dismissed the matter with a wave of her hand. "And you accepted my help – a vital part of the test. Your next trials will come in pairs. They are inseparable."

I had barely survived one test at a time, but I didn't argue with the witch. Better not to try and catch a river by its tail.

She'd come in through the door, but she left through the air.

I was well again, and now, I was hungry. I packed my bags and cleaned the room as best I could. Downstairs, the house was abandoned. I found only dust on the chairs and in the cupboards. I left some extra money on a table, just in case, and went in search of supplies in the village. But it had vanished, like it'd never been there at all. The house stood alone at the edge of the road, surrounded by a barren landscape of reed and stone.

I walked south along the road. The climate quickly became more arid than I'd remembered. I knew if I kept heading this way, I would come to a river, then to a fertile delta, and then to the Great Forests of the Low Down. At least, I thought that was my direction. The sun was too high for easy navigation. I'd have to wait for its descent to know for sure.

I moved slowly, weary from my second trial, and quickly growing ravenous. I chewed on long grass, and then, growing desperate for sustenance, stopped to dig up a few sparse dandelions. I sliced and boiled the roots and devoured these with their greens. My belly growled and then roared. Above me, the sun stood still in the blazing sky.

Another hour passed and then another. I realized, with horror, the nature of my new trials: Hunger and her sister, Fear. With the sun stuck at high noon, I had no way of knowing which direction I was heading, no knowledge of the time besides what my body could tell me, and no assurance of my next meal.

I surveyed the landscape for any kind of nutrition. Only rocks and parched land surrounded me. I could leave the road, but without the sun or stars to guide me, I'd lose my way.

My gut rattled and groaned. My throat constricted. I kept moving, but my thoughts were dark and desperate. I saw myself, kneeling in the dirt, swallowing stones. I saw my bones baking in the road. The way forward was suffering and death. The way back was nothing less.

Finally, after a long and desperate time, I came to a single pinyon pine at the edge of the road. I cried for joy at the sight of it. If death was coming for me, she wouldn't find me alone. I harvested three handfuls of pine nuts and ate them slowly, sparingly, saving the rest in my pockets. With a small knife, I chose an area of the trunk, stripped away the rough outer bark, and then peeled ribbons of the soft inner flesh. I fried these with the oil of a few mashed nuts over a crackling fire. I chewed my meal in silence, watching the smoke rise towards the stubborn sun.

As vitality infused my blood, I felt the smallest stirrings of hope. Despair was a lie. There might be another tree, or several more, just a few miles down the road. There might be a village. Surely, the sun would have to set eventually. I must go on, I told myself. The way out is through.

After resting and eating again, I walked on and saw a figure down the road. I thought at first it might be another pine, but it was Ullah Du. She was dressed in brown robes now, and cooked a rich soup over a cheerful fire. She offered me a bowl. I hesitated. The last time I'd eaten her food, I'd been sick almost to death. But she offered the bowl again and I took it. I knew better than to refuse a witch's gift. I might as well refuse the wind.

I ate and was nourished. I felt strong, awake, and alive again. I thanked her. I wanted to ask her questions and study her face, but she turned away from me and reached into the bag at her side. From it, she pulled a bronze and leather belt.

"Wear this," she said.

I took the belt and strapped it around my waist.

"You've passed Hunger and Fear," she said with a voice deep as the night sky.

"And what now?" I asked.

But she was gone, of course, faded into a shiver of smoke.

I covered her fire as the sun began to set. Time, at least, was moving again. Perhaps I should as well.

***

"Why did you keep moving, Mama? Why didn't you turn around or go back home?" The child sat up in her bed, bright-eyed, eager to perform her part in the story's ritual.

Her mother smiled and nodded. "That's a fine question, Little Fish. I'll answer if you lay back down."

The child did and her mother closed her eyes, remembering.

"My feet were on a path. I'd come so far and faced so much. More than anything, I wanted to arrive. I wished to finish what I'd started."

***

I traveled south again, wary of what new trap or trouble would ensnare me. Only the landscape and weather had changed. The ground began to loosen and then soften. The skies darkened and rained. New plants with broad, flat leaves began to crowd the sides of the road. Trees, some old and wide, stood with their vast canopies darkening the world above and beyond as countryside gave way to a dense, dripping forest.

Food, at least, was easy to find. Wild oranges and tangerines hung over the road. Bananas and mangoes were abundant. Avocados crowded their branches.

I didn't know it yet, but the Great Rain was coming. If I'd known, I might have been more careful. I might have prepared myself. Instead, I whistled as I walked and braided grass bracelets. After a few days of idle thoughts and unbothered steps, I let myself imagine Ullah Du had gone easy on me this time. Maybe she'd forgotten our deal entirely. Maybe I was free.

But a witch's memory is an owl's clutch; strong as iron and sharp as a blade.

The rain began. Thunder rolled through the canopy as the belt around my waist tightened and grew heavy with an invisible weight. I tested its buckle and sure enough, I could not remove it.

Water found its way to the forest floor. My boots sank deep into the soil. Muddy boots are heavy and my clothes sagged with water, but these were nothing compared to the weight of my belt. Each step was a labor. The storm consumed me. All I could see, or hear, or feel, or taste, was rain. Maybe, I thought, I should sit until the storm passed. Find a place beneath one of those sturdy trees and wait out the deluge. I stopped in my path, considering, and as I did, the weight of my belt tripled. My hips and knees ached in protest. My ankles buckled inside my mud-wrecked boots. It was Will, then, and Weight. These were my new trials. I moved forward again. Slowly. I gritted my teeth and closed my eyes. One step more. Each time. One step more. And again.

Time, immeasurable and unrelenting, passed with no relief. I ate in the rain. Slept in the rain. Water fell and collected until the forest became a swamp. At last, the weight of my belt fell so heavy that my legs gave out. I kneeled in the mud and raised my face to the rain.

"What must I do?" I called to the Great Rain.

No answer came, but I found my own: the way out is through. I shed what I could of my outer clothing. I dropped my supplies. I kept only my staff and crawled forward on hands and knees. When I finally stopped to rest, I vowed I would go on at morning light.

When I woke, the Great Rain had stopped and my belt was gone, replaced with a sore back. Ullah Du stood over me in pale blue robes. I lifted myself from the mud, leaving behind a clear impression of my curled form. Ullah Du's shape, in contrast, was still wavering and indistinct, like an object sunk to the bottom of a lake, or a figure at the end of a sun-baked road.

"Three trials left," she said, as if this was good news.

I couldn't answer. I spat out mud and wiped filth from my face and arms.

"You need a wash," she observed.

"I know," I grumbled.

"There's a spring half a mile from here."

"Will it boil me alive?"

"No," she said and I could hear the frown in her voice. "You're almost through."

"We'll see," I said. "There's not much left of me."

"More than you think."

She was gone again and I rolled my eyes. Her mystery was getting old and my mood was foul.

I made my way down the road and found the spring, a crystal green pool. Its still waters mirrored the sprawling trees and green moss of the swamp. I stripped away what remained of my clothes, hid my staff beneath the ferns, and stepped slowly into the water. I washed and hung my clothes to dry in a patch of sun, then swam and floated, rejoicing in my body's hard-won freedom.

I dressed, retrieved my staff, and traveled down the road until I came to LeReve, a small village near to bursting with life. Colorful flags, banners, and streamers hung from every tree and building. Puppet masters and musicians played on the street, dancers and cooks could be spied through door-ways, storytellers and children yammered on every side. The crossroads were bustling with vendors, hagglers, and buskers.

I had no money left and I must have looked a pitiful sight, because an old woman approached me and tut-tutted in sympathy.

"Oh dear me," she said, "you've been in the rough, hav-en't cha, young lady? You need a hot meal and a lie down. Come, come, let Gran comb your hair."

My newfound cynicism had the best of me; I suspected her of trickery.

"I think I better not," I said. "I'd rather be alone."

"Well, well," said Gran, "that's right and fine, but there's not much solitude 'round here. We're a bunch of nosy swamp rats, all of us." Her eyes twinkled and I had to smile. "What's your name, deary?" she continued. "Where you from?"

I couldn't answer. I had no earthly idea of the answers. My memory stretched to just before the last test and that was all. And so my seventh trial began: Self.

The old woman saw the worry in my face and tut-tut-ted again. "That's alright, my love, that's alright," she said. "You've seen trouble. You need a rest."

"Yes," I said. "I... I... think I'm being tested. I can't remem-ber anything else."

"Well, let's see," she said, "you carry a fighting staff, so you must be a soldier. Or you took the staff, which would make you a thief."

"Yes," I said, considering the staff in my hand, "one or the other."

"You're traveling, you're alone, and you seem to be carrying no money or supplies. Do you know where you're going?"

"No, I don't think so."

"Well then, we have what we can find. You are poor, lonely, traveling, and lost. And you're either a soldier or a thief. You're a woman in need."

"I suppose," I said.

"Only one would change my offer," she said and smiled. "I don't think you're a thief, do you?"

"No," I said, "but I can't be sure."

"I'll take that risk," said Gran and pointed across the road to a small cottage.

I followed her into her home and let her comb my hair and feed me. That night I slept soundly in a soft bed, but when I woke the next day I was tormented by my lack of memory.

"What am I to do?" I asked my host, desperate for a clue. "Where am I to go?"

"Those are your decisions," she said, "but you're welcome here until you know. Tomorrow may be better."

"Thank you," I said, though I felt little gratitude.

Day after day I woke up angry and afraid. I didn't know my own name. I couldn't remember my family or my purpose. I chewed my nails at day and ground my teeth at night. I refused to leave the old woman's cottage except to help with firewood and water. She was patient. I was not.

"You need to get on with it," she said one morning.

"On with what?"

"With living," she said. "There's no point in waiting for your memories. They'll come or they won't."

"But if they never come, I won't know who I am."

"Wrong," she said. "You won't know who you were." She patted my shoulder and left the door open behind her.

She was right, of course. I was not so lost that I couldn't recognize wisdom. I breathed deeply and set my intention to live the day as myself in the here and now. The self that woke up in the cottage of a kind old woman, in a merry town, in the vast wilds of the Low Down.

I stepped outside with new hope, but instead of the happy sounds of children playing and vendors calling, I was greeted by angry shouts and terrified screams from the far side of the village. I lunged back in the house for my staff and raced towards the struggle.

A small pack of rough folk had infiltrated the village. They slashed with thick crude swords and laughed as they kicked over stalls and children. Their purpose seemed only to scare us, until I noticed one of them catch a young girl and rip a silver chain from her neck. It was treasure they wanted, and they'd use brute force to get it.

It wouldn't be easy to stop so many, but I couldn't stand idly by and watch the casual abuse of my new home. I raised my staff and, in a flash, remembered who I was.

I howled the war cries of my training and ran headlong toward the brutes.

I disabled three of them before the fourth managed to punch me hard in the lower ribs. The damage would be deep, but the energy of battle blocked my pain. I swung my staff backwards and bludgeoned the fourth while a fifth managed to pierce my hip with a dagger. I pulled the foul thing out and turned, ready now to attack with two weapons. The fifth rogue cowered and took off running.

The sixth and final villain was larger than the others and wielded an ax as well as a sword. I managed to twist the ax from his hand, but his strength quickly got the better of me. He landed a kick in my gut. I folded forward, unable to defend myself as his massive elbow slammed down on my lower back. I crumpled to the ground, momentarily without control of my legs. I summoned all my upper body strength and launched to the side. His sword came down and sank deep in the clay that might have been my back. I hurled my dagger and it planted in his shoulder. He howled, abandoned his sword, and staggered off into the brush.

I lay in the road, bleeding and broken. I watched the sky above me. Regal towers of soft white moved lazily through the piercing blue. Gentle, they seemed to say, gentle now.

The old woman and a group of young people came and fussed over me. They moved me tenderly back inside Gran's home. They cleaned and dressed my wounds. The old woman offered me tea, but I couldn't drink. I lay on my good side, quiet, focusing on my breath, observing rather than enduring the pain of my injuries.

Late that night, the cackling of an owl woke me. I tried to sit up, but the stabbing pain in my gut and back reminded me to be still.

Gran was sitting near me, watching me sleep.

"I know who you are," I said.

"And who's that?"

"You're Ullah Du. You're the witch who's testing me."

"No," she said. "Never heard of her."

"But you must be. I have one test left," I said.

"That right?"

"I've passed eight," I said breathlessly. "One more. I have one more."

"Hmmm. Well, sleep while you can," she said. "I don't know about a test, but you're lucky to be alive. Foolish of you to run into a fight in your condition."

"I remembered who I am," I protested. "Just before the fight, I remembered."

"That's good news," she said, "but I meant about the baby."

"The baby?"

"Your baby. She's lucky to be alive and now she's on the way."

She was. I felt a contraction, warm and fierce, spread through my middle.

"I'm having a baby," I said, incredulous.

"Yes," said the old woman, smiling. "Time to choose a name."

I understood then, for the first time, the nature of my trials. The reason for their being: Sleep, Illness, Hunger & Fear, Weight & Will, Self, and Pain. They all lined the path to a single and ancient door. Ullah Du was with me and had been all along.

"Yes," I said.

My labor was long, and my injuries complicated the process. My new friends worked wonders with heated stones and careful massage, but because it took so long, Gran fretted that the baby might not survive. Near the end she told me that the infant was in grave danger.

"Now," said the old woman, "you must get her out now!"

I pushed with all the strength left in my body and howled again the war cries in my heart. The baby came. Pink and wailing and wondrous as a star. She laid on my chest, a warm little fish, and I held her. We trembled and cried. She was mine and I was hers. My little Ullah Du.

***

"And what did you pick, Mama? What reward did you pick for passing the trials of Ullah Du?"

"I chose nothing," said her mother. "I already had the light to my path and the key to our door."

"What was the answer to your question?"

"It was you, Little Fish."

The child of seven snuggled her pillow happily and sighed with pleasure. Her mother smoothed her hair.

"And now all witches must sleep," said her mother, gently, "even the most wonderful and wicked."

Feathers and Thread

Jennifer Adam

No one talks about the way the scent of blood coats the back of your throat with the slick taste of sick long after the carrion crows have claimed the field of battle. You never hear about the stink of shit and piss and sweat, or the sound a body makes when a sword spills the life out of it. No one sings the screams of wounded men and women.

Fix your eyes instead on the fluttering pennant, the banners snapping in the wind, the gleam of sun on steel. Pretend it's for the greater good, the noble cause, the call of justice. Quiet your conscience by calling every death a destiny, cling to your faith in fate.

Battle songs and epic poems gild brutal gore with glory, turning butchers to heroes. But I'm no hero.

I'm Corva Greenwitch, bound to the trail of battle until I find what I never should have lost.

And I've sworn to tell the truth.

***

Surya stretched, feeling the pull of sore shoulders and a stiff back. Bruises ached along her forearm despite her leather wrist guard. Fresh callouses marked the ends of her fingers. How many times had she drawn her bow in today's battle? How many hundreds of arrows had she let fly, shooting so fast the bow runners could barely keep her quiver filled?

And every arrow would have found its mark, taken a soul.

Pressing her hands to her eyes, she crouched before her fire and listened to the hiss and pop of the embers, the gentle bubble of the stew simmering in the cast iron pot. Bone-deep weariness settled over her like a weighted blanket.

Boots scuffed the ground. A throat cleared. "Commander, the Field Marshall wants to see you. Immediately."

Surya stifled a groan and rose to her feet. "Very well. Then you can watch my fire. And if my supper scorches I'll hold you personally responsible."

The soldier—just a boy really, still too young to grow anything but peach fuzz on his chin—touched two fingers to his brow and nodded. "I'll have it ready and waiting when you return," he promised.

She could have told him she was only teasing but he looked so earnest she didn't have the heart to dismiss him. Instead she said in all seriousness, "Thank you, soldier."

Weaving around fires, past canvas tents and picket lines of horses, Surya hurried to the command pavilion in the center of camp, its blue-and-gold banner snapping in the evening breeze. Two soldiers in dented breastplates stood at attention before the tent flap, but they didn't offer Surya a challenge. She was easily recognizable even in the purple dusk.

"Commander Surya Tori reporting," one of the men announced.

"Enter!" Field Marshall Brey called, and Surya ducked inside.

Lady Ann Brey had already changed out of her armor and now wore a simple yellow tunic with pale green embroidery at the neck and hem. Her copper skin gleamed in the flickering glow of oil lanterns and her hair, freshly washed, smelled of roses. Surya tugged at her filthy tunic and wished she'd at least taken time to rebraid her own tangled hair.

But the Field Marshall barely looked at her. "Two cohorts failed to return this afternoon. I've sent scouts out but they report no sign."

Surya hesitated before asking, "And the battle crows?" Though she understood the necessity of identifying and retrieving bodies left on the field of battle, she'd always found something distasteful in the sight of ragged people dressed in black cloaks, stooping over the fallen and scavenging their weapons.

The Field Marshall shook her head. "They did not find any of the missing soldiers."

"I'll be back at midnight then, with my feathers."

✳✳✳

My daughter was seven summers old when she first killed a man.

We'd walked to the market fair, I remember, and I was worried that she might be tired. I led her to a shaded alley between the stalls and bought her a wooden skewer of sizzled meat and vegetables. As she nibbled bites off the steaming stick and licked grease from her fingers, I stepped away to look at a booth with pieces of ribbon and tiny boxes of glass beads on display.

I heard a scuffle, a muffled grunt, and I looked up to see a young woman wrapped in the arms of a much larger and older man. She tried to wrestle free, kicking at his shins and twisting from side to side, but he had one hand in her hair and the other around her throat. He held her too closely for her to get any leverage, and his overpowering bulk had her at a disadvantage. "Stop being such a tease!" he growled in her ear. "If you weren't so pretty I'd never have noticed you."

"Please!" she cried. "Leave me alone! I don't want any trouble."

"It's not trouble I'm going to give you," he chuckled, shoving her against the stone wall of a building.

A blaze of fury scalded my chest and I sucked in a breath, muscles tense as I prepared to fling myself against him.

A heartbeat before I lunged, nails ready to claw the smug leer from his face, a streak of motion at the corner of my eye startled me to stillness. He screamed and threw himself backwards, away from the trembling woman. Without looking behind her, she raced away-- quickly losing herself in the maze of stalls and shoppers.

A second scream climbed from his throat and dwindled as he collapsed. I took a step forward, then another... A wooden skewer protruded from his left eye, spilling crimson tears down his face.

A shard of ice as cold as frozen moonlight on a midwinter night pierced my heart and I turned to stare at my wide-eyed daughter. Her hands were empty. A half-eaten mushroom, two chunks of meat, and part of an onion lay in the dust at her feet. "What did you do, Surya?" I whispered.

"He was going to hurt her," she said, her voice sweet as spring syrup. "He was a bad man."

"But how—?"

There was no time for talk—a bystander must have alerted the guards because the drumbeat of pounding boots rumbled through the alley and a moment later a dozen armed men surrounded us.

"She didn't mean—" I started, but one of them knelt in front of my daughter. He wore the badge of the Queen's High Guard on his chest, with a purple and white armband around his right arm.

"You are a brave and talented little girl," he said. "And the Queen needs girls like you in her army. Will you come with me, please? I know she would like to meet you and show you all the things you could learn."

"She's just a child!"

Again I was ignored. The man held out a hand to my daughter and she took it, eyes shining with excitement and face glowing with pride. "Tell your mother goodbye," he said gently. "It may be some time before you see her again, but the Queen will make you a woman of great renown."

She waved to me, blew me a kiss. "Bye Mama," she said. "Don't be sad! I'll make you proud."

"No!" I clutched the arm of the guard nearest me. "I won't allow you to take her."

Bending down, speaking so softly she couldn't hear, he said, "If you do not she'll be burned as a witch for her murderous impulse and uncanny aim."

"But she was only trying to—"

"I speak for the Queen. Do you deny me?" His voice was a low growl in my ear, the threat clear as cold rain.

The penalty for treason was death and then he'd take Surya anyway.

I ask you, what could I have done?

***

Surya shared her stew with the young soldier and then headed to the river to bathe the stink of battle off her skin. She dressed in a clean tunic and combed her hair, and then sat before her fire to compose herself as the moon rose and the stars wheeled slowly through the sky.

When the flames had burned to dark red embers and most of the camp lay sleeping, the constellation of the Archer finally climbed directly overhead. Surya returned to the command pavilion with a silk-lined sack full of feathers.

The Field Marshall waited just outside the tent staring at the stars. "Commander Tori," she said when Surya approached.

You can call me Surya, she thought but wouldn't say. "Yes, Field Marshall Brey."

"You have your feathers?"

Surya raised the sack and the Field Marshall slapped her palms on her thighs. "Excellent," she said. "Let's get started." Surya followed her inside the tent.

Kneeling on a brightly woven carpet, Surya loosened the strings holding the bag closed and tipped a pile of feathers onto the ground. Eagle for victory. Hawk for truth and clear sight. Pigeon for home and a safe return. Swan for loyalty. Peacock for illusion and deception. Swift for speed. Heron for luck. Owl for secrets. Cardinal for warning. Woodpecker for persistence. Bluejay for theft, killdeer for loss, and crow for death.

Surya flushed under the pressure of Lady Ann's gaze but did not falter as she gently stirred the feathers with her finger. She couldn't remember when she'd first learned to read feathers--at first it had been a simple thing, guessing who would fall in love with whom, or which woman would carry a baby before the year's end. But when she'd been appointed Commander of Archers and Armored Horses to Lady Ann's army, she'd used her trick to keep her soldiers and their horses out of unnecessary trouble. And when the Field Marshall heard of her odd ability she'd become one of Lady Ann's chief strategists.

Closing her eyes, she breathed on the feathers and raised both palms. Without looking she stirred the air with her hands, sensing the feathers lifting and spinning around her. *Where have the missing cohorts gone? What has happened to them?*

Sharply dropping her hands, she opened her eyes. Three feathers fell directly before her knees, the others scattered in a wide circle around her.

Peacock, owl, and cardinal.

"The soldiers in both cohorts live," Surya said, gathering the three feathers. "But they are caught in some sort of trap... They are in danger and attempting a rescue might threaten our entire objective." She held up the owl feather. "Our cohorts are part of someone's secret plan."

The Field Marshall met Surya's eyes.

"Lord Caius has left his Rock," they said together.

***

My own mother tried to warn me. "Our people are Travelers, Corva," she'd said, sweeping off the steps of her brightly painted wagon. "We're not meant to put down roots. Without the wind of wandering against your cheeks, the feel of new ground beneath your feet, your spirit will wither."

"He loves me."

"Ah, child, he barely knows you. What will he think when he discovers what you can do, what you are? Come away with us and I'll introduce you to Brendin's son. He's a Traveler from afar, and if you're looking for a man to grow a family with he'd be a good match."

Oh, but I was stubborn and the handsome blacksmith had already caught my eye. I let him put a bonding brace-let around my wrist and an apron around my waist, and I moved into his little white cottage with blue shutters and a red door. For a time, the novelty of a house that didn't roll on wheels and a garden of vegetables I grew myself kept me satisfied. He was a kind man and he treated me well. And when our baby girl was born he was as proud a father as you'd ever hope to see.

But secrets cast long shadows and we both had too many.

His were hidden in the bottom of the bottles he drank too often, flickering in his eyes when he thought I couldn't guess where he stayed so late on nights the innkeeper's pretty sister was home alone.

Mine though...

I fought to keep my magic quiet. I fought with every shred of strength and willpower I possessed. And when it sizzled beneath my skin or sparked along my fingertips I ran to the woods so no one would see the things I could do.

But whispers hissed behind me, rumors swirled around me, and I knew he suspected I was more than I appeared.

Still, the life we shared with our daughter, our sweet Surya, was mostly pleasant. Until the day I ran from the market fair to tell him what had happened.

He was already home, eyes like two dark coals in a face gone hard as steel. "Witch!" he spat at me the instant I stepped through the door. "Had I known you would birth a monster I would never have taken you to bed. I want you out of my house. And, if you know what's good for you, you'll leave this town and never return."

"You don't understand. She was trying to save—"

"Not a word," he growled. "Just *get out.*" He turned away but changed his mind and glanced back at me. "I didn't want to listen when they told me you were a witch. When they said you danced in the woods like a demon made of starlight I called them drunken fools. When they said you could call lightning, read minds, trace memories, I called them liars. But Surya *murdered a man* because she has your damned blood. I should let the village elders kill you at the crossroads but I don't want a worse curse to fall on me. So... just *leave.* Leave, witch, and never show your face again."

***

When Surya reached the command pavilion at dawn, Samin, the Commander of Footsoldiers, was already sitting on a camp stool, his twisted leg stretched out to ease the pain in his swollen knee. "I'm guessing news of the missing cohorts wasn't good?" he said, but before Surya could answer, the Commander of Field Weaponry, Edder, burst through the tent flap.

"Told my engineers three times not to use green wood for the catapults but did they listen? Of course not..." he muttered.

The Field Marshall entered a heartbeat behind him. "We have a problem," Lady Ann said. The commanders fell silent, attention focused on her. "Evidence suggests Lord Caius has left his Rock and that he's captured our cohorts."

Samin cursed and smacked a fist on his good leg. "If the weather hadn't slowed us we could have taken the pass and kept him pinned in that damned fortress until his forces fell apart."

"No army in the world of the living could hold him," Edder said, scrubbing a hand through his graying hair.

Lady Ann paced the tent. "I'd hoped the allied forces and the battle mages would keep him occupied along the coast a while longer but that doesn't seem to be the case."

"What is the bone mage up to?" Samin asked.

"If Caius has captured our cohorts, he'll use his magic to give his undead army the likenesses of our own people," she said.

"What does that mean?"

"It means your warriors will be fighting legion upon legion of the undead—and they'll all be wearing the faces of our friends. Try to prepare them."

✻✻✻

When my husband named me witch it was as if a weight lifted from my shoulders. I didn't have to hide anymore. I didn't have to lie, so I embraced the truth. I was free in a way I hadn't been since I'd left my own people.

I was free to find my daughter.

I wove a seeking spell and followed Surya to the Queen's barracks, where I cloaked myself in shadows and slipped through the iron gate around the training complex. I caught a glimpse of her in a courtyard full of other children, tossing knives and throwing spears at straw-filled dummies. Even then, even from a distance, it was clear she had an uncanny talent. When a tall man in a leather breastplate handed her a slim curved bow, she held it like an extension of her own arm—and she never missed a shot.

The Queen herself came to watch and the pride on my daughter's face when she split the Master Archer's arrow pierced my heart.

I waited until after dark to return, intending to take my daughter away with me. But I couldn't make it past the perimeter—someone must have noticed my incursion and set a magic ward I couldn't break.

The Queen's mages wielded magic far more powerful than my own, but I was a mother. I wouldn't give up.

***

Surya had spent years training with the Queen's army and, after joining Field Marshall Brey's forces, had seen more battles than she could count.

But this... this was a horror she'd never imagined.

Soldiers stared at the faces of their friends and hesitated a heartbeat too long, wondering if the warrior before them was an animated corpse or a member of one of the missing cohorts. Even if they did manage to strike first, the bone mage's undead were notoriously hard to destroy.

Surya's arms ached and her fingers throbbed as she fell into the rhythm: grab an arrow, nock, draw, release. Grab, nock, draw, release. Grab, nock, draw, release. Once she chose a target she never missed, but she had to hit the undead directly between the eyes to fell them. Watching arrow after arrow strike familiar faces shook her spirit.

And still the armies of Lord Caius poured through the valley, spreading like a plague.

Grab, nock, draw, release.

***

I've spent years tracking my daughter, tracing stories of Surya--the archer who never misses. Peddling magic cures and healing ointments from one town to the next, I've followed the trails of battle trying to find her. Small skirmishes mostly—rebel lords looking for trouble, barons fighting over borderlands... Surya and the legendary Lady Ann swoop in with their well-trained soldiers, win quick victories, and fly swiftly away, cloaked in secrecy and hard to pursue.

But I've seen the aftermath, the waste and ruin left behind.

Lately the conflicts have widened, deepened, stretched. War drapes its ugly black wings across the land and I know I must be getting close to my girl.

The innkeeper sets a wooden plate of roasted chicken and potatoes on the table before me but hesitates when I hand her two copper rings and an iron bit. "Beg pardon for bothering you, Goodie," she mumbles, "but I'm wondering if that's the mark of a greenwitch." She points a gnarled finger at the leather thong around my neck, the amulet suspended from it.

"What can I do for you?" I ask.

Hope lights her face. "Come to the kitchen when you're finished eating." She drops the copper and iron pieces on the table and smiles. "Supper's on me. Eat all you want now."

The food is good—hot and filling—but I'm too curious to linger over it. Is it a cure she needs? A charm for fertility? A hex on a neighbor's milk cow? When I finish eating, I make my way behind a narrow wooden door and find the kitchen. She grabs my elbow and steers me to a window overlooking the stable yard. Breath warm on my cheek, she whispers in my ear, "There's a shambleman been bothering our horses.

Only my man doesn't believe me. He says it's a soldier gone soft in the head from the blood he's seen but I *know* it's a shambleman. How do I get rid of it?"

Shambleman. There's a word I haven't heard in a long, long time. I consider ways I might soothe her superstition, but when I peer through the murky glass I catch a glimpse of the figure she means.

His armor is missing and the shirt he wears is ragged and dirty, but in the last blush of sunset I see the blue-and-gold badge on his chest. He is one of Lady Ann's then... or was. He would know my Surya.

He lurches toward the barn door, spins about, stumbles to the pasture gate, collapses. Climbing to his feet again, he tries to turn to the kitchen but falls. Through the glass I hear a low, dismal moaning that raises the hair at the back of my neck.

Magic prickles along my skin, foul and greasy. The innkeeper is right. This is a shambleman. One of the undead.

"There are others," she whispers. "Lisha, my kitchen girl, saw three heading through the woods like they were lost yestereve. What do we do?"

"If you can hit it between the eyes with something," I tell her quietly, "you can destroy it. A pebble from a slingshot might work but an arrow is better. You can try lighting it on fire but if it runs for the barn you'll just bring yourself more grief. They're slowest at noon but sunlight makes them more aggressive, too."

"Can you help us, Goodie Greenwitch?"

"I'll do my best," I promise. But the only way to save her village is to find the one responsible, otherwise more shamblemen will come—and eventually they'll get hungry.

The only man I know with the skill—and stupidity—to raise a shambleman is Lord Caius, the bone mage, and if he's raised one shambleman, he's raised an army.

My daughter is in grave danger and even though I know she's a soldier now, all I can think about is saving the little girl she was. The little girl I lost.

✳✳✳

Surya was exhausted, but Lady Ann asked her to read the feathers again so she washed her face in a bucket of stale water and rubbed foul-smelling ointment on her blistered fingers. She hurried to the command pavilion, nearly stumbling in the dark.

"Thank you for your courage and calm focus, Surya," the Field Marshall told her when she stepped inside. *She called me Surya.* "Without your steady aim we would have been overrun already."

Cheeks flushing at the praise, Surya ducked her head. "I'm only sorry I can't do more. We've lost too many..." And every soldier that fell offered another corpse for Lord Caius to animate.

"What do the feathers say?" Lady Ann asked.

Surya closed her eyes, cast the feathers in the air, and let them settle. Three again: swan for loyalty, woodpecker for persistence, and crow for death. She ran her fingers over them, blinked and shook her head. For the first time the message was not clear. All she said was, "We must persist."

✳✳✳

I twist a spark of magic around a sharp-edged stone and cast it at the shambleman, hoping my aim is good enough to fell him. I'm a far cry from my legendary daughter, but he sinks to the ground with a sad sigh as the energy animating him spills back into the earth. The power that raised him leaves a dark trace I can almost taste so I follow it.

I find the battlefield two days later.

***

Surya sat back on her heels and rubbed her neck. Though a small crowd of warriors-in-training—her bow runners—were responsible for collecting and replacing her arrows and filling her quiver, she still did most of the feather fletching herself. It was long and tedious and as she watched the stacks of finished arrows grow beside her, she couldn't help thinking of the lives she'd already taken. The weight of so much death was a heavy burden but she'd been trained to protect and defend. The Queen needed her. Lady Ann needed her.

She sighed and picked up an arrow, testing the point with her thumb and sighting along the shaft to make sure it was straight and true. Someone called her name and she dropped the arrow.

"Surya!" the voice called again. A voice she recognized from memory.

She stood, shading her eyes with one hand as she scanned the hillside. There—a woman in a tattered green cloak, gray hair blowing like smoke in the wind... "Ma?" Surya whispered in disbelief. Had exhaustion finally caught her? Was she now dreaming even while awake?

But the woman reached the crest of the hill, laughing and sobbing as she ran to Surya. "My daughter! Oh, my daughter! I've spent years searching for you, always days behind your battles. At last I'm not too late!" She flung her arms around Surya with surprising strength.

Surya pulled back to look at her mother. "Is it really you?"

Tears shimmered in her mother's eyes. "I am sorry it took me so long to find you. I'm sorry I had to let you go – the Queen's Guard threatened to kill you and I didn't know what choice I had..." She clutched Surya to her, stroking Surya's hair with a shaking hand.

"I wrote you letters but never received any replies... I was afraid you were angry with me, for what I did that day at the market fair," Surya mumbled against her mother's shoulder.

"Never, child. Never! Since the day they took you from me I've been trying to get you back. And now I have! Now we can go home..."

Surya was already shaking her head. "But I can't. Lady Ann—the Field Marshall—is depending on me. Lord Caius..." she swallowed. How could she tell her mother about the army of undead wearing the faces of friends she'd fought beside for years?

"Raised an army of shamblemen," her mother said. "I know. But the only way to win this war of yours is to kill Lord Caius himself, else he'll just keep raising corpses until your forces are all dead.

Surya caught her breath. She'd suggested as much to Lady Ann but they hadn't managed to get close enough to Caius to threaten him.

"It's not a job for you," her mother tried to argue. "Come away with me and let the Field Marshall defeat him." She touched the jagged scar running down Surya's cheek and said, "You've given enough already."

"No, Ma," Surya said. "It has to be me. No one else can get close enough, but if I can just snatch one clear shot..."

"He'll kill you! I haven't spent all these years looking for you just to lose you now!"

"If I don't try, his... shamblemen, did you call them? will destroy this realm, one town, one village at a time. The Queen trusted us to defend this border. I swore an oath and I won't break it."

Her mother sighed and nodded, as if she'd hoped to convince Surya otherwise but hadn't actually expected to succeed. "Then I will help."

***

I wish she were still a child, young enough for me to drag her out of danger and back into the safety of my arms. The scar along her cheek rips my heart to shreds—what wounds lie hidden below the surface?

But I know she's right. No one else has her aim. No one else can kill Lord Caius and end this war.

This is what she's spent her life training for. I just have to keep her safe long enough for her to loose her arrow and then it's done.

My magic has always been a small and quiet thing—I'm a simple greenwitch, not a mage—but I've had years to practice and love has a power of its own. So while Surya and her fellow soldiers meet to discuss strategy, I ask one of the camp followers to fetch a small loom from the closest town and set it up near my daughter's tent. And then, concentrating harder than I ever have before, I head out to collect the things I need.

First I gather armfuls of summer grass, sweet and green. I shred the stems with my nails and spin the fibers into thin green thread. I use my magic to sift strands of sunshine from the heat of the day, and when I sit at the loom I weave this light in between the green grass threads. I make my daughter a vest imbued with the powers of light, life, and healing. It will offer more protection than any coat of armor ever could.

Next, I make my way along the picket lines of horses. I murmur softly in their ears and they agree to let me take a few long hairs from each of their manes and tails. I tease out thin wisps of wind and weave it with the horse hair until I've made shin guards that will grant Surya unmatched speed and stamina.

Then I wander far afield, long after the sun sets, collecting cobwebs. I spin moonbeams into shining silver thread and weave it with the spider silk, creating a cloak that will give my girl the power of invisibility.

I've never tried anything so complex, but I pour my love into every strand and pray it is enough.

It's nearly dawn before I'm done and when I present my gifts, Surya cries. "I will never forgive myself for losing you," I tell her. "I didn't know how to protect you back then, but maybe now…"

"Oh, Ma, you've never been to blame for what happened. Sometimes I've wished that I could go back and change that moment… I didn't know what I was doing. I only wanted to help."

She scrubs her cheeks with her fists like the little girl she used to be. Then she sucks in a breath, straightens her shoulders, steadies herself. The brave soldier back to the business at hand. "There's no time to waste. Lady Ann will create a diversion," she tells me. "She and two of our remaining cohorts will try to draw Lord Caius away from his camp and I'll sneak in as close as I can. When I can take a shot, I will. You stay here, stay safe, until I return."

She kisses me on both cheeks and strides away, the storybook legend the Queen has made her. "Wish me luck!" she calls, glancing back at me over her shoulder.

***

Surya tied the shin guards around her legs, above the soft leather boots she always wore. She adjusted the green vest— it smelled of fresh-cut hay and lazy summer afternoons—and then settled the cloak around her shoulders. Her skin tingled with the buzz of magic and when she took an experimental step she felt as if her feet barely touched the ground. If her mission weren't so desperate she would have laughed with delight. Her mother was a wonder.

Running to the edge of the woods that separated the Queen's army from Lord Caius's forces, she looked back to wait for the signal.

There—a single burning brand tossed high in the air.

Surya darted into the trees, weaving between the trunks

and leaping from one patch of shadow to the next. Behind her trumpets blared the call to battle and she knew Lady Ann led the cohorts to the field.

She fervently hoped Lord Caius would take the challenge.

The trees ended at the base of a steep hill and Surya raced to the top, barely breathing hard. Crouching behind a boulder, she surveyed Lord Caius's camp on the plateau a mile away. He'd sent a large contingent of his shamblemen out to meet Lady Ann's attack, but... Surya's stomach twisted. Lord Caius sat astride a tall black horse, watching the fight from behind a ring of guards holding heavy shields.

Even perfect aim couldn't penetrate his protection. She had to get closer.

Raising the hood of her cobweb cloak, she slipped down the far side of the hill and ran for the plateau. She hoped her mother's magic was strong enough to keep her hidden from sight.

The clash of weapon meeting weapon, the cries of the fallen, and the shouts of soldiers rose behind her. The clamor drew flocks of crows who added their own harsh chorus.

Surya reached the first line of sentries and dropped to a crouch. Holding her breath, she eased behind the first man, ducked around the second, and crept past the third. They didn't react.

Gaining confidence, she hurried toward the center of Caius's camp, her bow and quiver of arrows a comforting weight across her back. She couldn't risk drawing it until she was close enough to take the shot.

A fallen log blocked the way to the main tent, apparently used as a bench by weary soldiers. Surya breathed a sigh of relief and knelt behind it. Her cloak would keep her hidden from anyone approaching behind and the log offered the perfect cover for anyone watching this direction. Without hesitating she pulled her bow from beneath her cloak. In one smooth motion she rose, nocked an arrow, drew, and let loose.

The arrow sped toward Lord Caius, still calmly sitting in the saddle and watching the battle raging along the floor of the valley below.

He never saw it coming.

The instant he toppled from his horse, the shamblemen collapsed in a clatter of bones. Lord Caius's living soldiers threw down their weapons, weeping in relief at being allowed to surrender.

Surya raced back to her people, a glad smile on her lips. "Lady Ann, we've"—she started to call, but the Field Marshall pressed a hand to a blooming crimson rose at her side.

"We've won," Lady Ann coughed, trying to smile. "No," she corrected. "*You've* won." And then she fell.

***

I see the grief on my daughter's face when the Field Marshall dies and understand the love she carried.

As soon as I can reach her through the throng of cheering soldiers, I put my arms around her. "You've done well," I say. "And you've earned the chance for a new life. Come with me. Let me teach you what the Queen could not."

"All I know is killing," she whispers, turning her hands over as if she can see them stained with blood.

"And I can teach you healing, to balance the lives you had to take."

"How? I have no magic."

"If you had no magic the feathers would not show you glimpses of the future."

"How did you hear about that? It's just a trick…"

"If you had no magic your arrows would not fly so sure," I tell her.

She lifts her face to mine. "Is it really true?"

"I'm a witch, and I swore I'd always tell the truth."

Participant Bios

Jennifer Adam
Author, Copy Editor

Jennifer Adam lives on a farm in the heartland. When she's not riding wild mustangs, hiking through the woods with her dogs, or planting wildflowers for honeybees, she can be found surrounded by books and fountain pens. Her work has appeared in *Six Hens, The Edge of Propinquity, As You Wish, New Myths Magazine*, and two anthologies. She received Honorable Mention in Glimmer Train's 2017 Very Short Fiction Contest and is now working on another novel.

Jessica Aelwood
Author

Jessica Aelwood is a writer, reader, artist, Viking, and supernatural creature. She's also a practicing hedge witch with a degree in creative writing from Colorado State University. Her talents include accepting rejection letters, finding bones in strange places, and unintentionally taking the long way. She lives in the wintry (and, in an irregular pattern, summery) climes of Northern Colorado with her best friend and a host of familiar spirits.

Robyn Bennis
Beta Reader, Line Editor

Robyn Bennis spends her days working in biotech and her nights thinking up new curse words to adequately describe how horrible people are. Having met with limited success in either endeavor, she vents her frustrations through crime, yelling at clouds, and writing. Her debut novel, *The Guns Above*, is now available in hardcover, e-book, and audiobook fromTor Books.

Edith Hope Bishop
Author

Edith Hope Bishop is a writer, volunteer, and mother in Seattle, Washington. She grew up in South Florida, has degrees from Harvard and Columbia, and taught language arts for several years in a public high school. She was a finalist in the Pacific NW Writers Association Literary Contest in 2016 and 2013. Her work has recently appeared in *Mythic Delirium, Yellow Chair Review,* and *Lucia Journal.* She's represented by Sara Crowe of Pippin Properties and is online at www.ehbishop.com. Edie is most at home near, on, or in any body of salt water.

Kristen Blount
Author, Beta Reader, Editor, Formatter

Kristen works as a communication specialist and graphic designer for the local library. Since she's a lifelong book hoarder and obsessive reader, it's a good fit. Otherwise, she is too young to be parenting 20-somethings and too old not to have figured out more of life. She loves Orioles baseball, baking, and cross-stitch.

Jessica Corra
Content Editor

Jessica Corra is a professional freelance editor, formerly acquiring romance, science fiction and fantasy for Samhain Publishing. She believes in wonder, love and words, and is a fan of kittens, snowflakes and science. Her own writing is represented by The Bradford Agency. She eschews social media to keep her blood pressure down.

Nivair H. Gabriel
Author, Line Editor

Nivair H. Gabriel has written all her life, and feminist fantasy is her heart-home. At sixteen, she thought it would be fun to go to MIT and get a degree in aerospace engineering, so she did. Her work has been published in *Marvels & Tales*, *io9.com*, *Fantasy Magazine*, *Weird Tales*, *Pittsburgh Magazine*, *MIT's The Tech*, and the Sirens benefit anthology *Queens & Courtesans*. She is currently pursuing a dual-degree MA/MFA in Children's Literature and Writing for Children at Simmons College, while working in libraries and publishing companies whenever she can. She would do just about anything for Sirens.

Lyta Gold
Author

Lyta Gold writes fantasy, sci-fi, and political satire. You can find her living in Brooklyn with her husband and two of the world's wickedest cats.

Kallyn Hunter
Author

Kallyn Hunter is real estate researcher, writer and knight from Fort Collins, Colorado. She has been attending Sirens for six years and has no intention of stopping any time soon. When she isn't hunched over a laptop agonizing over her latest writing project (which is most of the time), Kallyn can be found adventuring through various Colorado lakes and rivers, reading to her Pomeranian Meister, honing her jousting skills with the Knights of the Tempest, or working on her latest chainmail creation.

Kate Larking
Author, Co-Creator

Kate Larking is a book buyer for an independent bookstore. In her off hours, between binge-watching anime and leveling-up game characters, she writes speculative fiction for both YA and adult markets. Her queer space opera comic, Crash and Burn, was a finalist for the 2016 & 2017 Aurora Awards for best English Graphic Novel. She cofounded Anxiety Ink, a community of writers dealing with the stress and challenges of writing. She resides in Calgary, AB with her wife, daughter, and six pets.

Tina LeCount Myers
Beta Reader

Tina LeCount Myers is a writer, artist, independent historian, and surfer. Born in Mexico to expat-bohemian parents, she grew up on Southern California tennis courts with a prophecy hanging over her head; her parents hoped she'd one day be an author. *The Song of All* (February 20, 2018, Night Shade Books) is her debut novel.

Amanda "Manda" Lewis
Artist

Manda holds a Bachelor of Science in aerospace engineering and a Masters of Tourism Administration, and served in the Air Force for seven years. She currently works for a children's museum in Raleigh, North Carolina, managing after-hours special events. Most days, she spends frolicking with her toddler and newborn trying to impart a love of fantasy and science fiction in them. Manda has always enjoyed creating art and loves themes far more than anyone really should. Manda has been a volunteer for Narrate Conferences for the last ten years and is thankful every day for its community.

Darian Lindle
Author

Darian Lindle is a playwright, novelist, coffee connoisseur, stargazer, and mother-of-twins living in Seattle, Washington. She's been published by Dramatic Publishing and has more than 60 productions nationally. Darian's passions for mythology, SFF, melodrama, science, geekery, family, and intersectional feminism are stoked by the fire that is Sirens.

Lola Lindle
Author

Lola Lindle lives in Seattle with her family. She is a wildly shy introvert who masquerades as a confident, independent extrovert for very short periods of time. She is active in local theatre, film, and writing critique groups. She received her BA from York University in English and is working on her Master's degree in Imaginative Fiction at Signum University. Lola is excited to be a part of such a worthy effort to support her favorite writing and reading conference, Sirens!

Cass Morris
Author

Cass Morris lives and works in the Blue Ridge Mountains of Virginia with the companionship of two royal felines, Princess and Ptolemy. She completed her Master of Letters at Mary Baldwin University in 2010, and she earned her undergraduate degree, a BA in English with a minor in history, from the College of William and Mary in 2007. She reads voraciously, wears corsets voluntarily, and will beat you at MarioKart. Her debut novel, *From Unseen Fire*, releases in April 2018 from DAW Books.

Cynthia Porter
Author, Beta Reader, Line Editor

Cynthia Porter spent over 25 years working in bookstores before suddenly deciding that a career in office management would leave her more time to write. She has the requisite patient husband, who enables her to spend time at her keyboard; one resident feline, who believes the keyboard is her pillow; and a stash of yarn for knitting and crocheting that is threatening to over-take her book collection. When not writing, she reads fantasy, science fiction, women's fiction, and mysteries. At heart, she will always be a bookseller.

Rook Riley
Author

Rook Riley is a writer, game enthusiast and veteran. The blog rookriley.wordpress.com details a few Rook mistakes she's made along the way.

Jennifer Shimada
Managing Editor

Jennifer Shimada (@JenShimada on Twitter) is an avid reader, world traveler, and academic librarian. She has loved Sirens since she first attended in 2015.

Paula Sutton
Beta Reader, Line Editor

Paula Sutton lives in Colorado with her man and her cat. She is an accountant by day, reader by night, and hiker on the weekends. She is currently trying to transform her house into a library, so she will never run out of reading material in case of apocalypse.